W9-APS-039

FRESHMAN

First published in 2011 by Zest Books LLC
35 Stillman Street, Suite 121, San Francisco, CA 94107
www.zestbooks.net

Created and produced by Zest Books, San Francisco, CA
© 2011 by Zest Books LLC

Teen Fiction / Comics & Graphic Novels

Library of Congress Control Number: 2010936581

ISBN-13: 978-0-9819733-6-4
ISBN-10: 0-9819733-6-1

CREDITS
EDITORIAL DIRECTOR/BOOK EDITOR: Karen Macklin
CREATIVE DIRECTOR: Hallie Warshaw
ART DIRECTOR: Tanya Napier
MARKETING ASSOCIATE: Nikki Roddy
MANAGING and PRODUCTION EDITOR: Pam McElroy

TEEN ADVISORS: Emma Herlihy, Celina Reynes, Diana Rae Valenzuela, Irene Xu

Manufactured in China.
LEO 10 9 8 7 6 5 4 3 2 1
4500283569

Every effort has been made to ensure that the information presented is accurate. The publisher disclaims any liability for injuries, losses, untoward results, or any other damages that may result from the use of the information in this book.

12.99

FRESHMAN

TALES of 9th GRADE OBSESSIONS, REVELATIONS, and OTHER NONSENSE

by Corinne Mucha

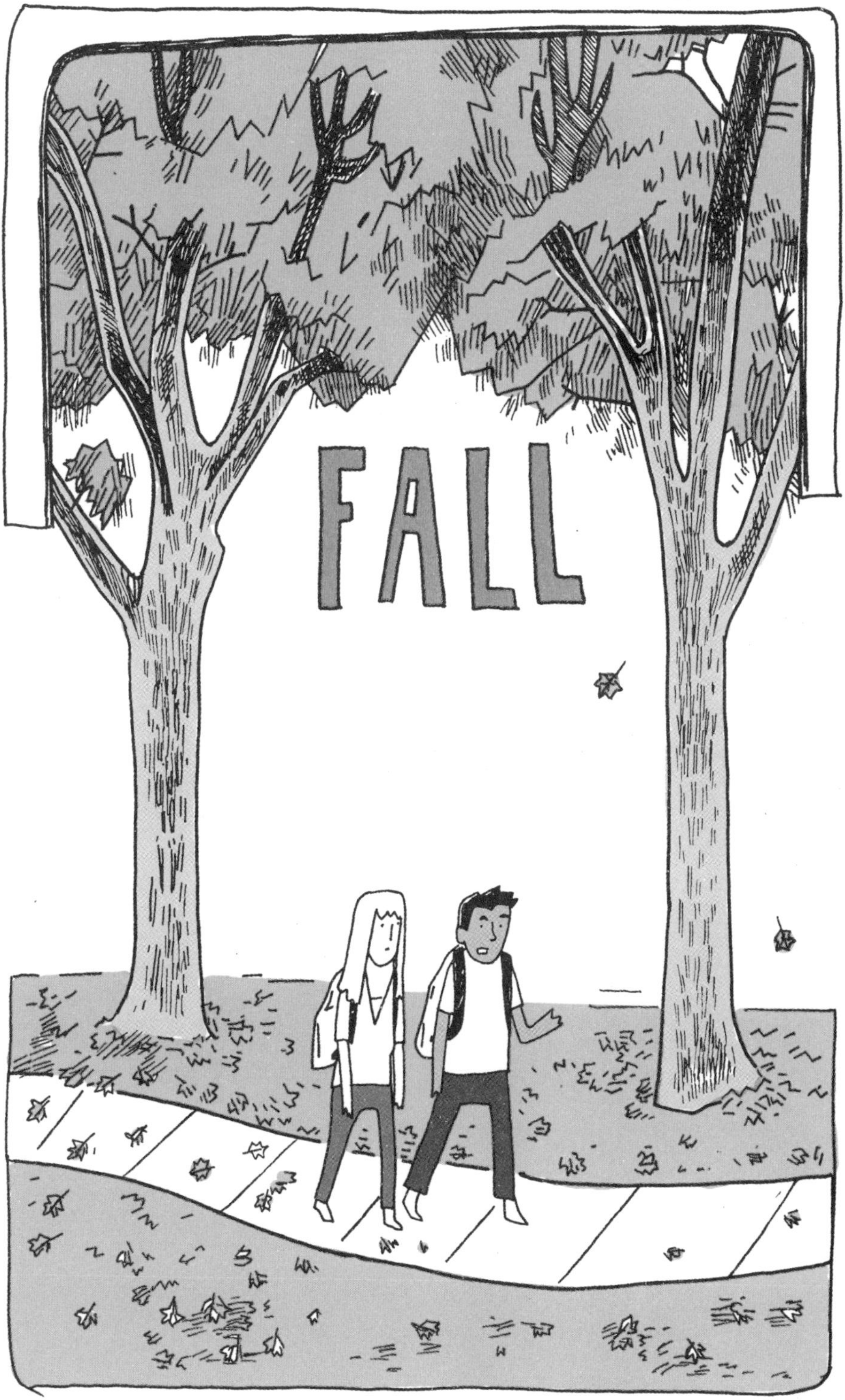
FALL

DAY ONE

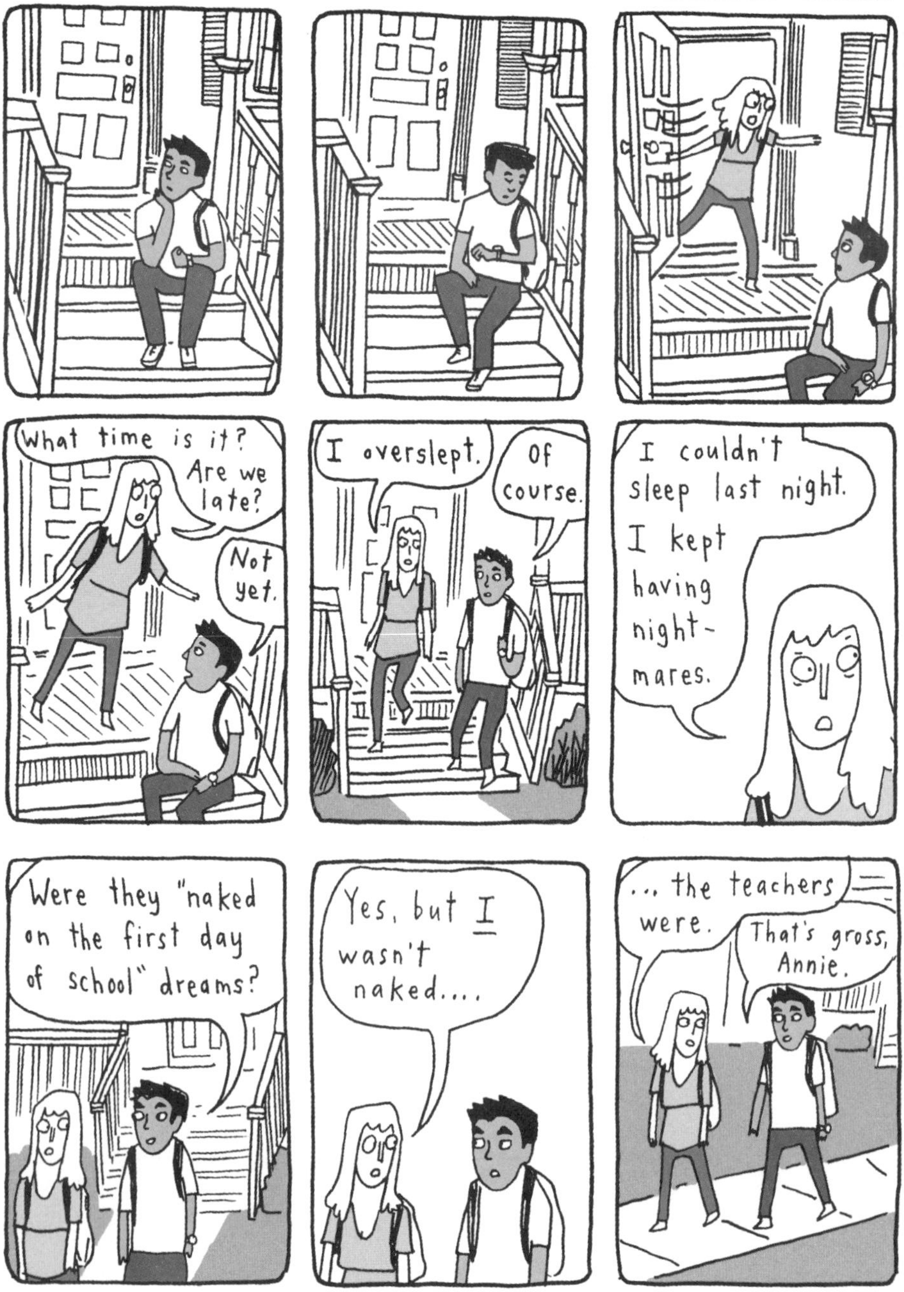
What time is it? Are we late?
Not yet.
I overslept.
Of course.
I couldn't sleep last night. I kept having night-mares.
Were they "naked on the first day of school" dreams?
Yes, but I wasn't naked....
... the teachers were.
That's gross, Annie.

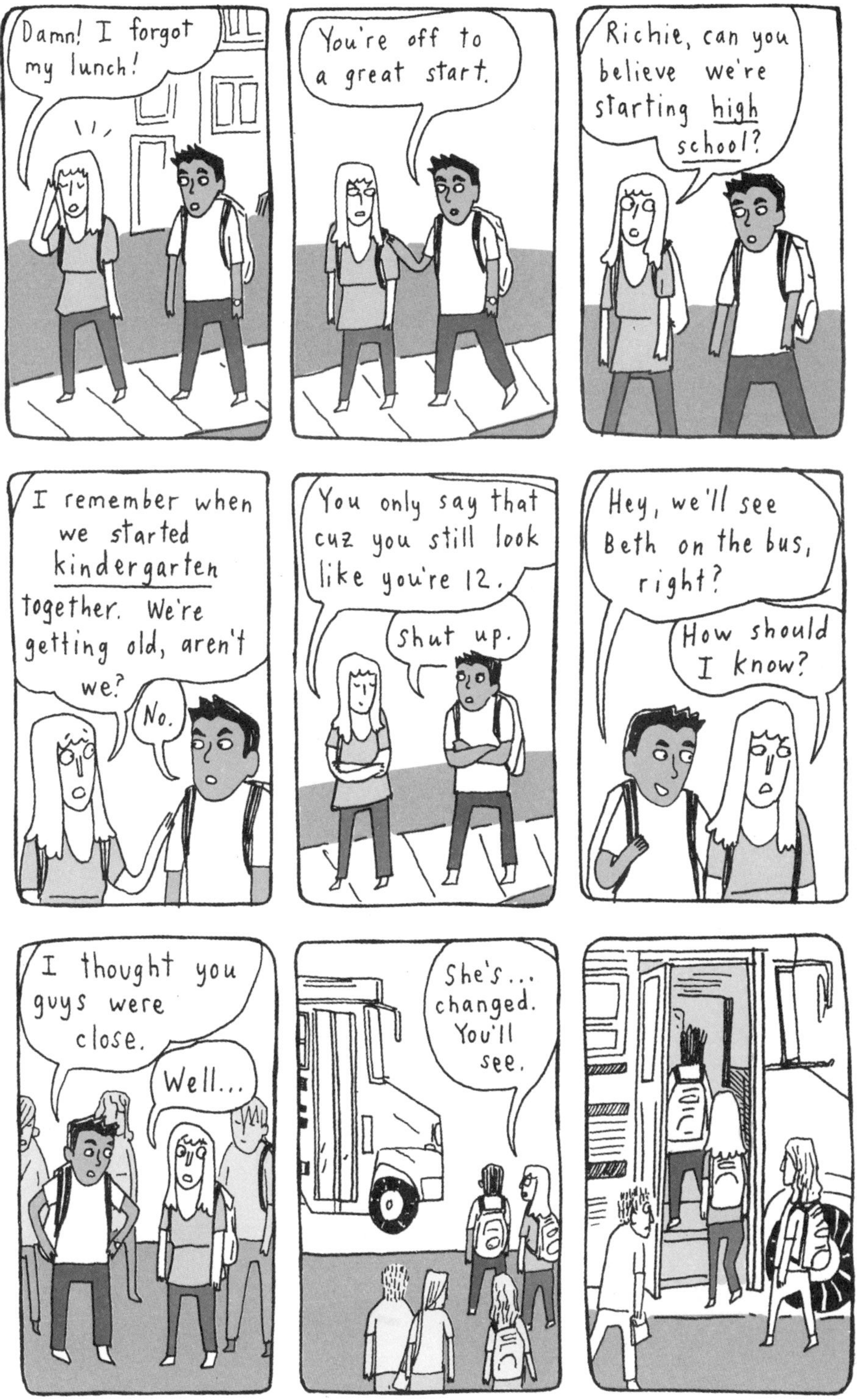
Damn! I forgot my lunch!
You're off to a great start.
Richie, can you believe we're starting high school?
I remember when we started kindergarten together. We're getting old, aren't we?
No.
You only say that cuz you still look like you're 12.
Shut up.
Hey, we'll see Beth on the bus, right?
How should I know?
I thought you guys were close.
Well...
She's... changed. You'll see.

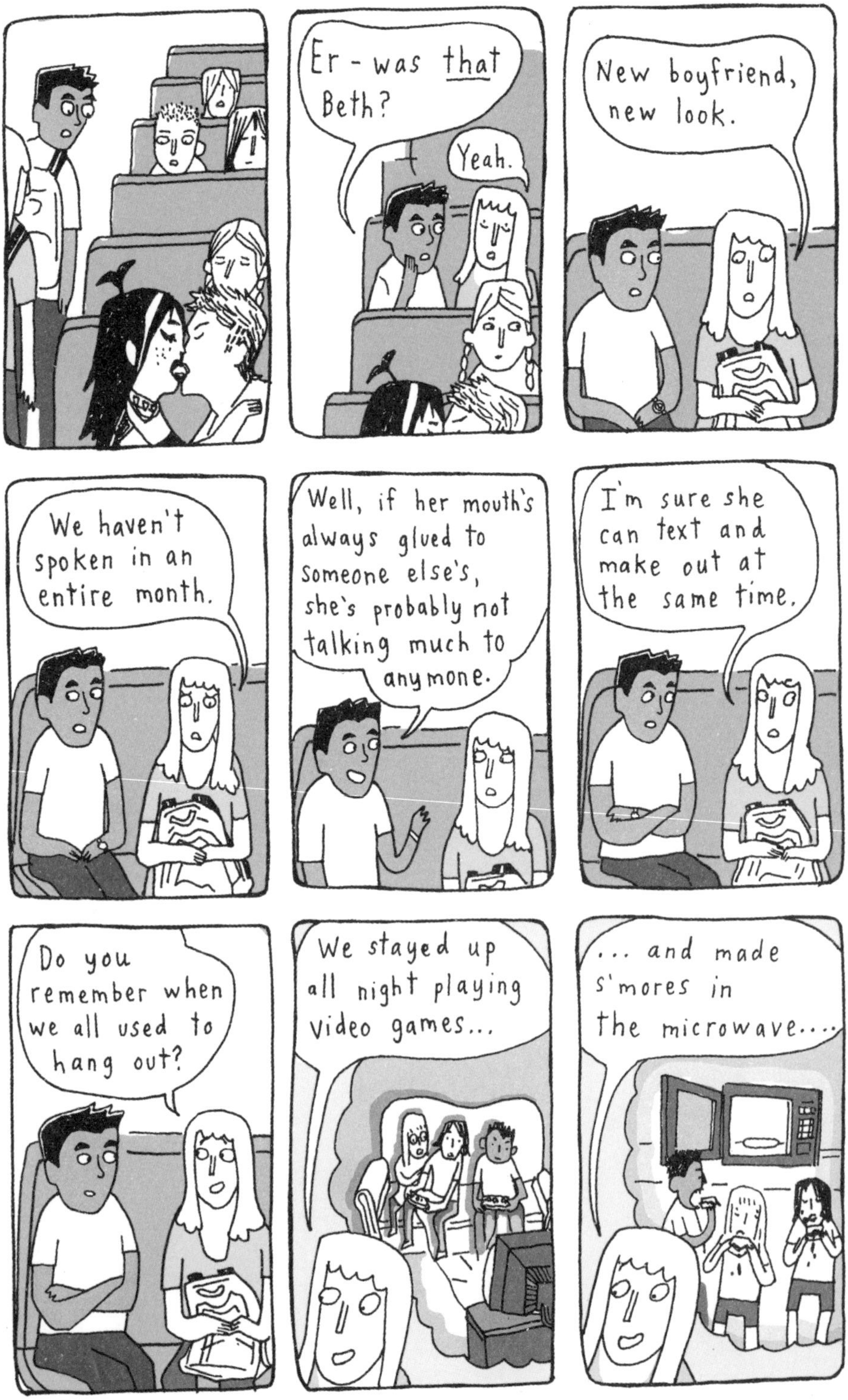
Er - was that Beth?
Yeah.
New boyfriend, new look.
We haven't spoken in an entire month.
Well, if her mouth's always glued to someone else's, she's probably not talking much to anymone.
I'm sure she can text and make out at the same time.
Do you remember when we all used to hang out?
We stayed up all night playing video games...
... and made s'mores in the microwave....

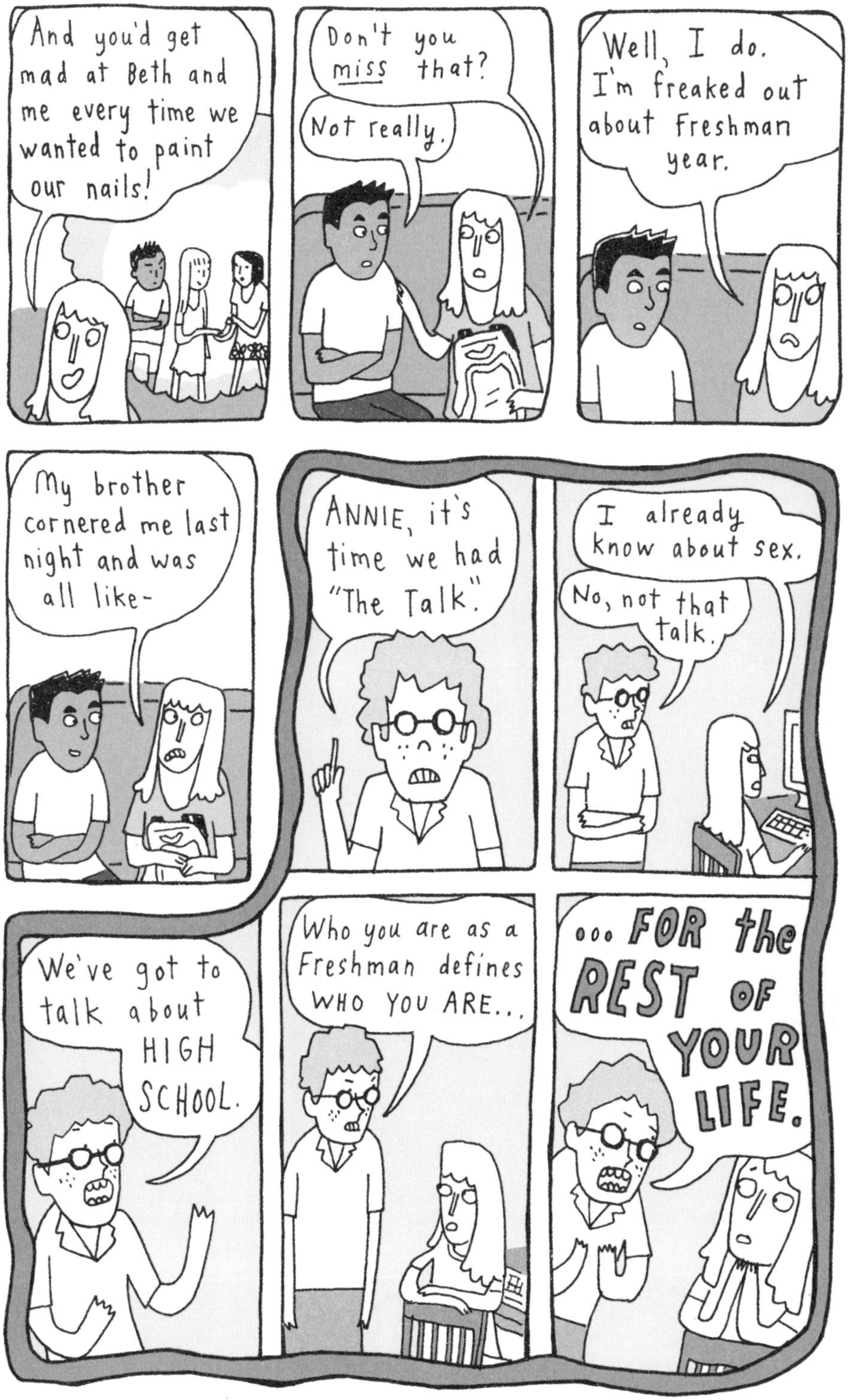
And you'd get mad at Beth and me every time we wanted to paint our nails!
Don't you miss that?
Not really.
Well, I do. I'm freaked out about Freshman year.
My brother cornered me last night and was all like-
ANNIE, it's time we had "The Talk."
I already know about sex.
No, not that talk.
We've got to talk about HIGH SCHOOL.
Who you are as a Freshman defines WHO YOU ARE...
...FOR the REST OF YOUR LIFE.

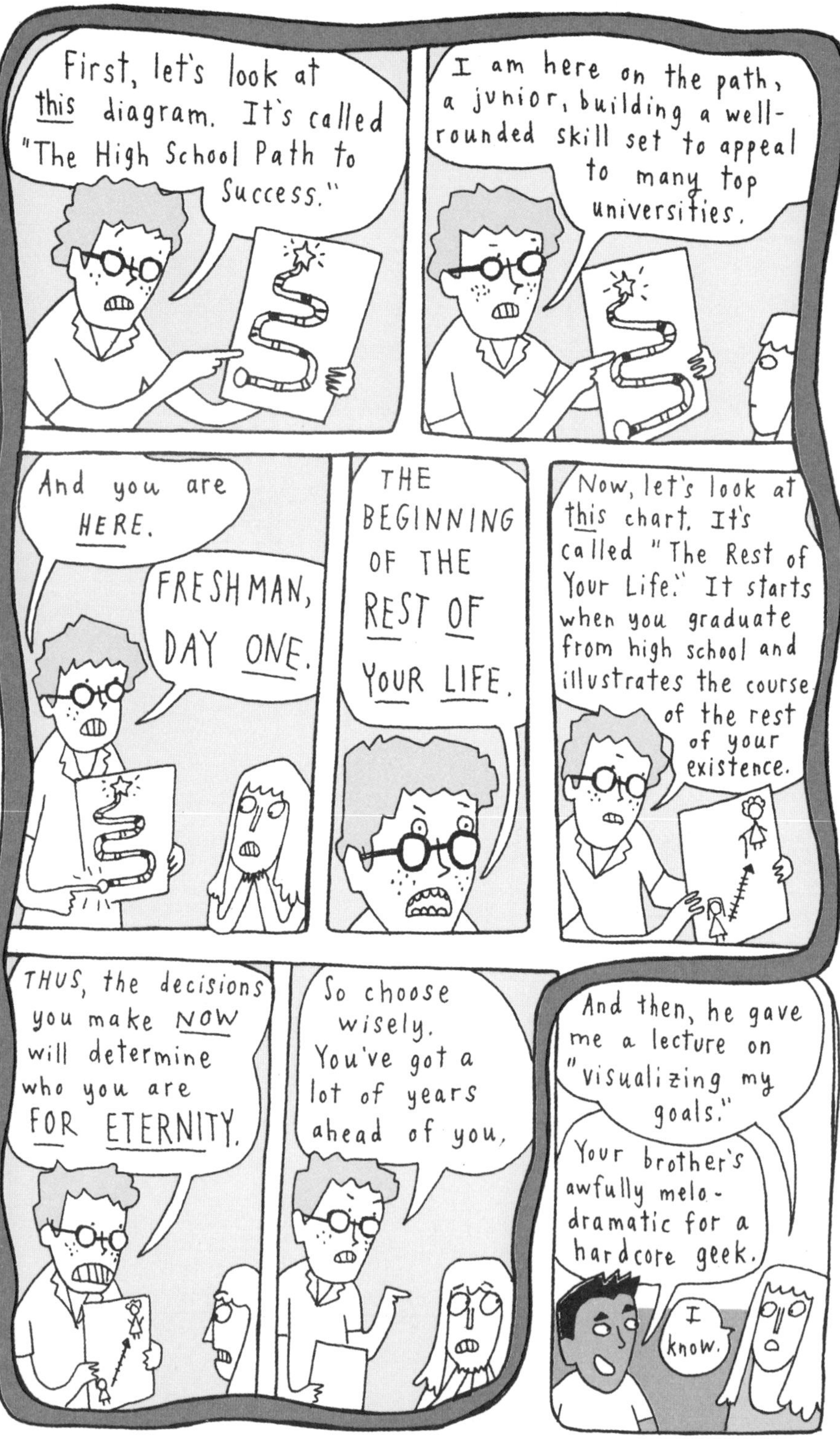
First, let's look at this diagram. It's called "The High School Path to Success."
I am here on the path, a junior, building a well-rounded skill set to appeal to many top universities.
And you are HERE.
FRESHMAN, DAY ONE.
THE BEGINNING OF THE REST OF YOUR LIFE.
Now, let's look at this chart. It's called "The Rest of Your Life." It starts when you graduate from high school and illustrates the course of the rest of your existence.
THUS, the decisions you make NOW will determine who you are FOR ETERNITY.
So choose wisely. You've got a lot of years ahead of you.
And then, he gave me a lecture on "visualizing my goals."
Your brother's awfully melo-dramatic for a hardcore geek.
I know.

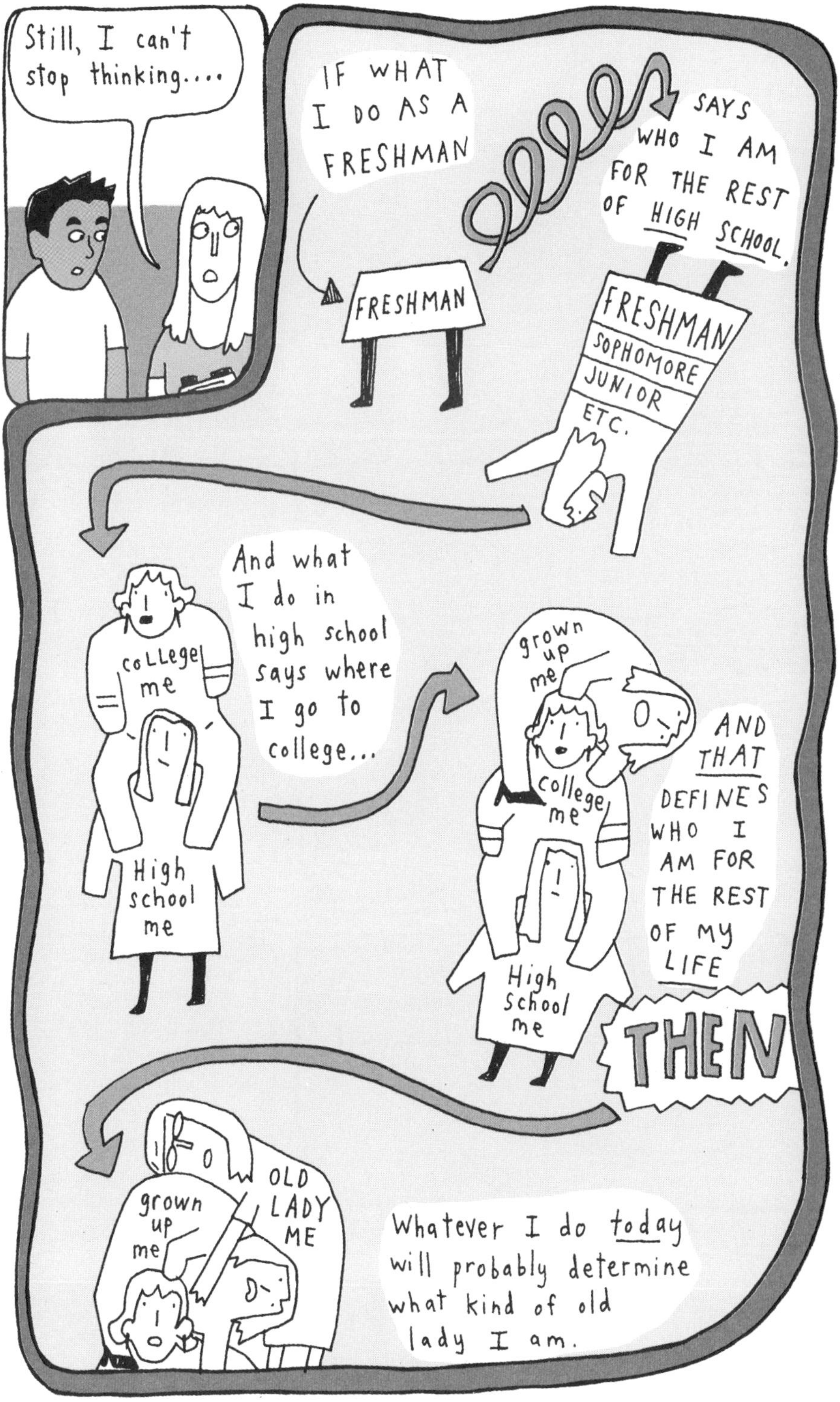
Still, I can't stop thinking....
IF WHAT I DO AS A FRESHMAN
FRESHMAN
SAYS WHO I AM FOR THE REST OF HIGH SCHOOL.
FRESHMAN
SOPHOMORE
JUNIOR
ETC.
And what I do in high school says where I go to college...
college me
High school me
grown up me
college me
High School me
AND THAT DEFINES WHO I AM FOR THE REST OF MY LIFE
THEN
OLD LADY ME
grown up me
Whatever I do today will probably determine what kind of old lady I am.

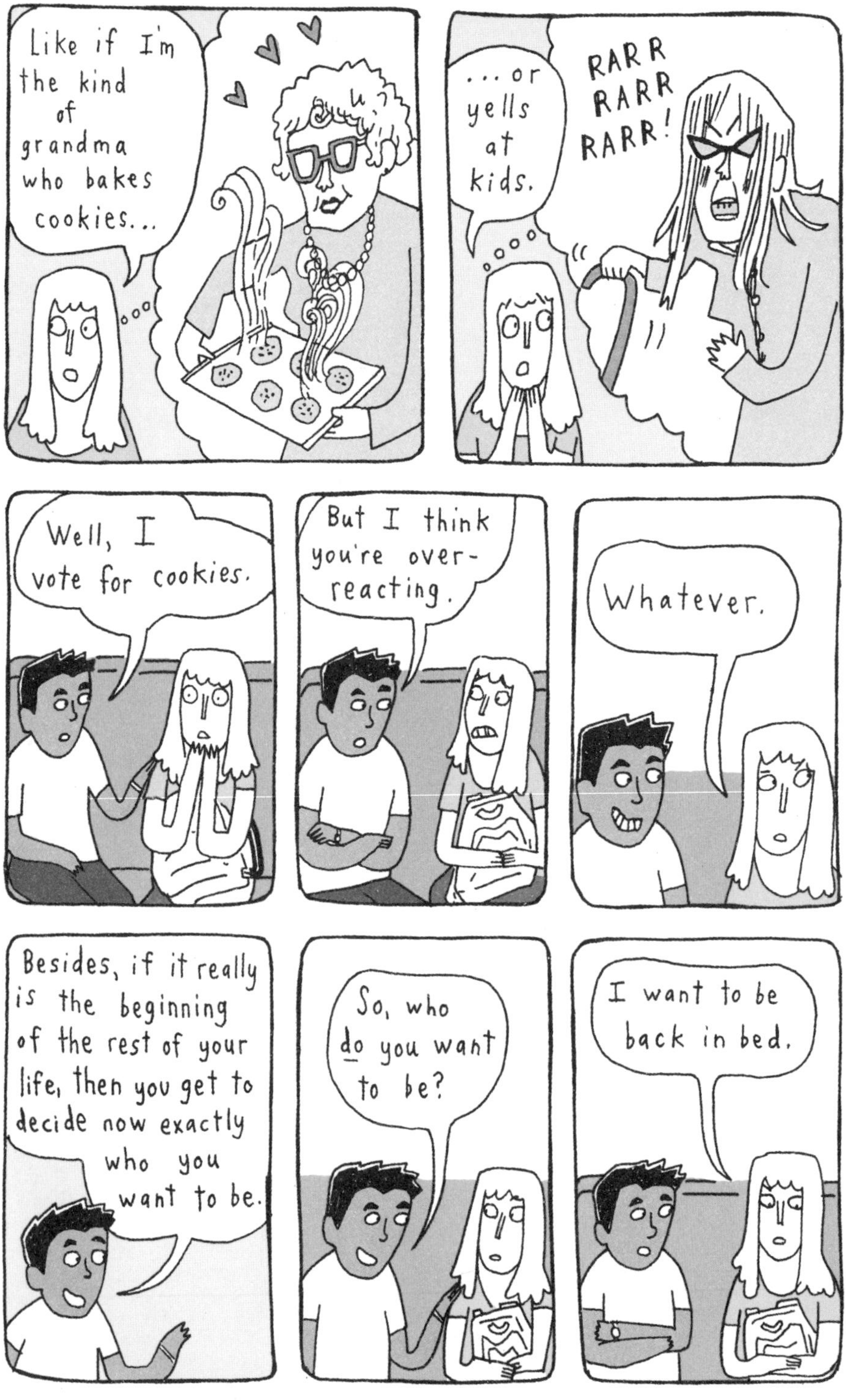
Like if I'm the kind of grandma who bakes cookies...
...or yells at kids.
RARR RARR RARR!
Well, I vote for cookies.
But I think you're over-reacting.
Whatever.
Besides, if it really is the beginning of the rest of your life, then you get to decide now exactly who you want to be.
So, who do you want to be?
I want to be back in bed.

HOME - RUINED

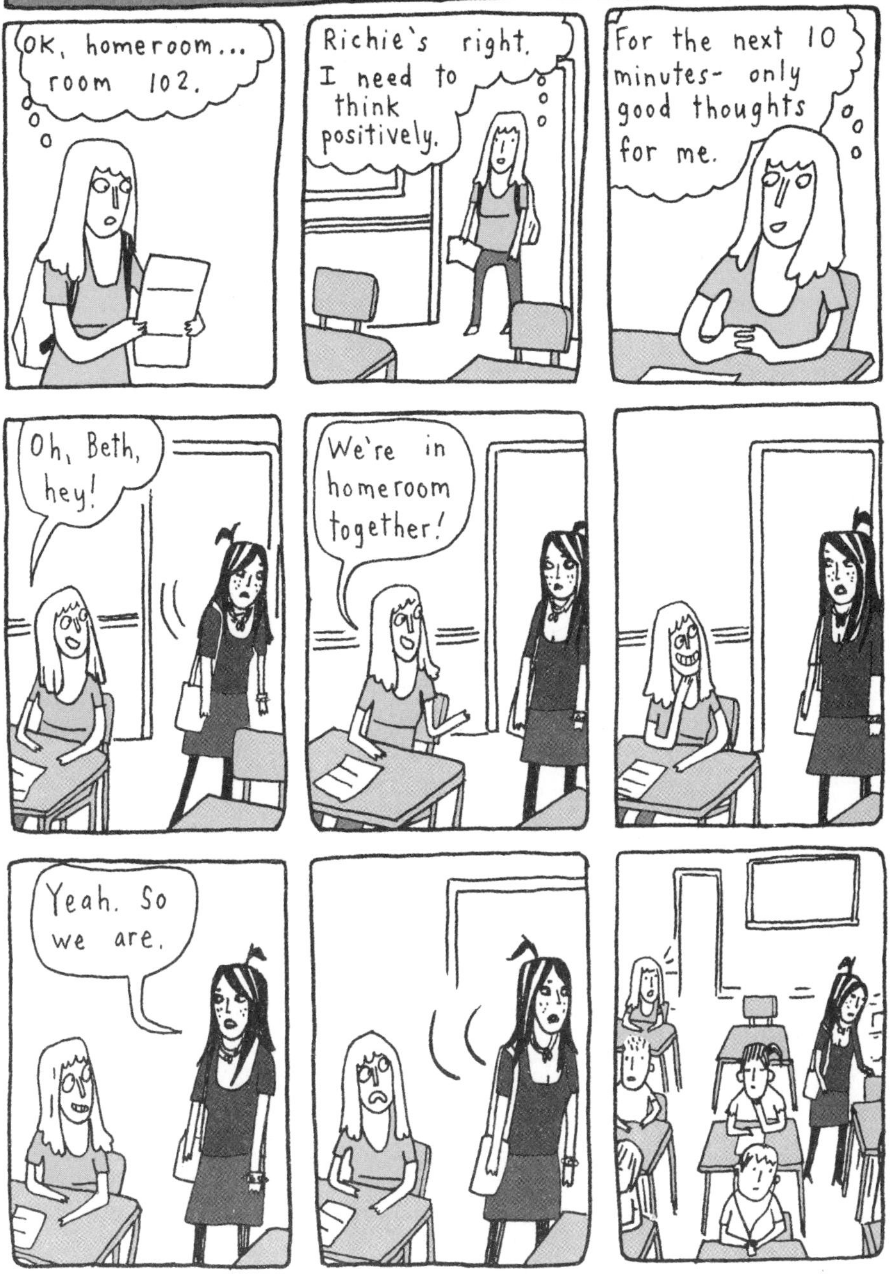
OK, homeroom... room 102.
Richie's right. I need to think positively.
For the next 10 minutes- only good thoughts for me.
Oh, Beth, hey!
We're in homeroom together!
Yeah. So we are.

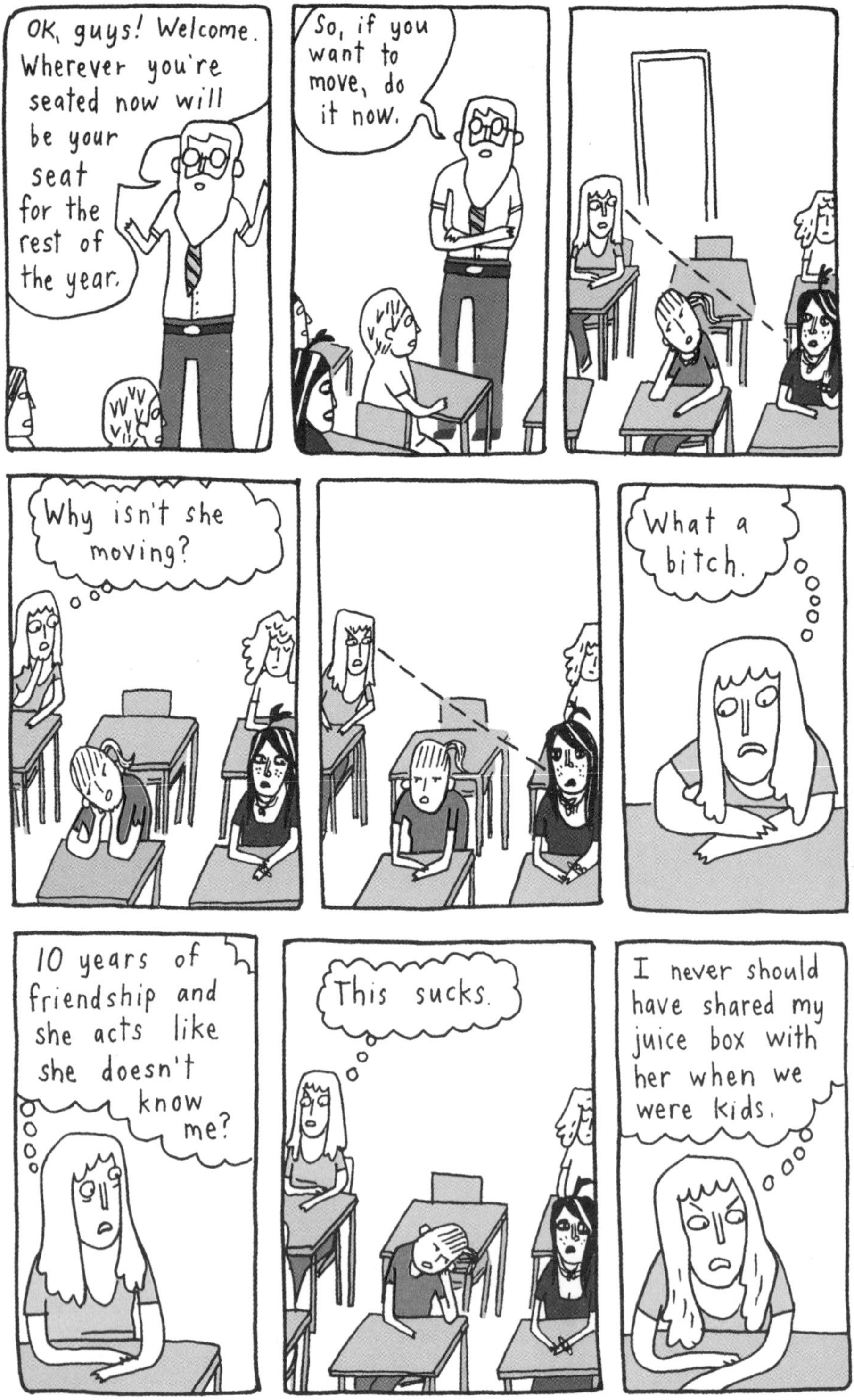
OK, guys! Welcome. Wherever you're seated now will be your seat for the rest of the year.
So, if you want to move, do it now.
Why isn't she moving?
What a bitch.
10 years of friendship and she acts like she doesn't know me?
This sucks.
I never should have shared my juice box with her when we were kids.

PENCIL, PAPER, PERIOD ONE

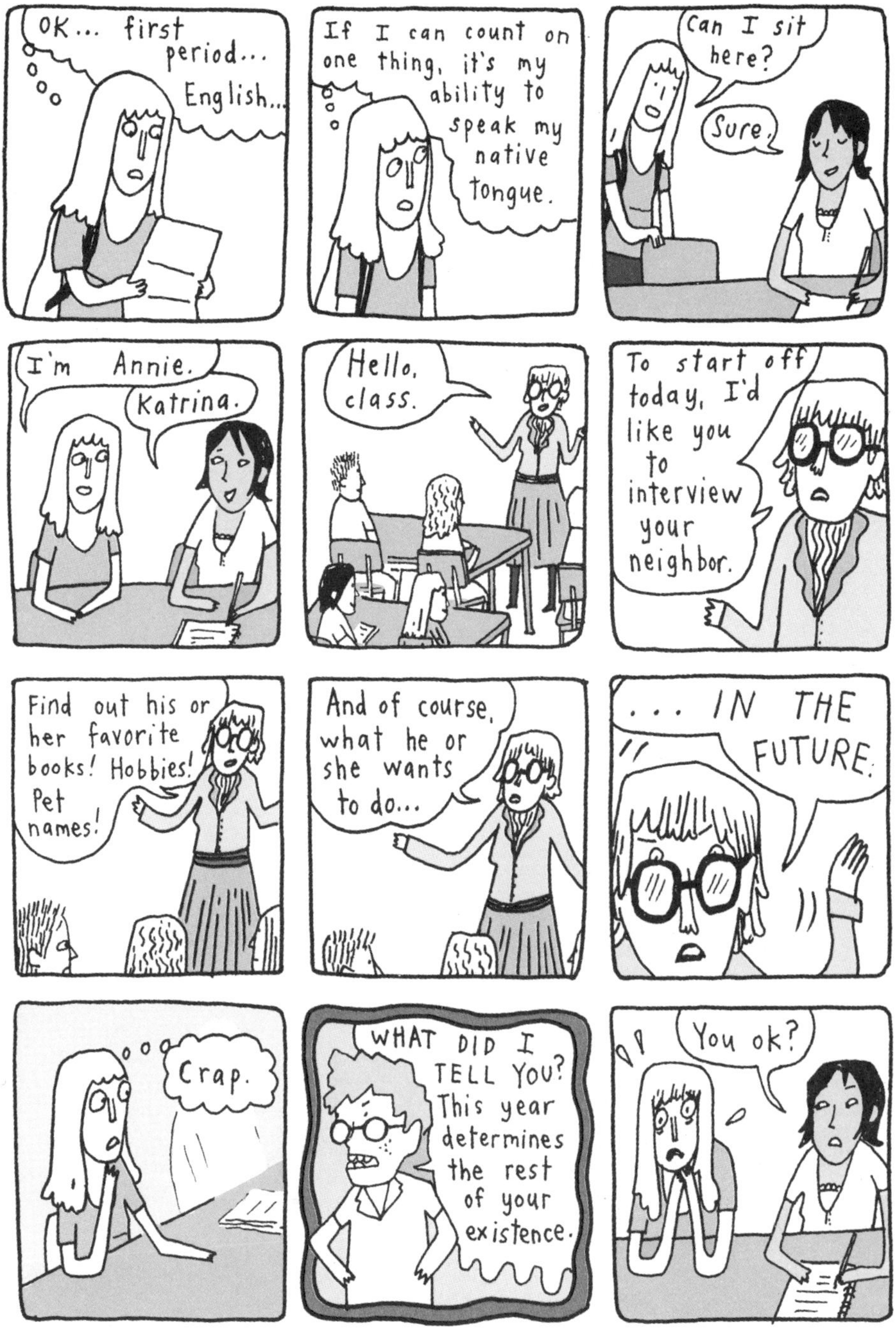

OK... first period... English...
If I can count on one thing, it's my ability to speak my native tongue.
Can I sit here?
Sure.
I'm Annie.
Katrina.
Hello, class.
To start off today, I'd like you to interview your neighbor.
Find out his or her favorite books! Hobbies! Pet names!
And of course, what he or she wants to do...
... IN THE FUTURE.
Crap.
WHAT DID I TELL YOU? This year determines the rest of your existence.
You ok?

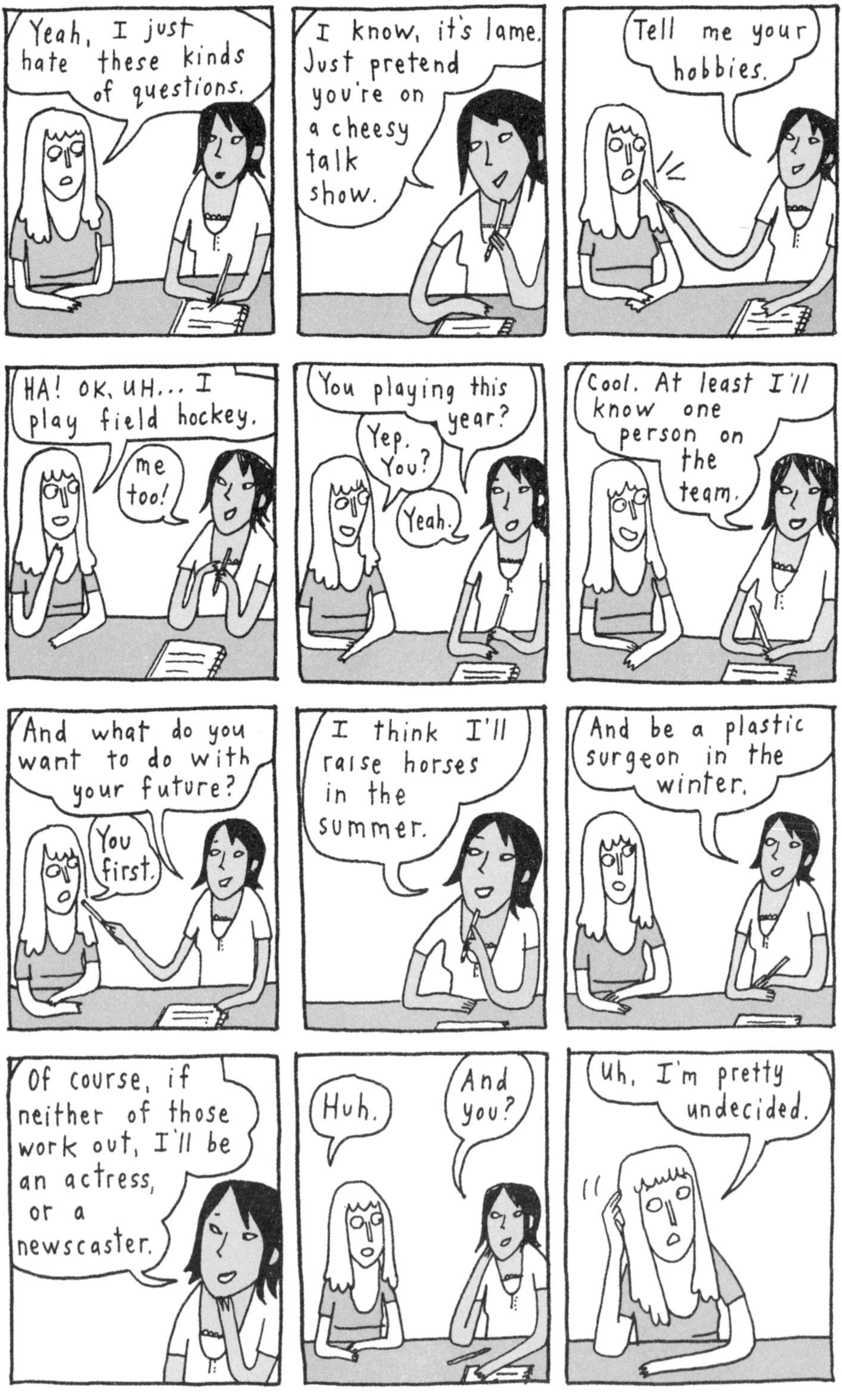
Yeah, I just hate these kinds of questions.
I know, it's lame. Just pretend you're on a cheesy talk show.
Tell me your hobbies.
HA! OK, UH... I play field hockey.
me too!
You playing this year?
Yep. You?
Yeah.
Cool. At least I'll know one person on the team.
And what do you want to do with your future?
You first.
I think I'll raise horses in the summer.
And be a plastic surgeon in the winter.
Of course, if neither of those work out, I'll be an actress, or a newscaster.
Huh.
And you?
Uh, I'm pretty undecided.

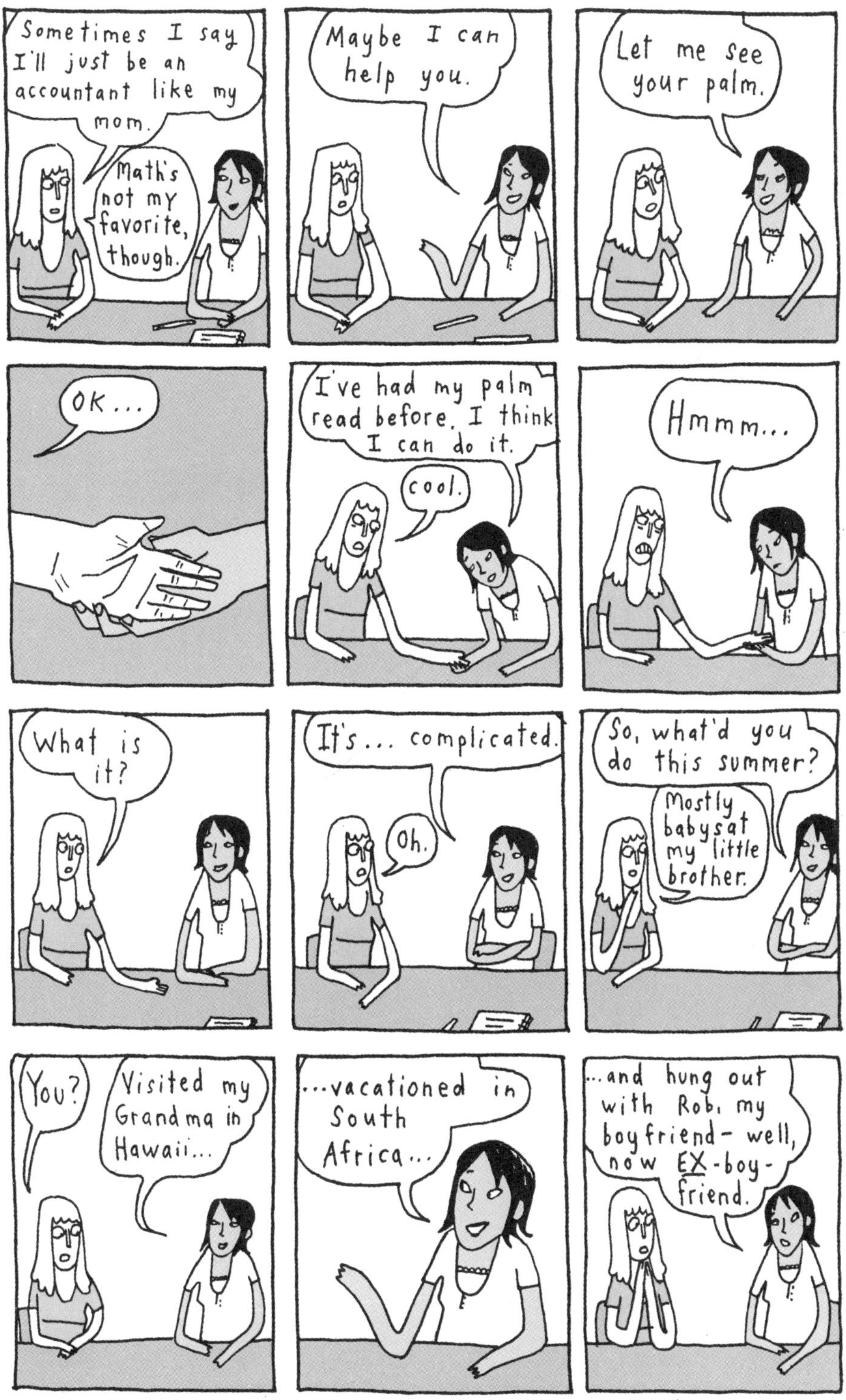
Sometimes I say I'll just be an accountant like my mom.
Math's not my favorite, though.
Maybe I can help you.
Let me see your palm.
OK...
I've had my palm read before. I think I can do it.
cool.
Hmmm...
What is it?
It's... complicated.
Oh.
So, what'd you do this summer?
Mostly babysat my little brother.
You?
Visited my Grandma in Hawaii...
...vacationed in South Africa...
...and hung out with Rob, my boyfriend - well, now EX-boy-friend.

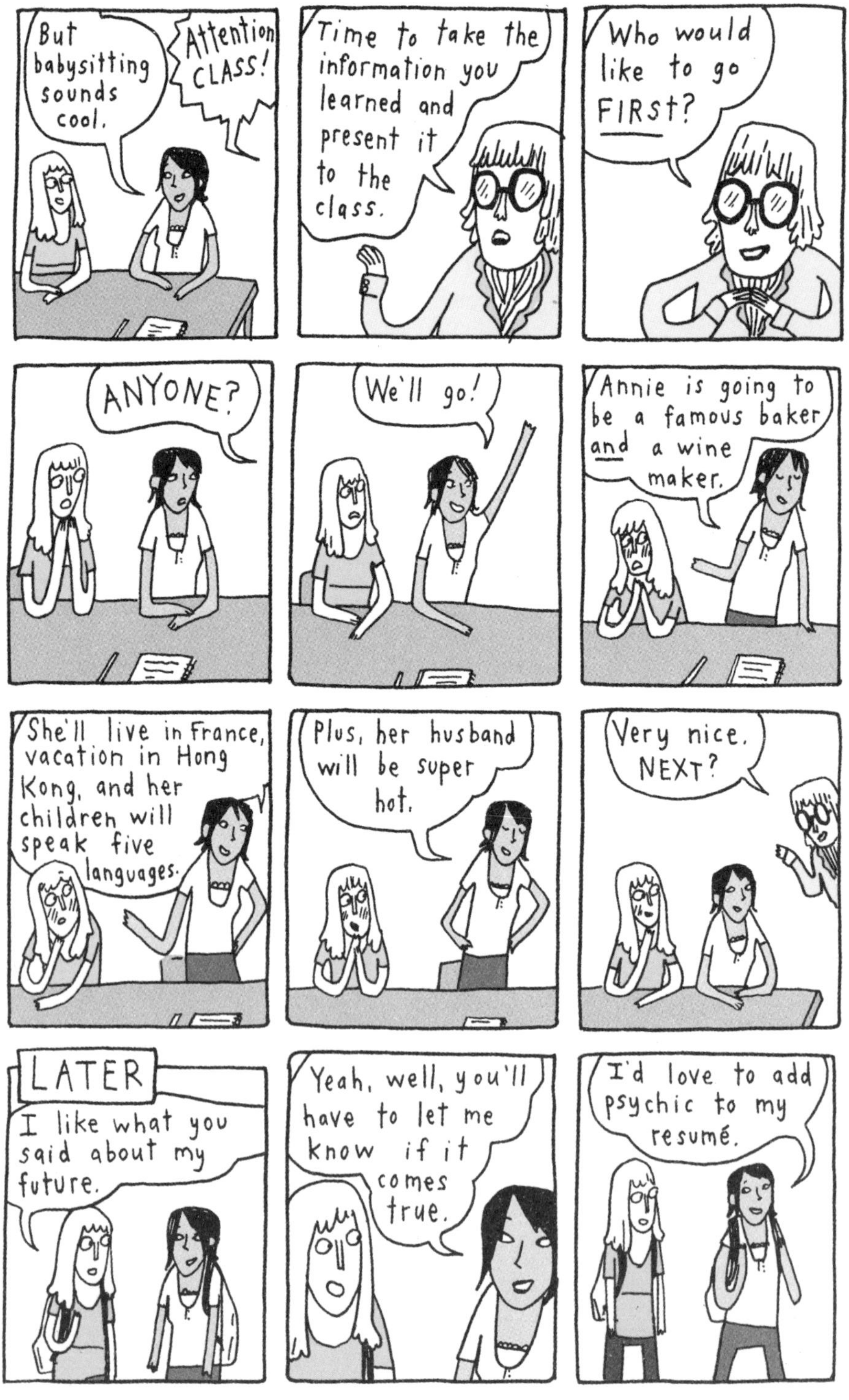
But babysitting sounds cool.
Attention CLASS!
Time to take the information you learned and present it to the class.
Who would like to go FIRST?
ANYONE?
We'll go!
Annie is going to be a famous baker and a wine maker.
She'll live in France, vacation in Hong Kong, and her children will speak five languages.
Plus, her husband will be super hot.
Very nice. NEXT?
LATER
I like what you said about my future.
Yeah, well, you'll have to let me know if it comes true.
I'd love to add psychic to my resumé.

THE RIGHT COMBINATION

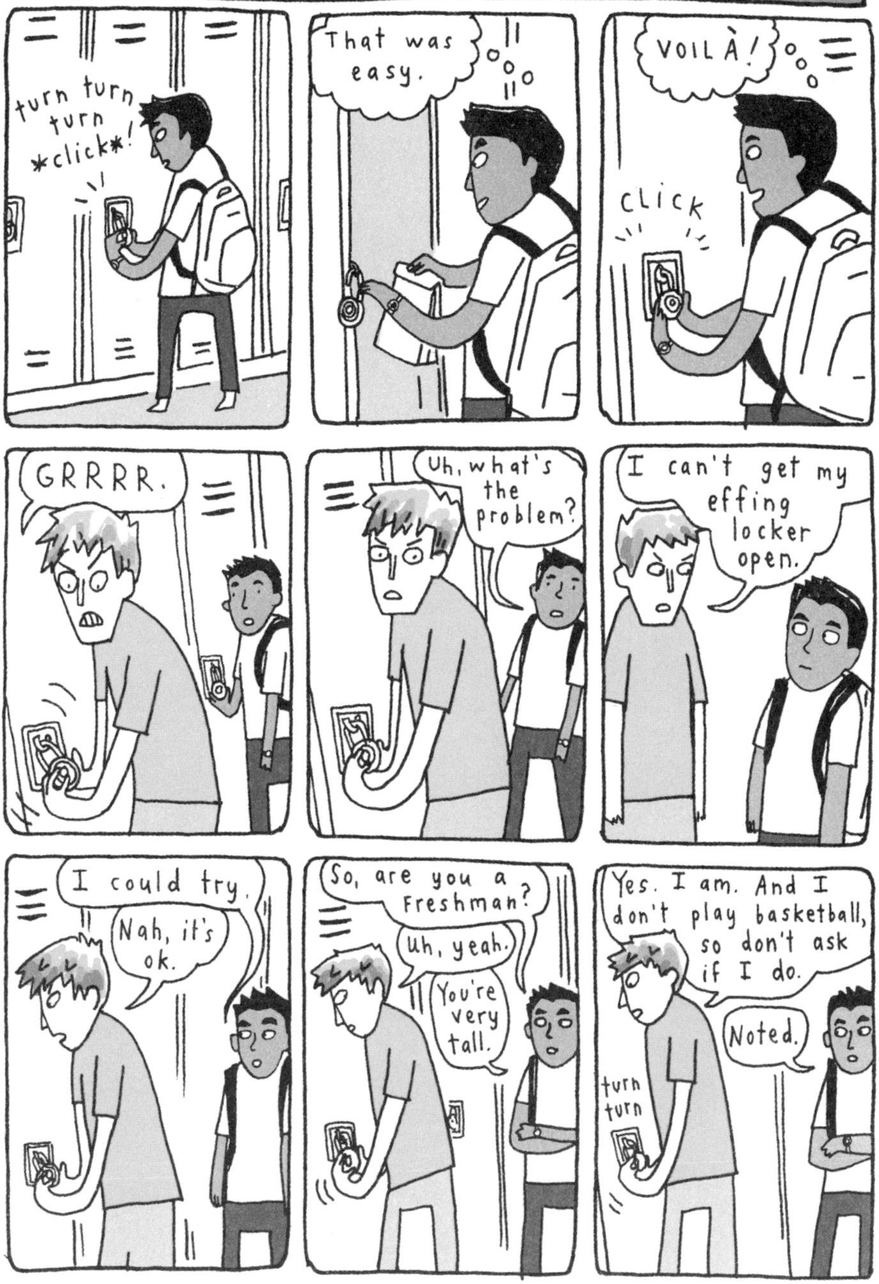
turn turn turn *click*!
That was easy.
VOILÀ!
CLICK
GRRRR.
Uh, what's the problem?
I can't get my effing locker open.
I could try.
Nah, it's ok.
So, are you a Freshman?
Uh, yeah.
You're very tall.
Yes. I am. And I don't play basketball, so don't ask if I do.
Noted.
turn turn

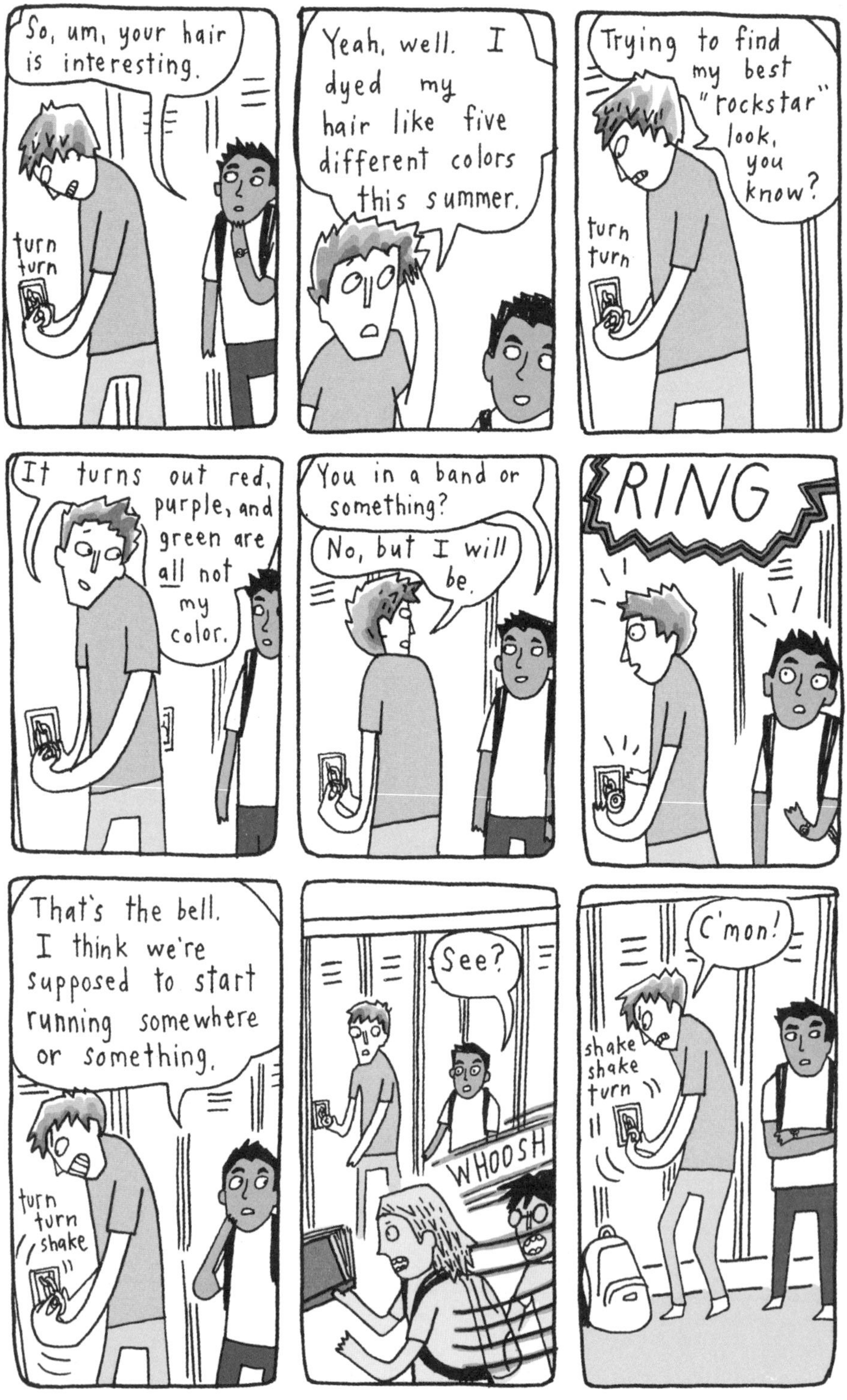
So, um, your hair is interesting.
turn turn
Yeah, well. I dyed my hair like five different colors this summer.
Trying to find my best "rockstar" look, you know?
turn turn
It turns out red, purple, and green are all not my color.
You in a band or something?
No, but I will be.
RING
That's the bell. I think we're supposed to start running somewhere or something.
turn turn shake
See?
WHOOSH
C'mon!
shake shake turn

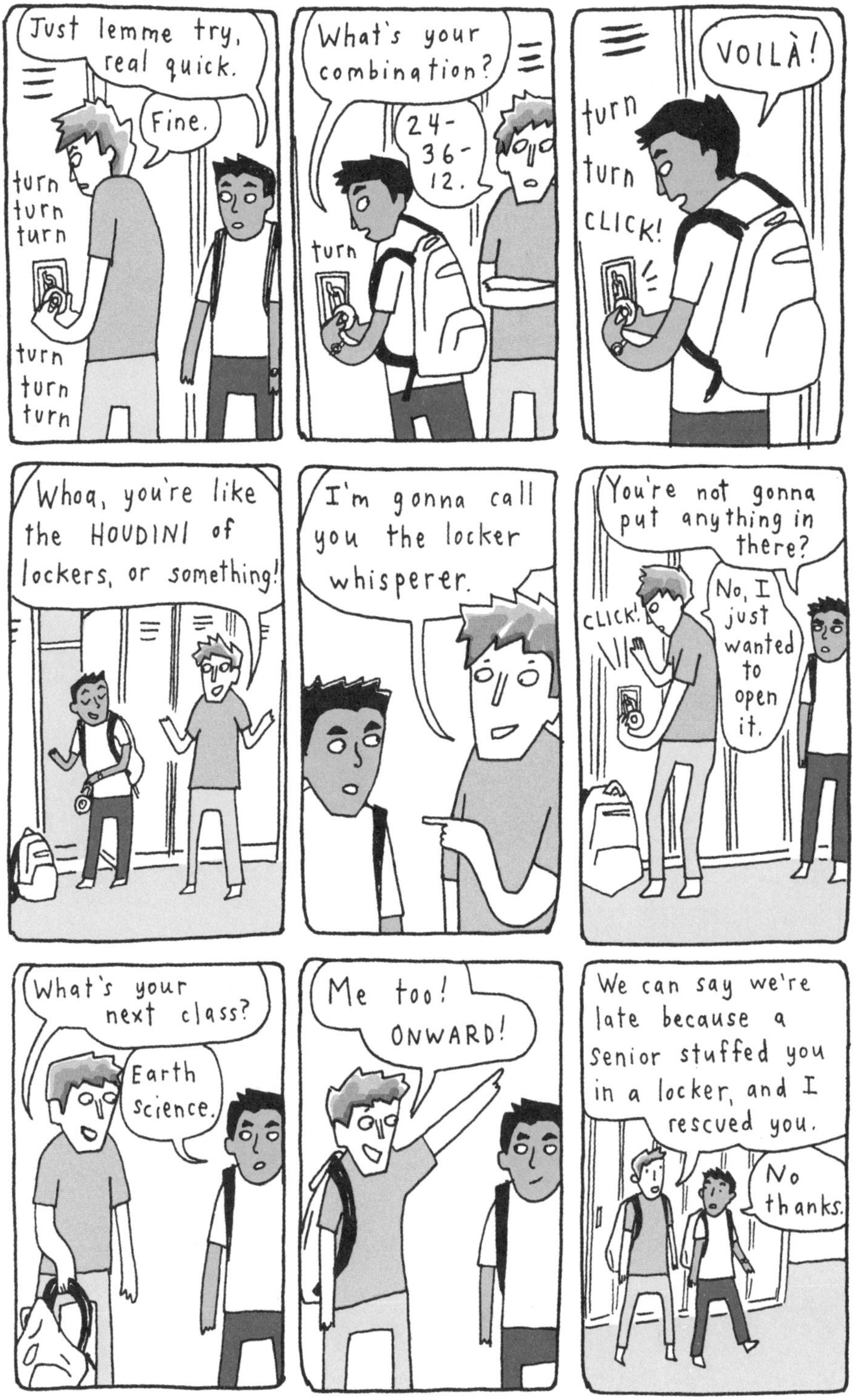
Just lemme try, real quick.
Fine.
turn turn turn
turn turn turn
What's your combination?
24-36-12.
turn
VOILÀ!
turn
turn
CLICK!
Whoa, you're like the HOUDINI of lockers, or something!
I'm gonna call you the locker whisperer.
You're not gonna put anything in there?
No, I just wanted to open it.
CLICK!
What's your next class?
Earth science.
Me too! ONWARD!
We can say we're late because a senior stuffed you in a locker, and I rescued you.
No thanks.

DON'T PRACTICE, YOU'RE PERFECT

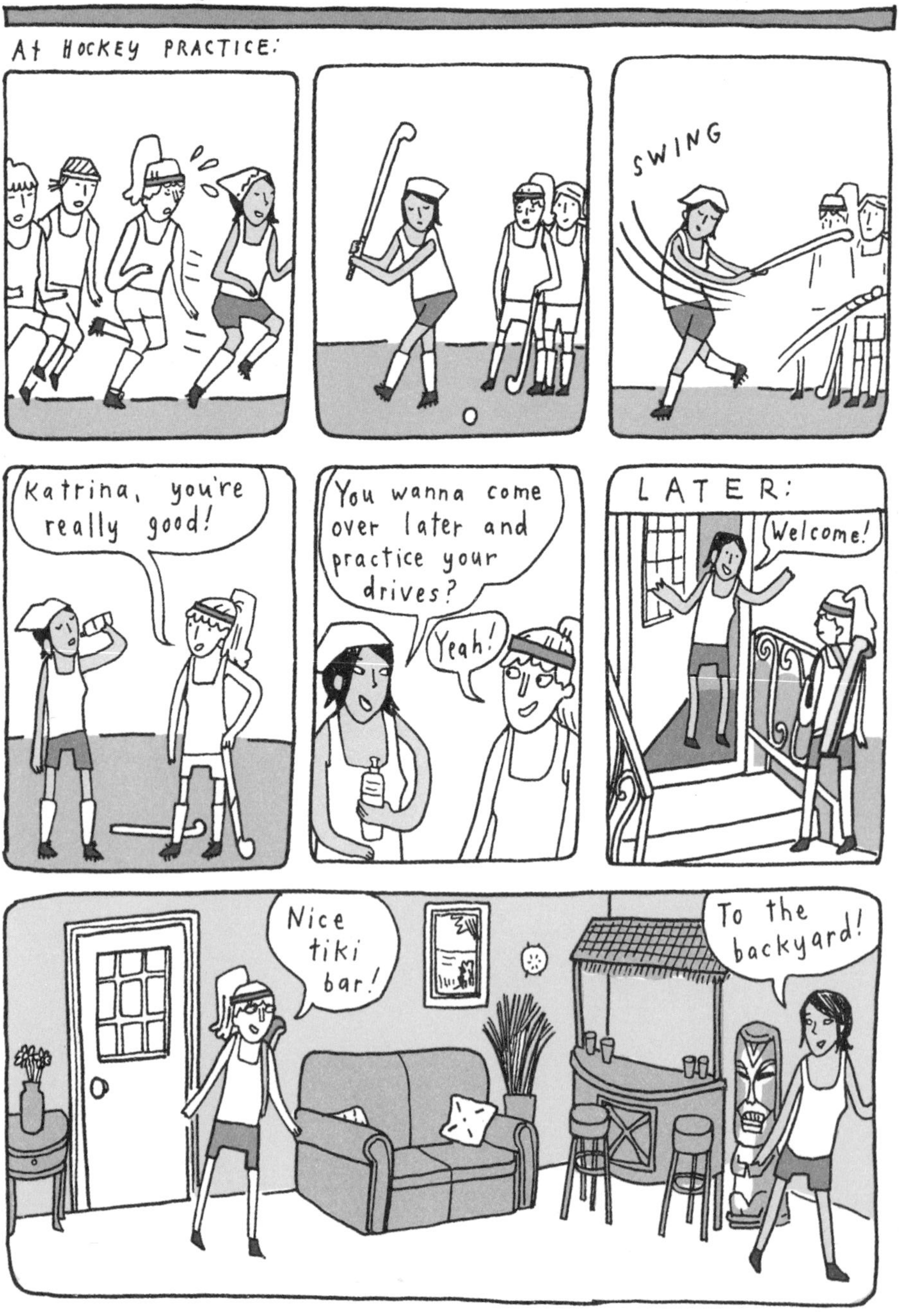
AT HOCKEY PRACTICE:
SWING
Katrina, you're really good!
You wanna come over later and practice your drives?
Yeah!
LATER:
Welcome!
Nice tiki bar!
To the backyard!

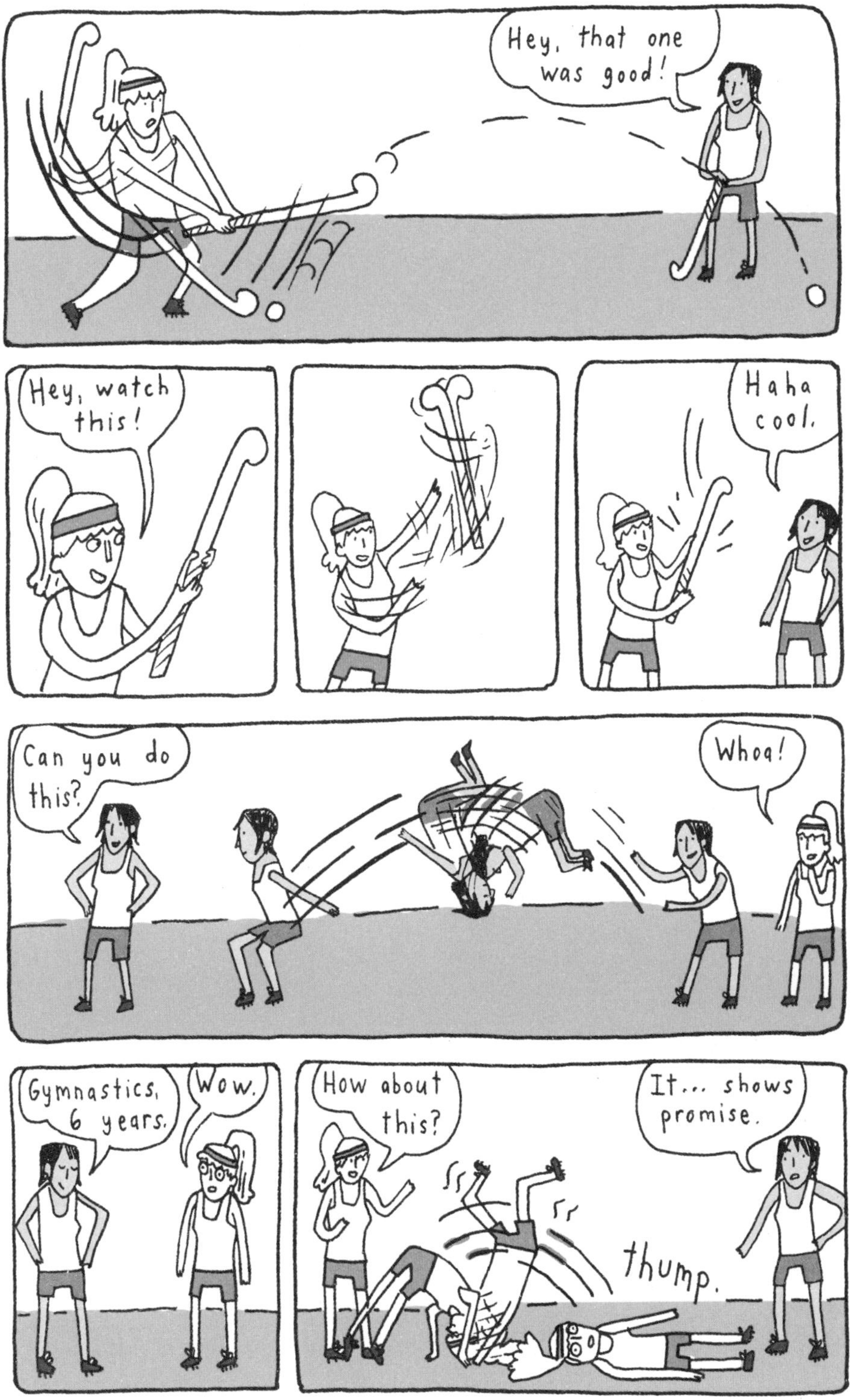
Hey, that one was good!
Hey, watch this!
Haha cool.
Can you do this?
Whoa!
Gymnastics, 6 years.
Wow.
How about this?
It... shows promise.
thump.

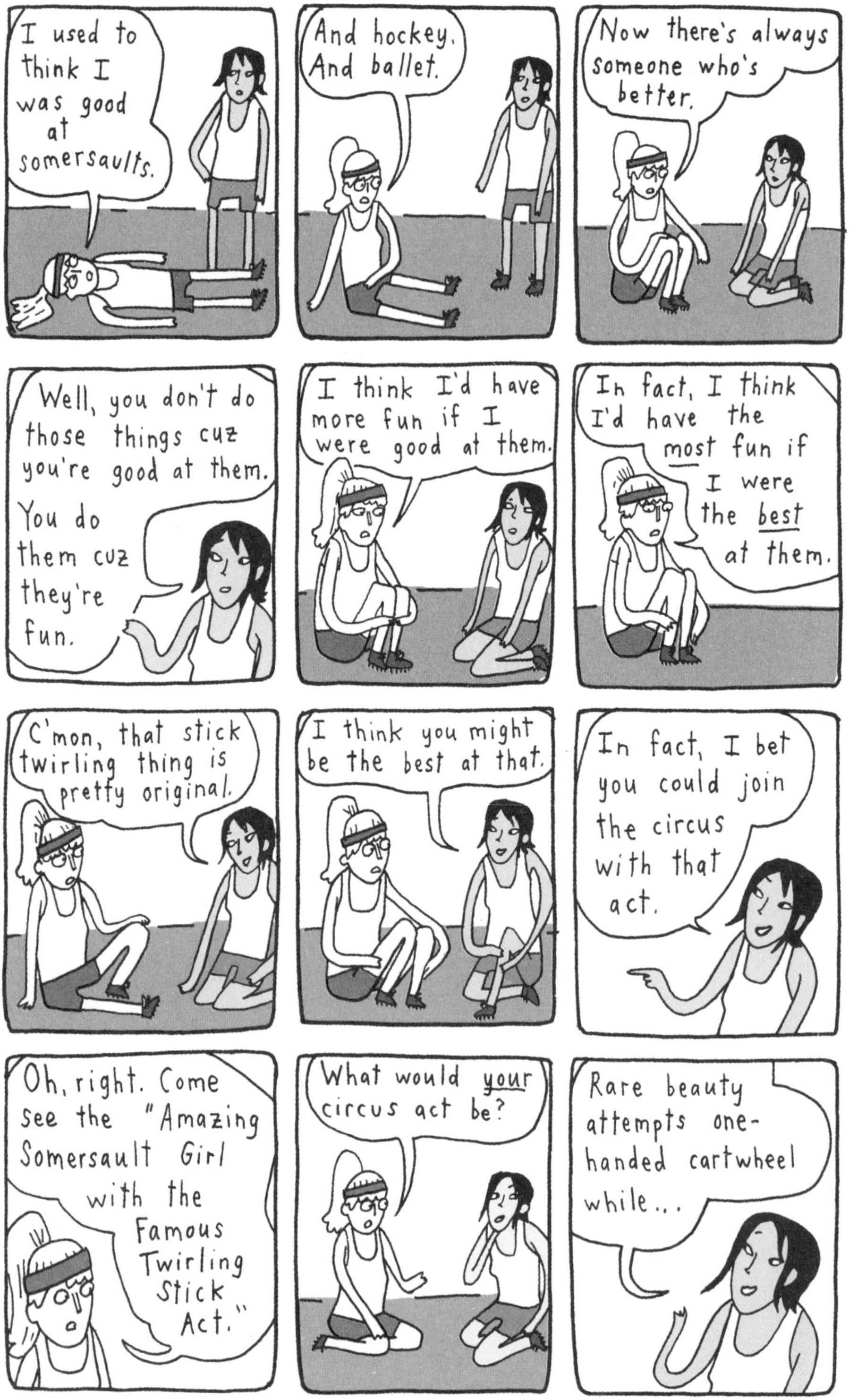
I used to think I was good at somersaults.
And hockey. And ballet.
Now there's always someone who's better.
Well, you don't do those things cuz you're good at them.
You do them cuz they're fun.
I think I'd have more fun if I were good at them.
In fact, I think I'd have the most fun if I were the best at them.
C'mon, that stick twirling thing is pretty original.
I think you might be the best at that.
In fact, I bet you could join the circus with that act.
Oh, right. Come see the "Amazing Somersault Girl with the Famous Twirling Stick Act."
What would your circus act be?
Rare beauty attempts one-handed cartwheel while...

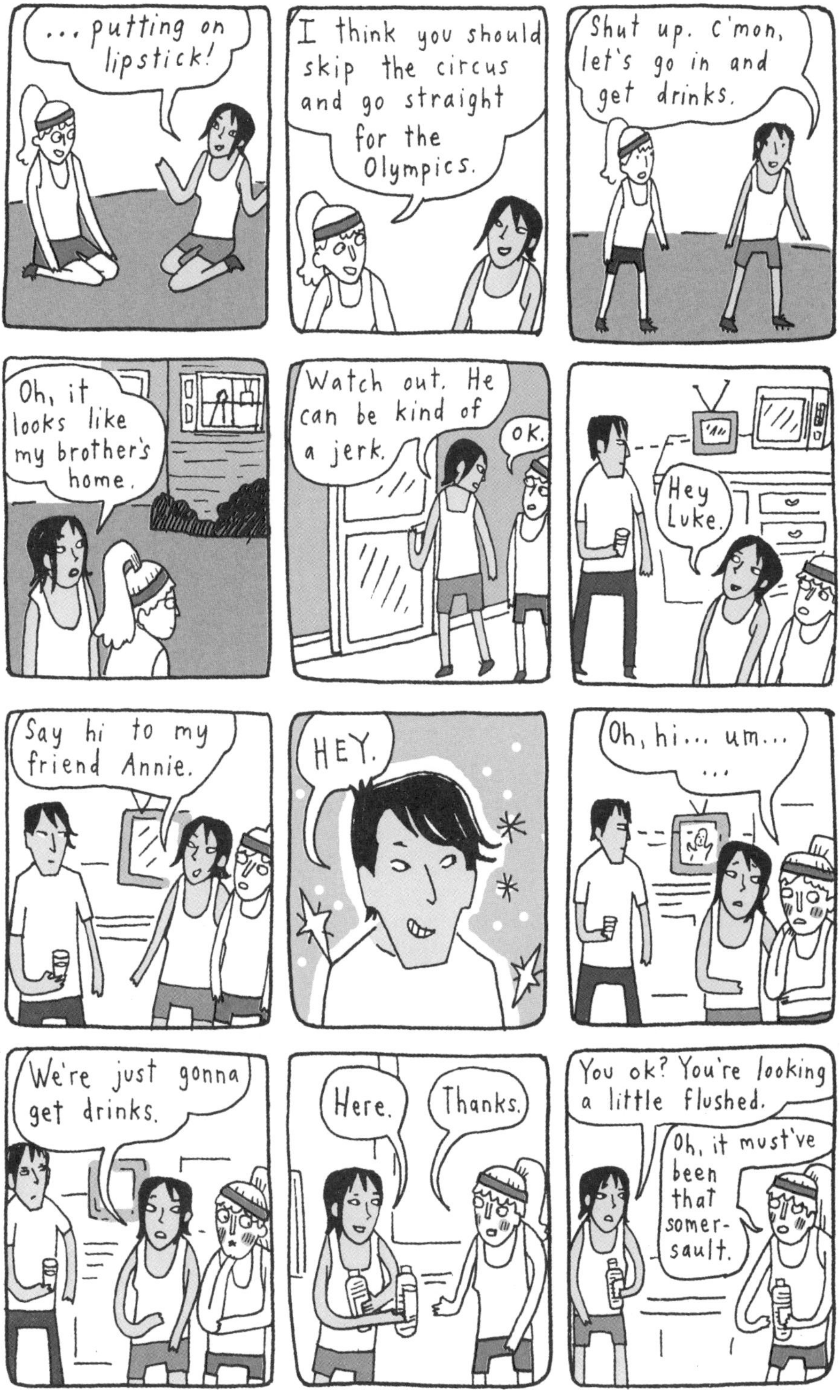
...putting on lipstick!
I think you should skip the circus and go straight for the Olympics.
Shut up. C'mon, let's go in and get drinks.
Oh, it looks like my brother's home.
Watch out. He can be kind of a jerk.
OK.
Hey Luke.
Say hi to my friend Annie.
HEY.
Oh, hi... um... ...
We're just gonna get drinks.
Here.
Thanks.
You ok? You're looking a little flushed.
Oh, it must've been that somer-sault.

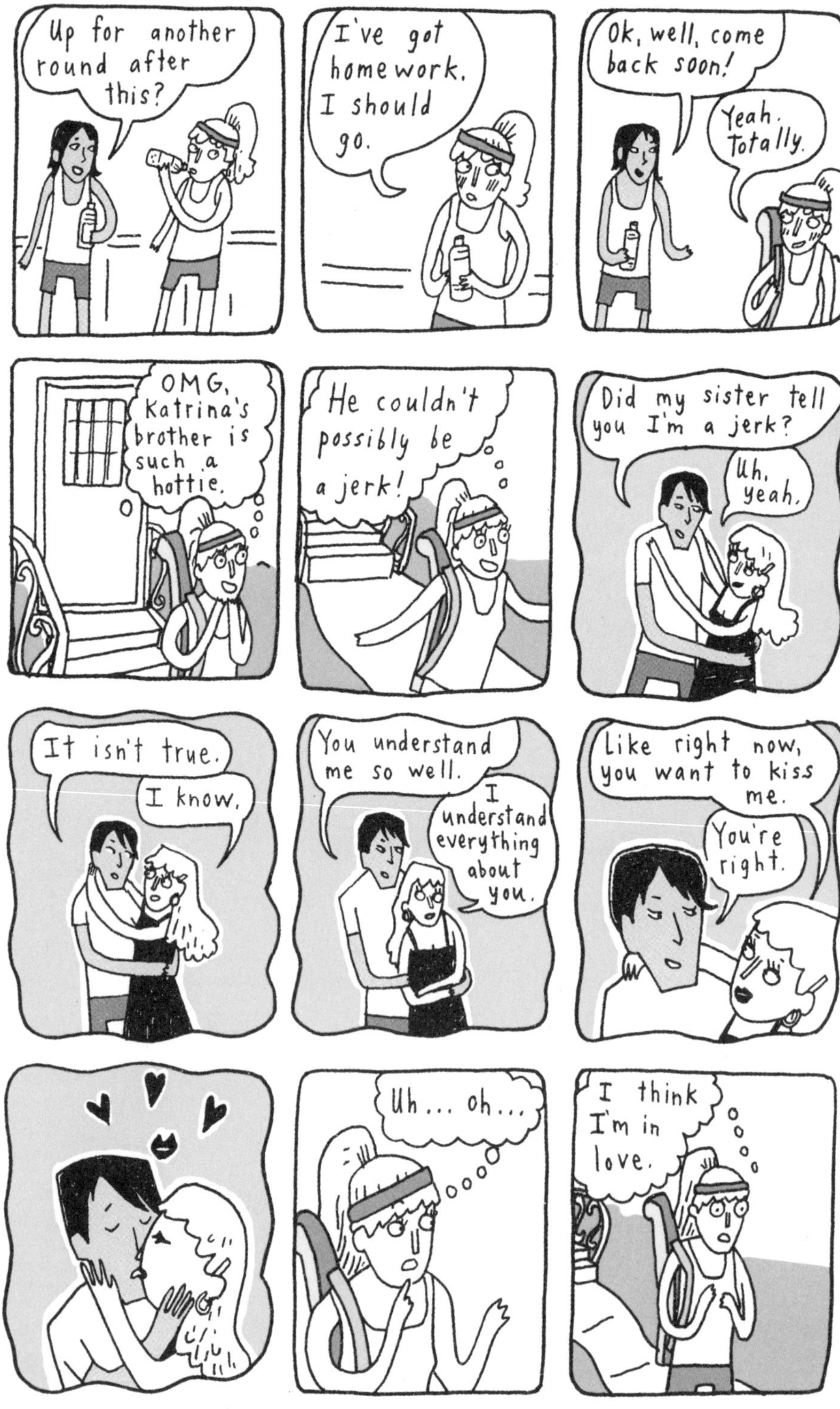
Up for another round after this?
I've got homework. I should go.
Ok, well, come back soon!
Yeah. Totally.
OMG, Katrina's brother is such a hottie.
He couldn't possibly be a jerk!
Did my sister tell you I'm a jerk?
Uh, yeah.
It isn't true.
I know.
You understand me so well.
I understand everything about you.
Like right now, you want to kiss me.
You're right.
Uh... oh...
I think I'm in love.

SPIRIT WEEK

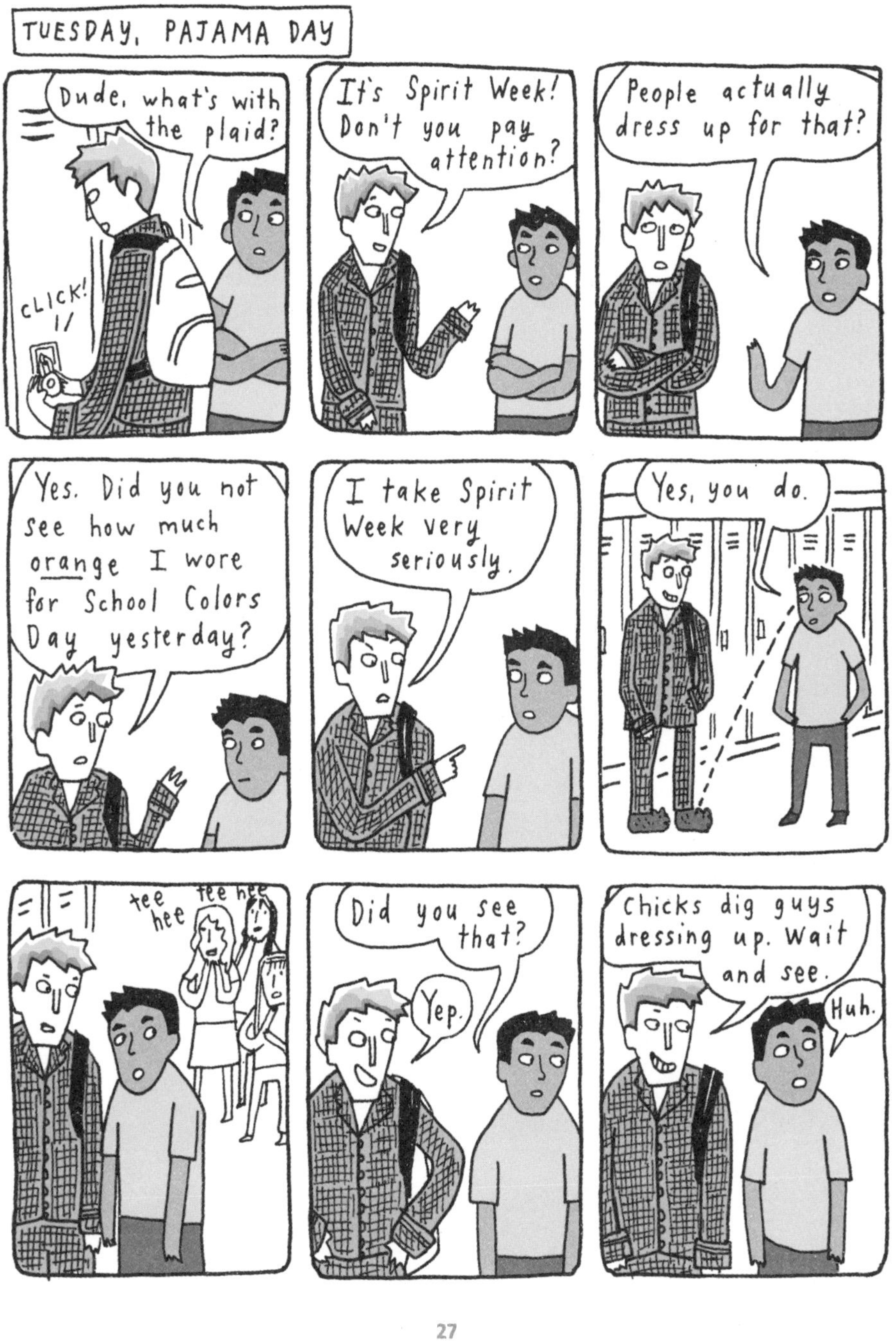
TUESDAY, PAJAMA DAY
Dude, what's with the plaid?
CLICK!
It's Spirit Week! Don't you pay attention?
People actually dress up for that?
Yes. Did you not see how much orange I wore for School Colors Day yesterday?
I take Spirit Week very seriously.
Yes, you do.
tee hee
tee hee
Did you see that?
Yep.
Chicks dig guys dressing up. Wait and see.
Huh.

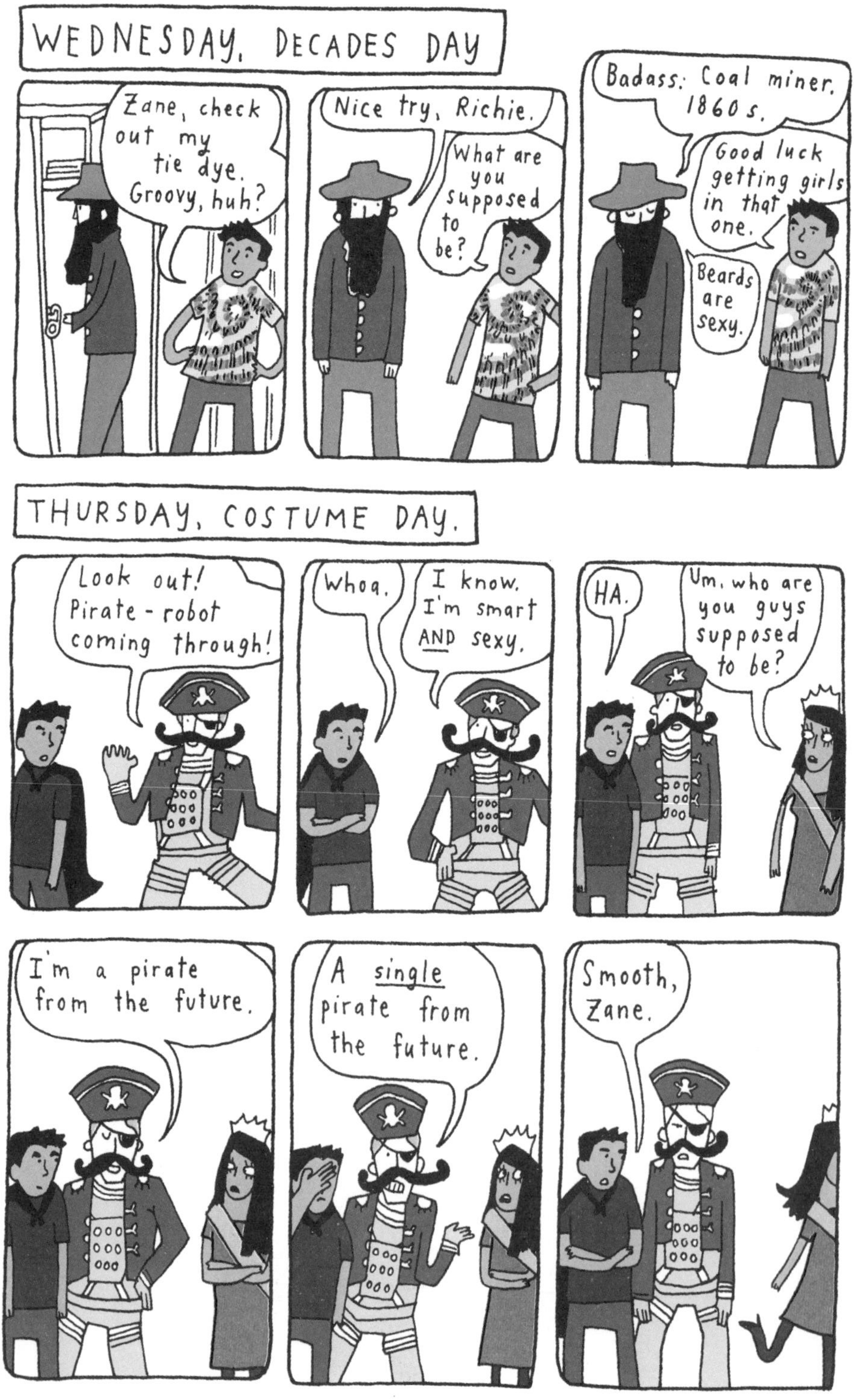
WEDNESDAY, DECADES DAY
Zane, check out my tie dye. Groovy, huh?
Nice try, Richie.
What are you supposed to be?
Badass: Coal miner. 1860s.
Good luck getting girls in that one.
Beards are sexy.
THURSDAY, COSTUME DAY.
Look out! Pirate-robot coming through!
Whoa.
I know. I'm smart AND sexy.
HA.
Um, who are you guys supposed to be?
I'm a pirate from the future.
A single pirate from the future.
Smooth, Zane.

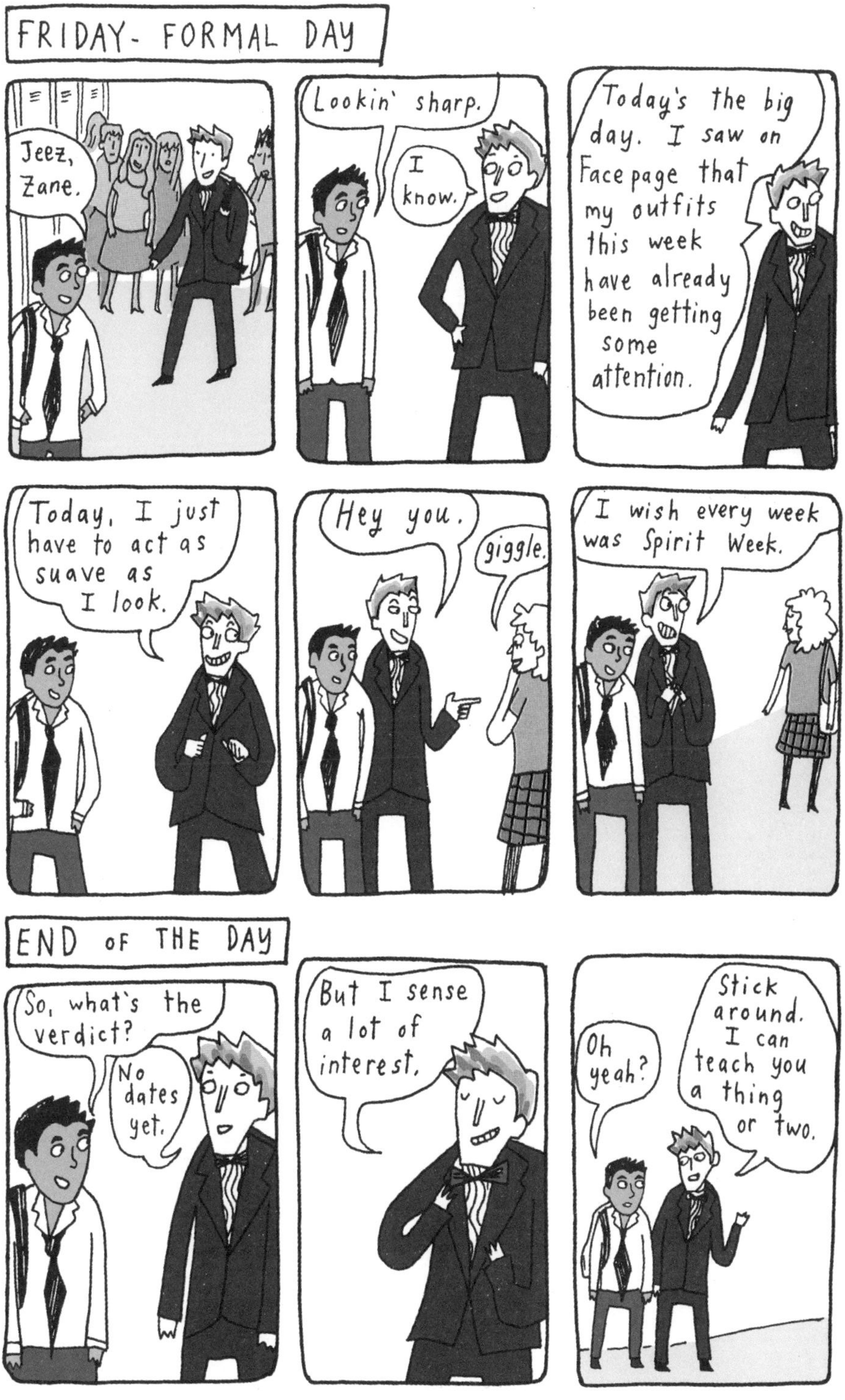
FRIDAY- FORMAL DAY
Jeez, Zane.
Lookin' sharp.
I know.
Today's the big day. I saw on Facepage that my outfits this week have already been getting some attention.
Today, I just have to act as suave as I look.
Hey you.
giggle.
I wish every week was Spirit Week.
END OF THE DAY
So, what's the verdict?
No dates yet.
But I sense a lot of interest.
Oh yeah?
Stick around. I can teach you a thing or two.

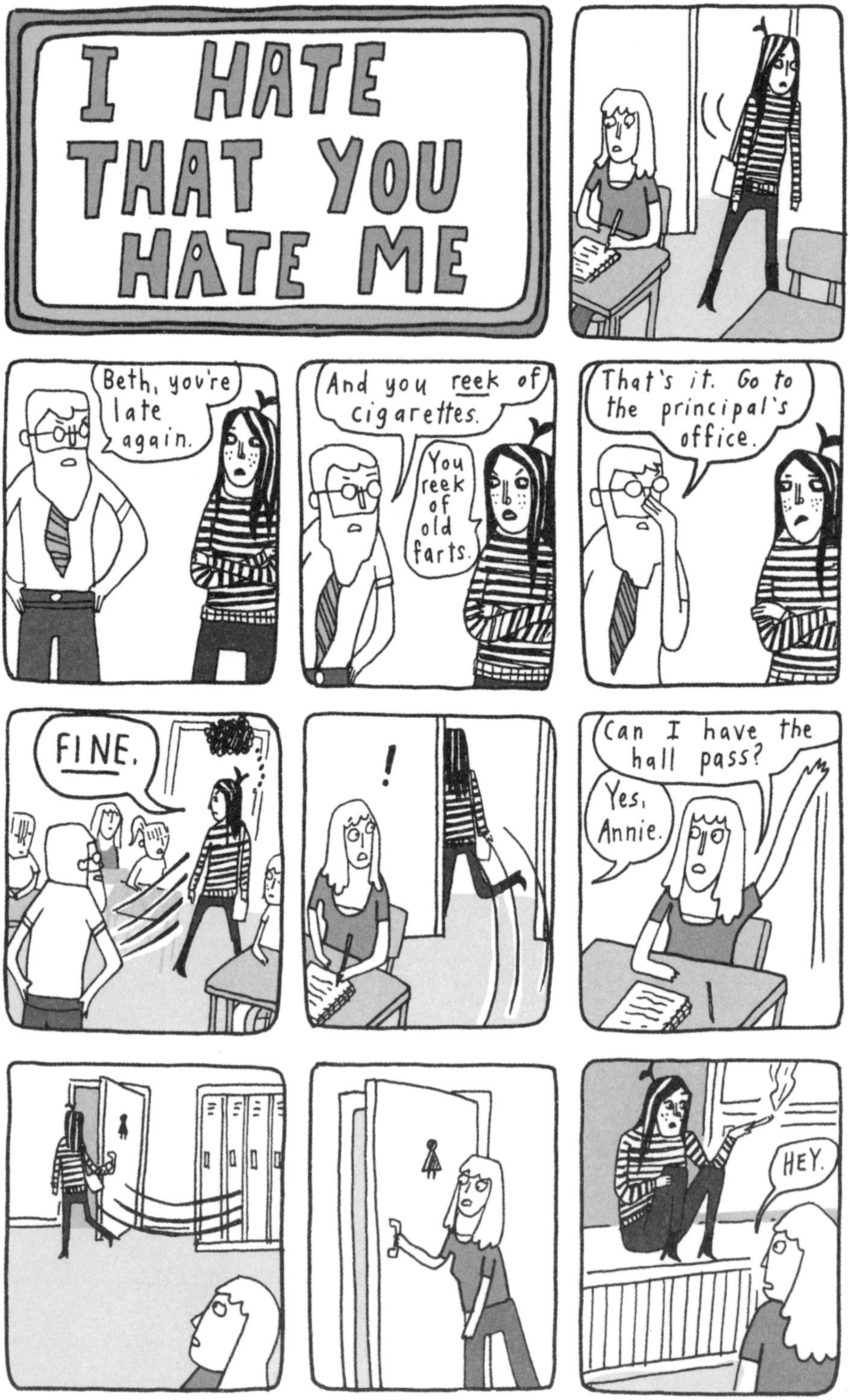
I HATE THAT YOU HATE ME
Beth, you're late again.
And you reek of cigarettes.
You reek of old farts.
That's it. Go to the principal's office.
FINE.
!
Can I have the hall pass?
Yes, Annie.
HEY.

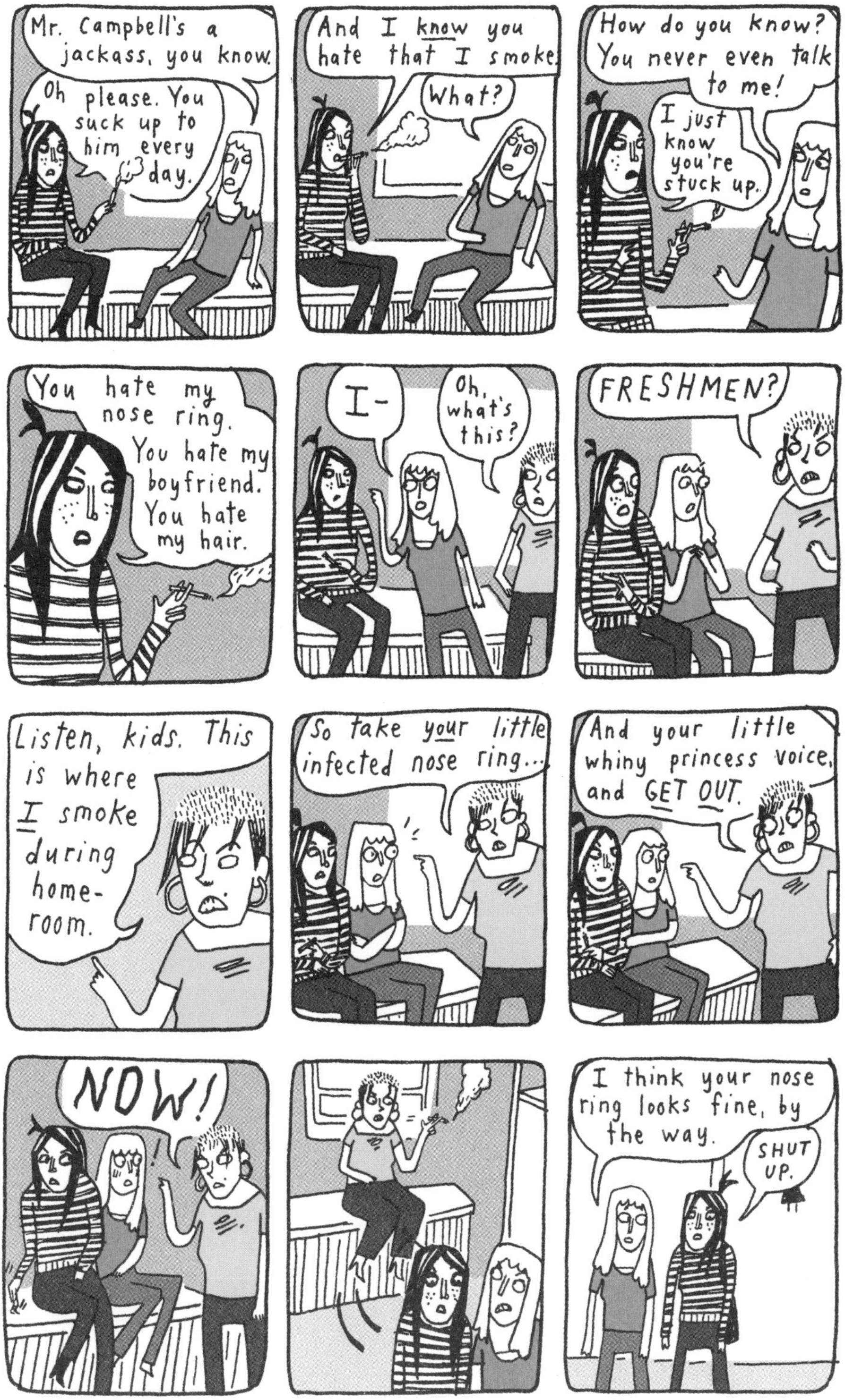
Mr. Campbell's a jackass, you know.
Oh please. You suck up to him every day.
And I know you hate that I smoke.
What?
How do you know? You never even talk to me!
I just know you're stuck up.
You hate my nose ring. You hate my boyfriend. You hate my hair.
I-
Oh, what's this?
FRESHMEN?
Listen, kids. This is where I smoke during home-room.
So take your little infected nose ring...
And your little whiny princess voice, and GET OUT.
NOW!
I think your nose ring looks fine, by the way.
SHUT UP.

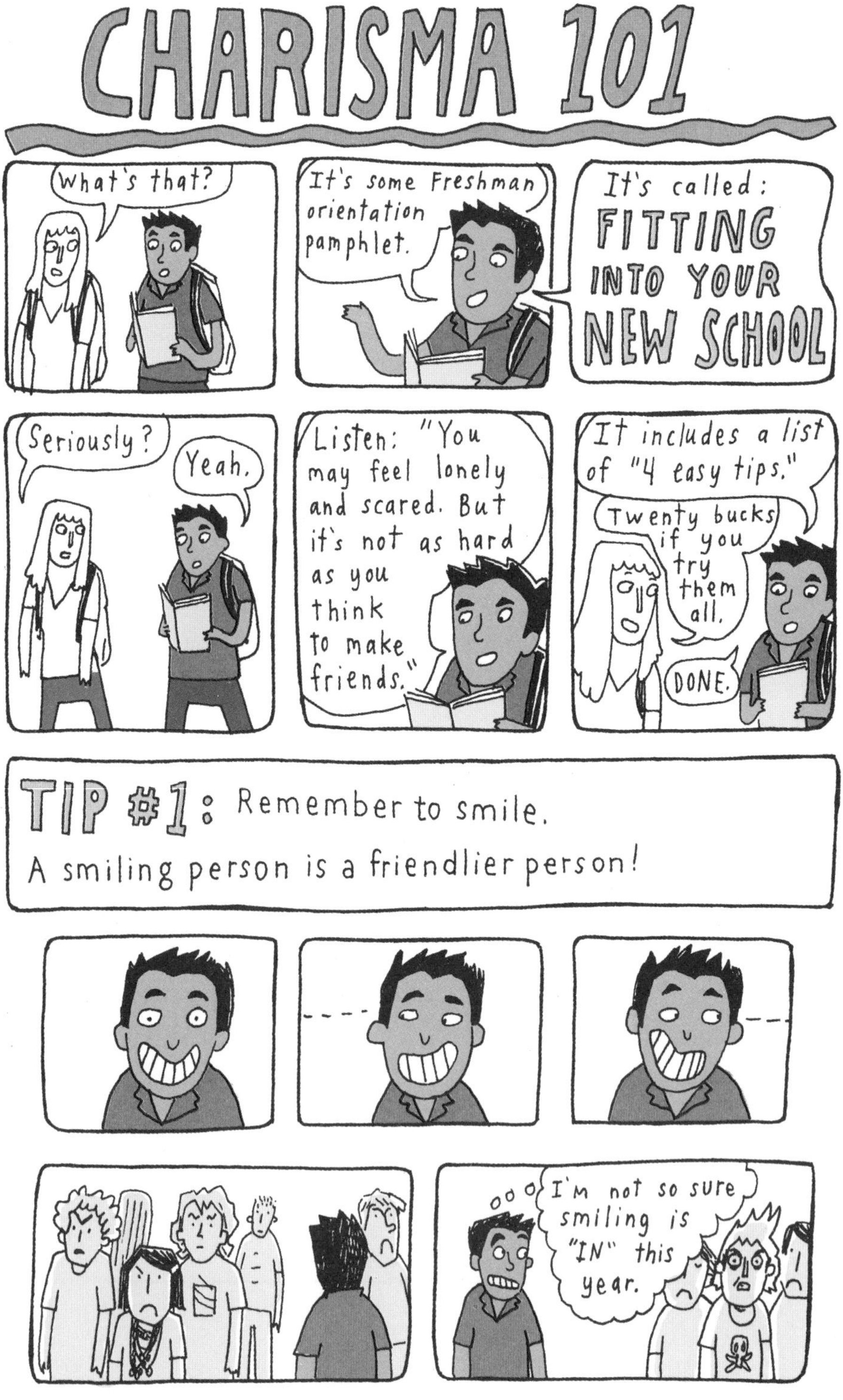
CHARISMA 101
What's that?
It's some Freshman orientation pamphlet.
It's called: FITTING INTO YOUR NEW SCHOOL
Seriously?
Yeah.
Listen: "You may feel lonely and scared. But it's not as hard as you think to make friends."
It includes a list of "4 easy tips."
Twenty bucks if you try them all.
DONE.
TIP #1: Remember to smile.
A smiling person is a friendlier person!
I'm not so sure smiling is "IN" this year.

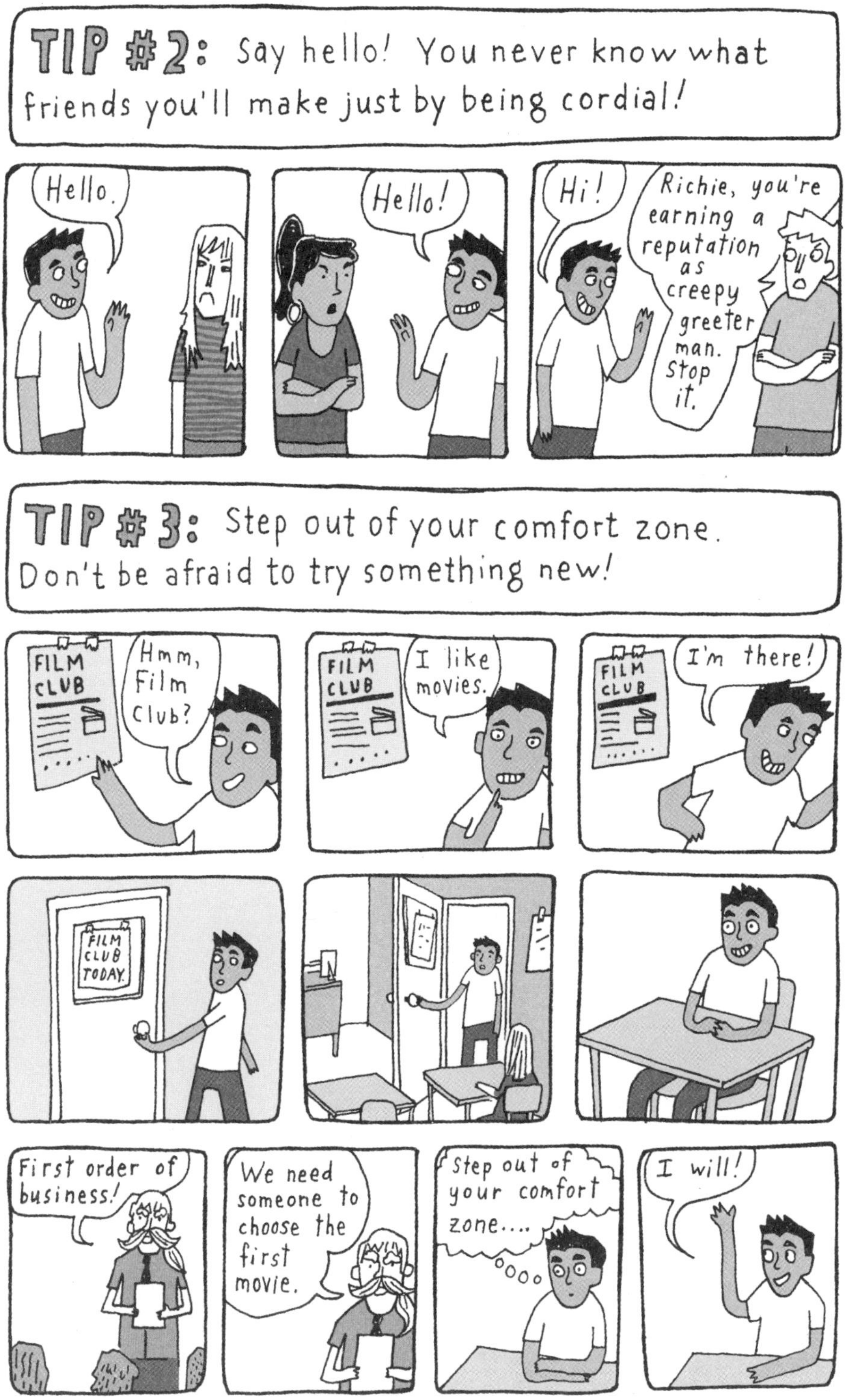
TIP #2: Say hello! You never know what friends you'll make just by being cordial!
Hello.
Hello!
Hi!
Richie, you're earning a reputation as creepy greeter man. Stop it.
TIP #3: Step out of your comfort zone. Don't be afraid to try something new!
FILM CLUB
Hmm, Film Club?
FILM CLUB
I like movies.
FILM CLUB
I'm there!
FILM CLUB TODAY.
First order of business!
We need someone to choose the first movie.
Step out of your comfort zone....
I will!

TIP #4 If you meet someone with common interests, don't be shy. If you like records, find out who else does, too!

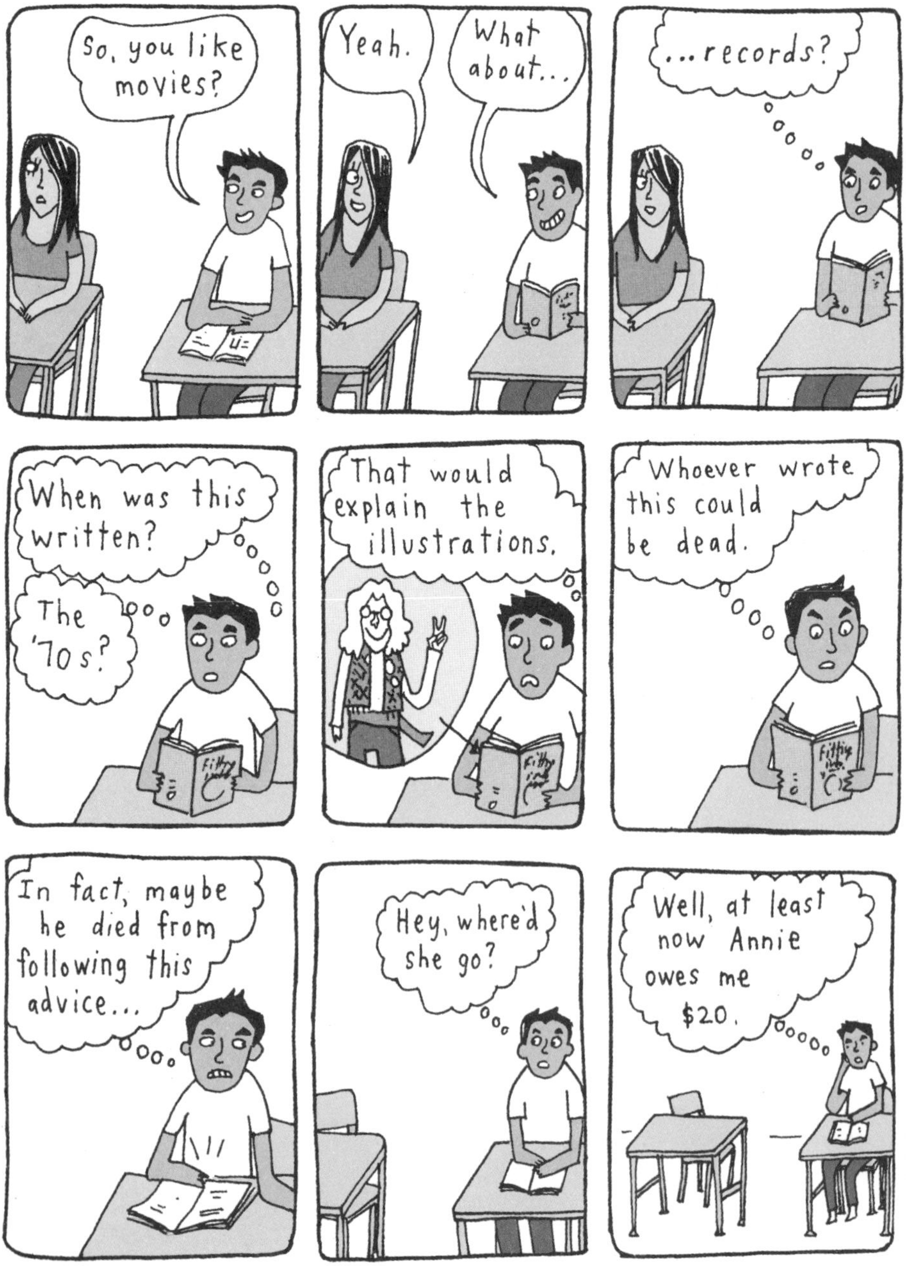

So, you like movies?
Yeah.
What about...
...records?
When was this written?
The '70s?
That would explain the illustrations.
Whoever wrote this could be dead.
In fact, maybe he died from following this advice...
Hey, where'd she go?
Well, at least now Annie owes me $20.

HOW to PLAN a Personal DEBACLE:

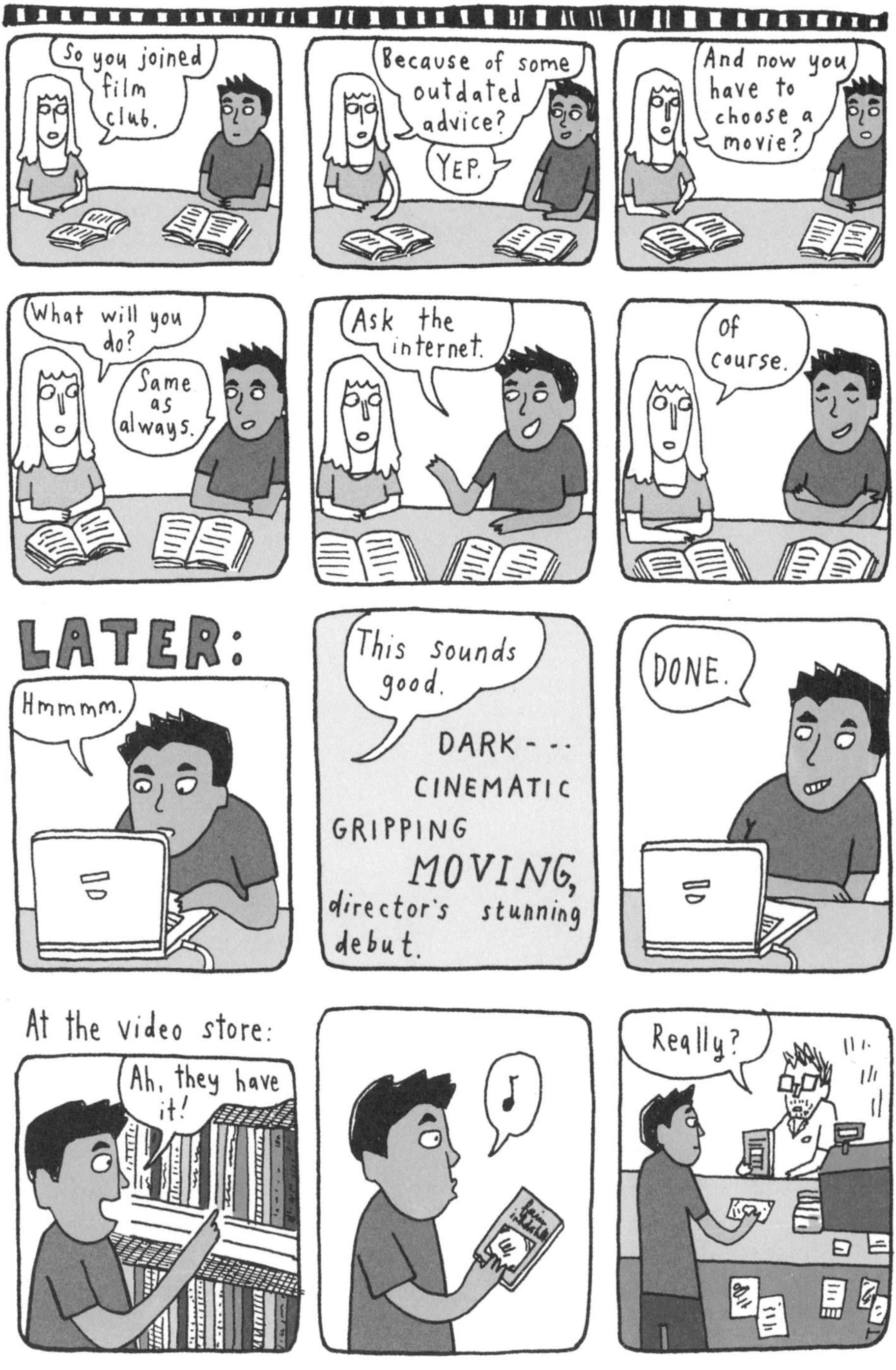
So you joined film club.
Because of some outdated advice?
YEP.
And now you have to choose a movie?
What will you do?
Same as always.
Ask the internet.
Of course.
LATER:
Hmmmm.
This sounds good.
DARK---
CINEMATIC
GRIPPING
MOVING,
director's stunning debut.
DONE.
At the video store:
Ah, they have it!
♪
Really?

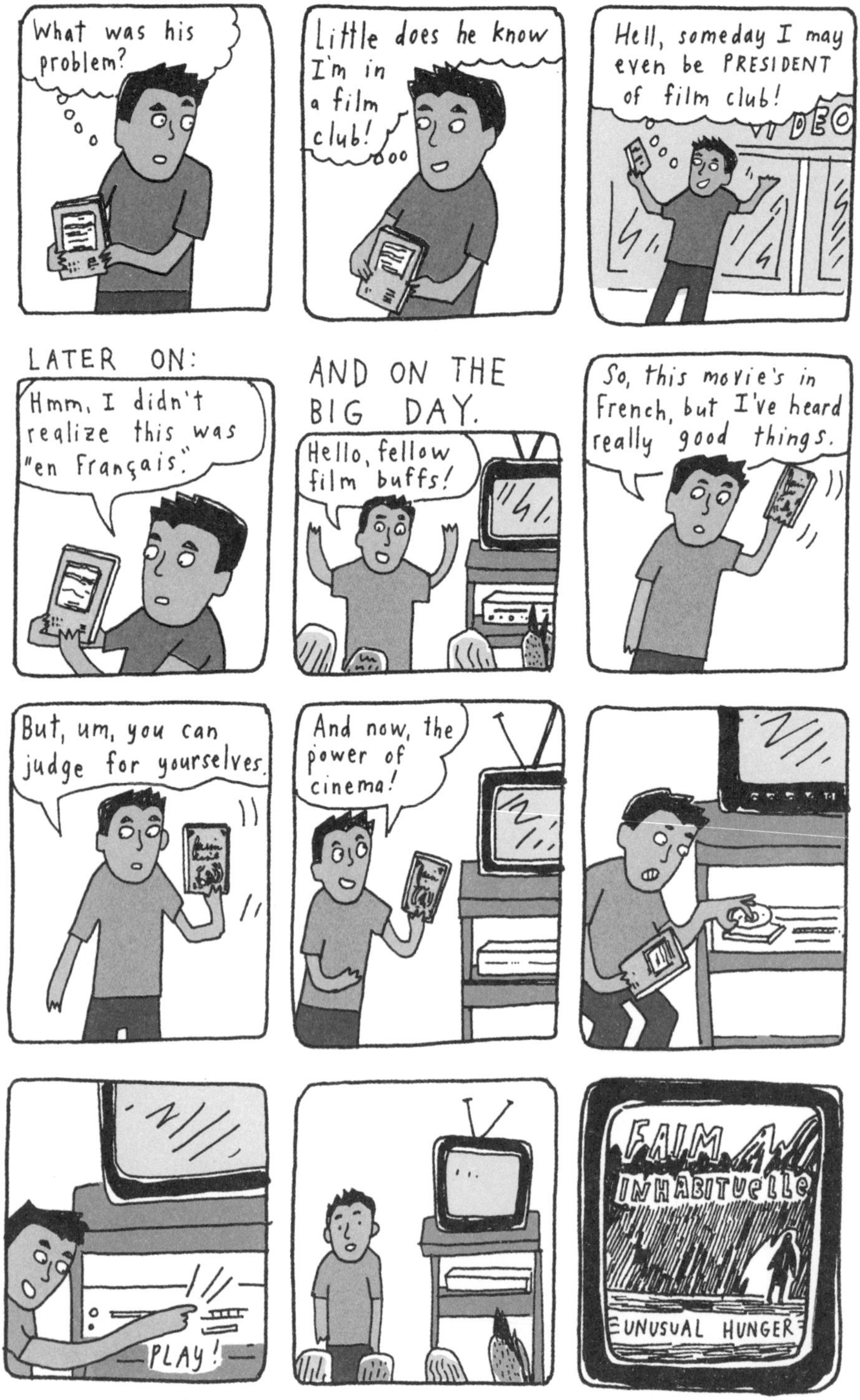
What was his problem?
Little does he know I'm in a film club!
Hell, someday I may even be PRESIDENT of film club!
VIDEO
LATER ON:
Hmm, I didn't realize this was "en Français."
AND ON THE BIG DAY.
Hello, fellow film buffs!
So, this movie's in French, but I've heard really good things.
But, um, you can judge for yourselves.
And now, the power of cinema!
PLAY!
FAIM INHABITUELLE
UNUSUAL HUNGER

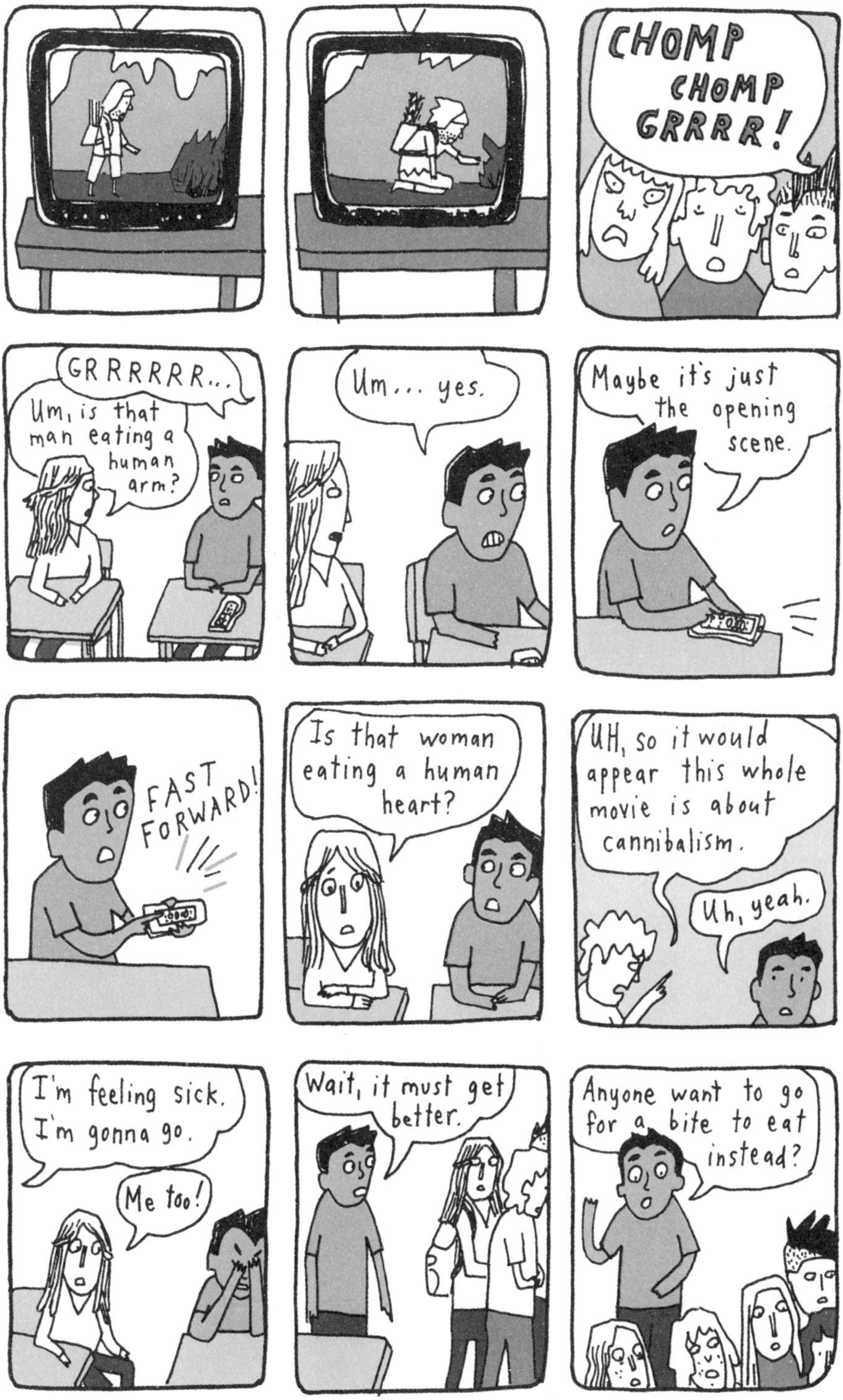
CHOMP CHOMP GRRRR!
GRRRRRR...
Um, is that man eating a human arm?
Um... yes.
Maybe it's just the opening scene.
FAST FORWARD!
Is that woman eating a human heart?
UH, so it would appear this whole movie is about cannibalism.
Uh, yeah.
I'm feeling sick. I'm gonna go.
Me too!
Wait, it must get better.
Anyone want to go for a bite to eat instead?

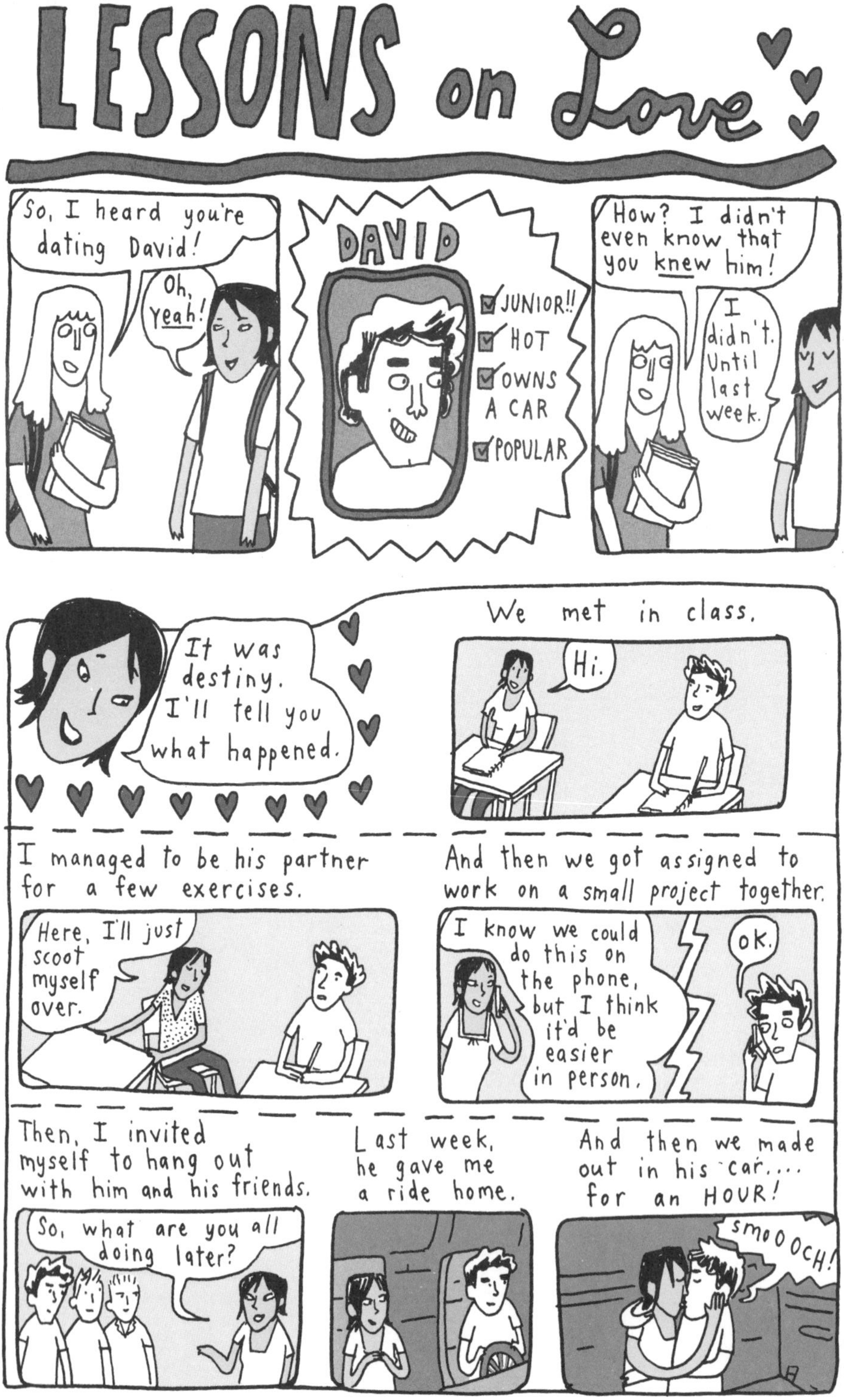
LESSONS on Love
So, I heard you're dating David!
Oh, yeah!
DAVID
JUNIOR!!
HOT
OWNS A CAR
POPULAR
How? I didn't even know that you knew him!
I didn't. Until last week.
It was destiny. I'll tell you what happened.
We met in class.
Hi.
I managed to be his partner for a few exercises.
Here, I'll just scoot myself over.
And then we got assigned to work on a small project together.
I know we could do this on the phone, but I think it'd be easier in person.
OK.
Then, I invited myself to hang out with him and his friends.
So, what are you all doing later?
Last week, he gave me a ride home.
And then we made out in his car.... for an HOUR!
SMOOOCH!

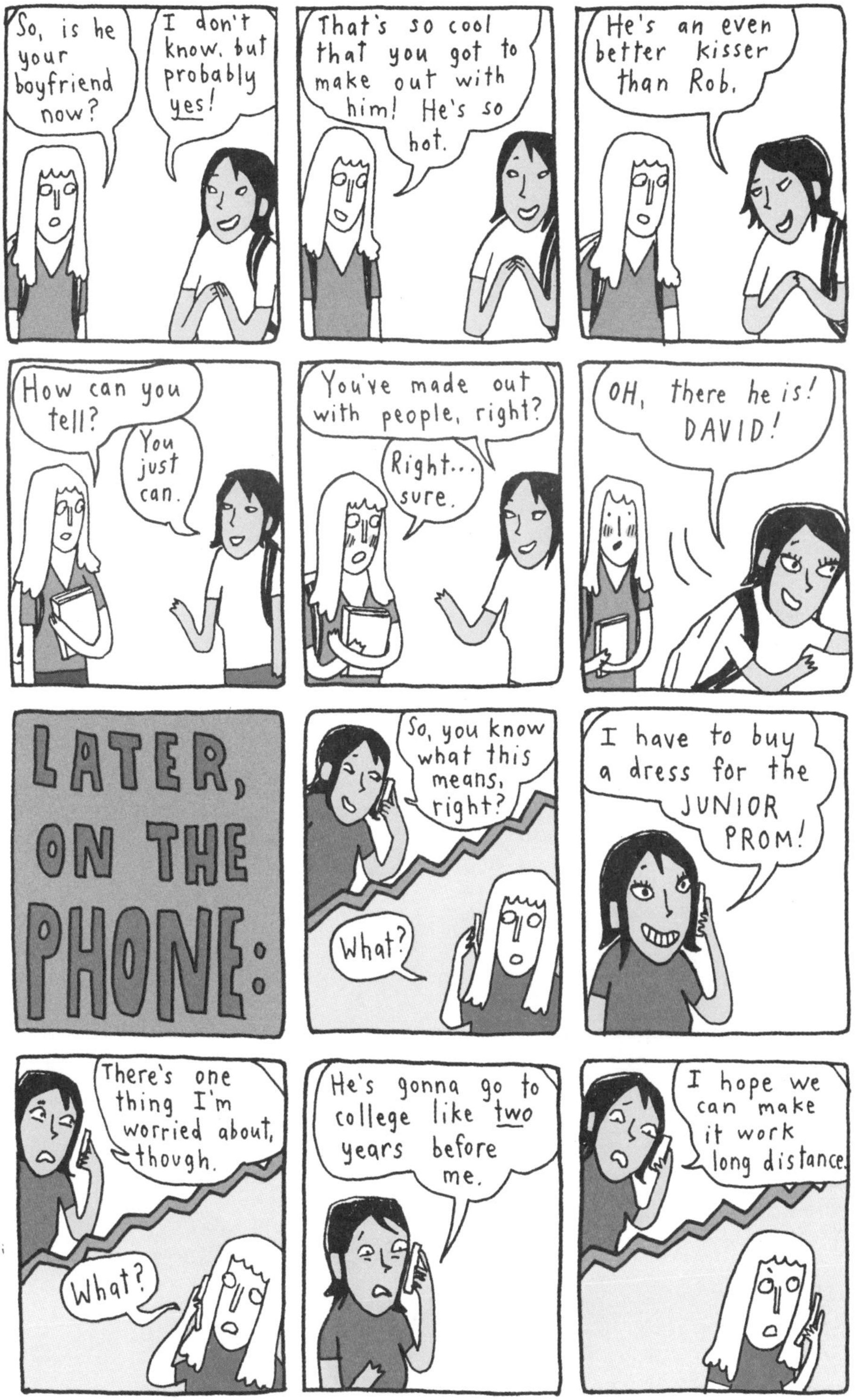
So, is he your boyfriend now?
I don't know, but probably yes!
That's so cool that you got to make out with him! He's so hot.
He's an even better kisser than Rob.
How can you tell?
You just can.
You've made out with people, right?
Right... sure.
OH, there he is! DAVID!
LATER, ON THE PHONE:
So, you know what this means, right?
What?
I have to buy a dress for the JUNIOR PROM!
There's one thing I'm worried about, though.
What?
He's gonna go to college like two years before me.
I hope we can make it work long distance.

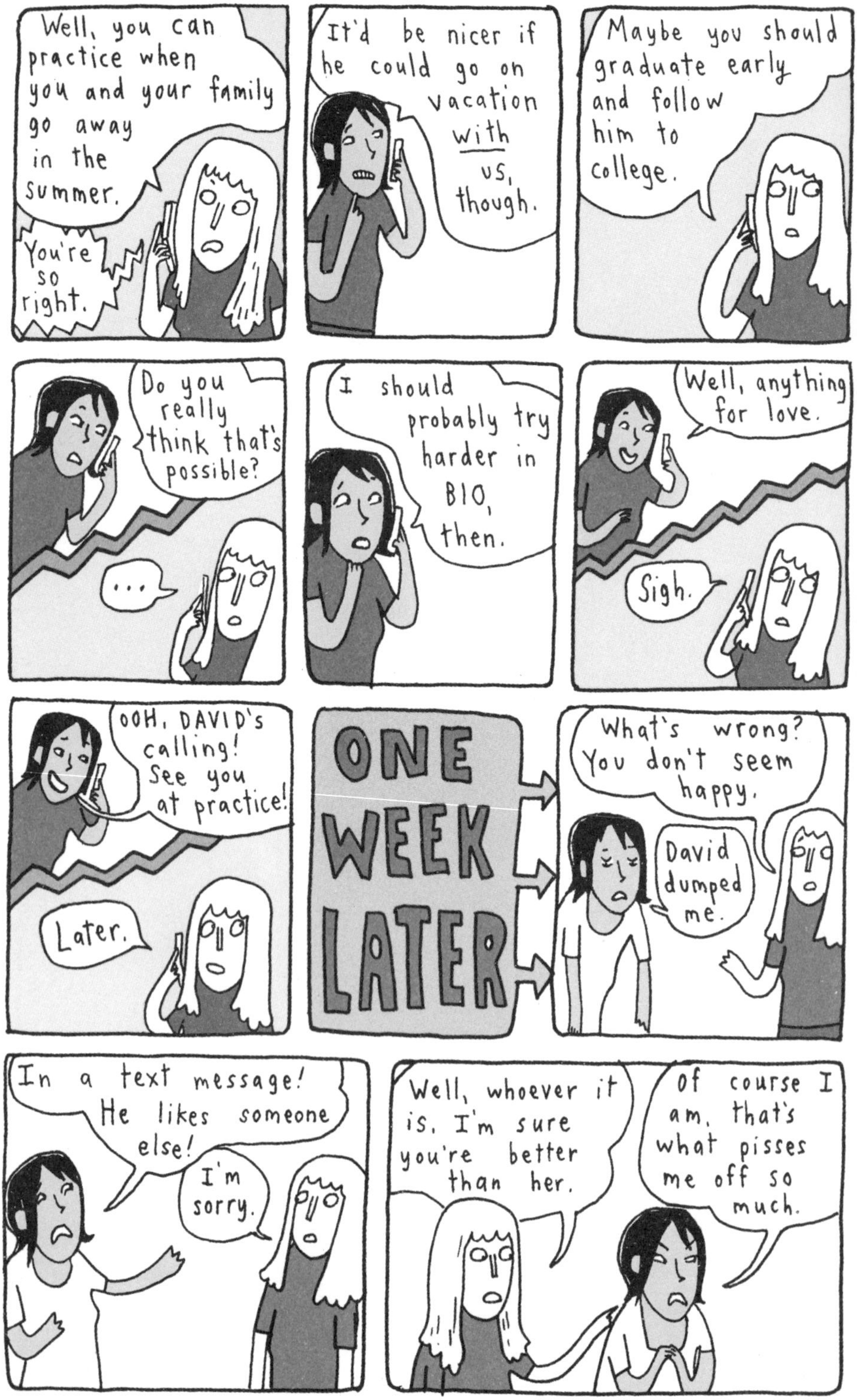
Well, you can practice when you and your family go away in the summer.
You're so right.
It'd be nicer if he could go on vacation with us, though.
Maybe you should graduate early and follow him to college.
Do you really think that's possible?
...
I should probably try harder in BIO, then.
Well, anything for love.
Sigh.
OOH, DAVID's calling! See you at practice!
Later.
ONE WEEK LATER
What's wrong? You don't seem happy.
David dumped me.
In a text message! He likes someone else!
I'm sorry.
Well, whoever it is, I'm sure you're better than her.
Of course I am, that's what pisses me off so much.

The END of HOCKEY

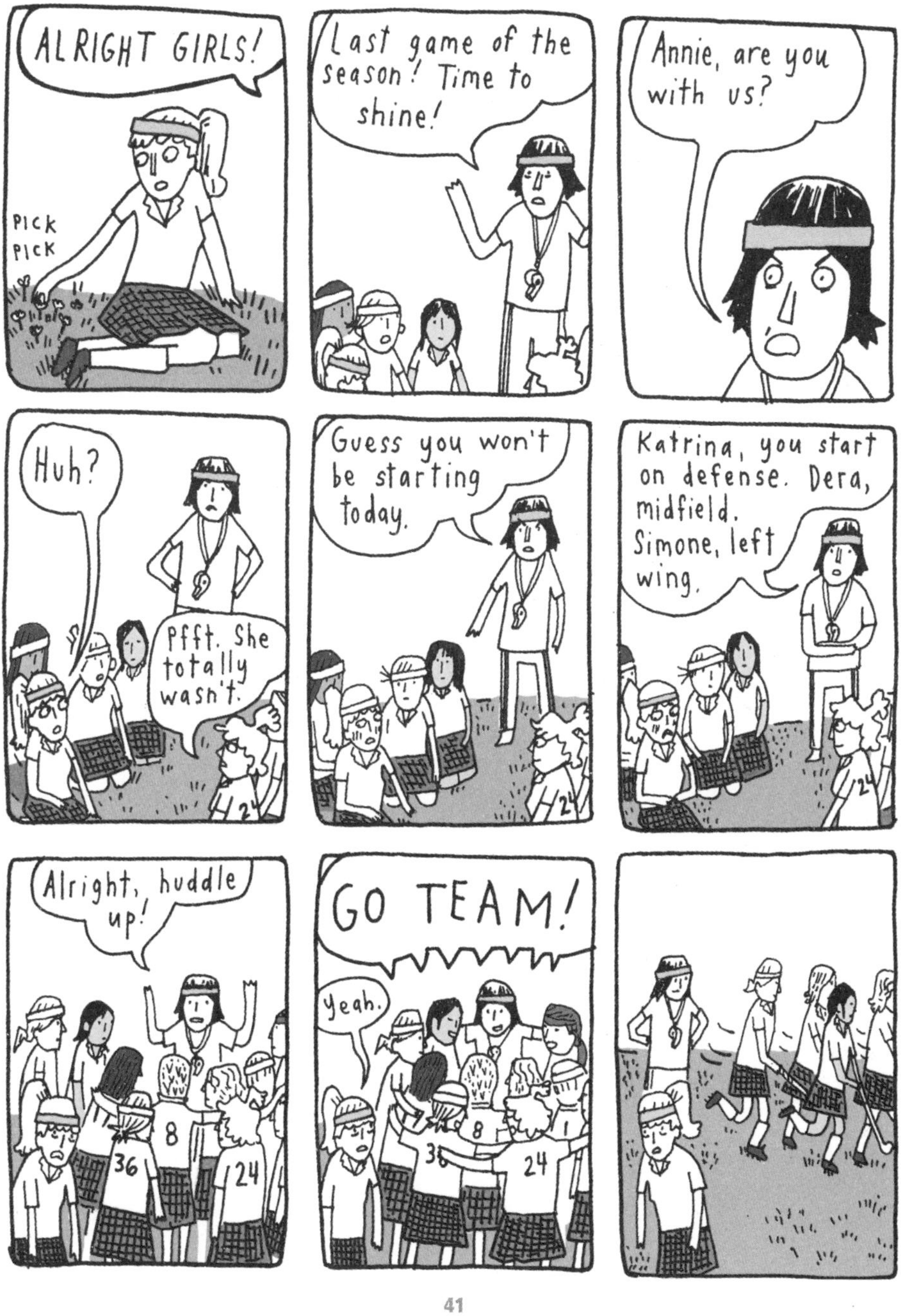
ALRIGHT GIRLS!
PICK PICK
Last game of the season! Time to shine!
Annie, are you with us?
Huh?
Pfft. She totally wasn't.
Guess you won't be starting today.
Katrina, you start on defense. Dera, midfield. Simone, left wing.
Alright, huddle up!
GO TEAM!
Yeah.

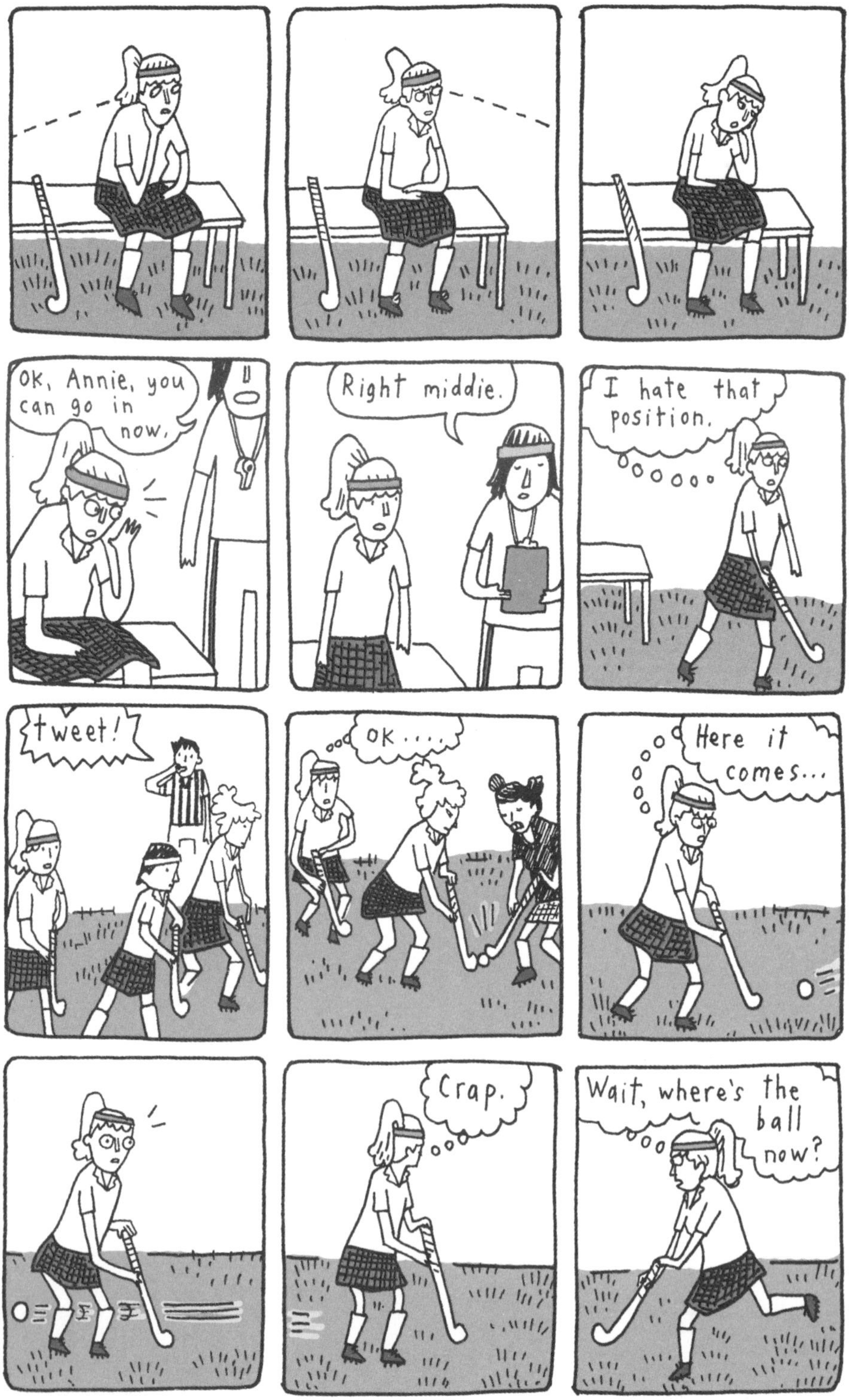

Ok, Annie, you can go in now.
Right middie.
I hate that position.
tweet!
OK....
Here it comes...
Crap.
Wait, where's the ball now?

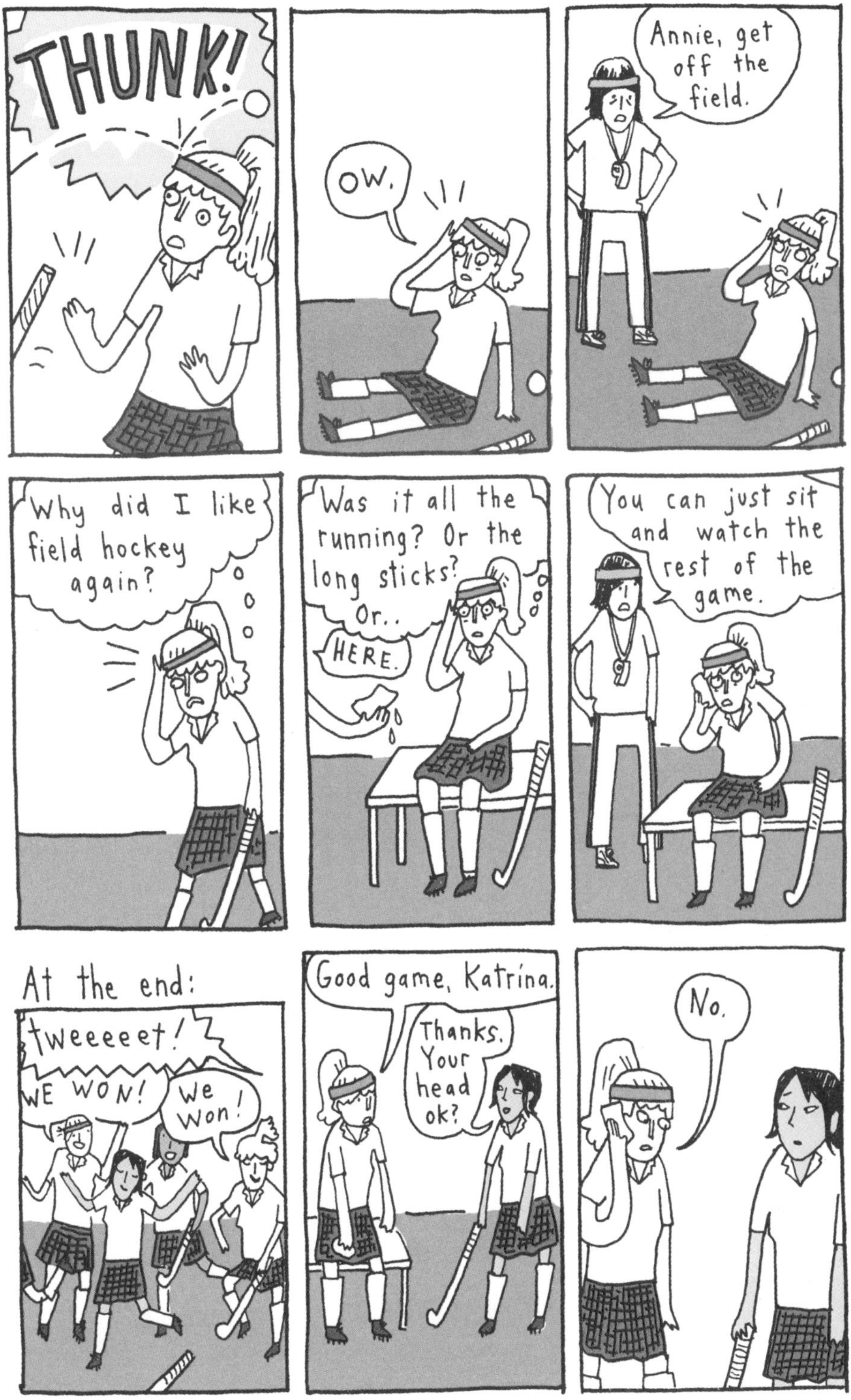

THUNK!
OW.
Annie, get off the field.
Why did I like field hockey again?
Was it all the running? Or the long sticks? Or..
HERE.
You can just sit and watch the rest of the game.
At the end:
tweeeeet!
WE WON!
We won!
Good game, Katrina.
Thanks. Your head ok?
No.

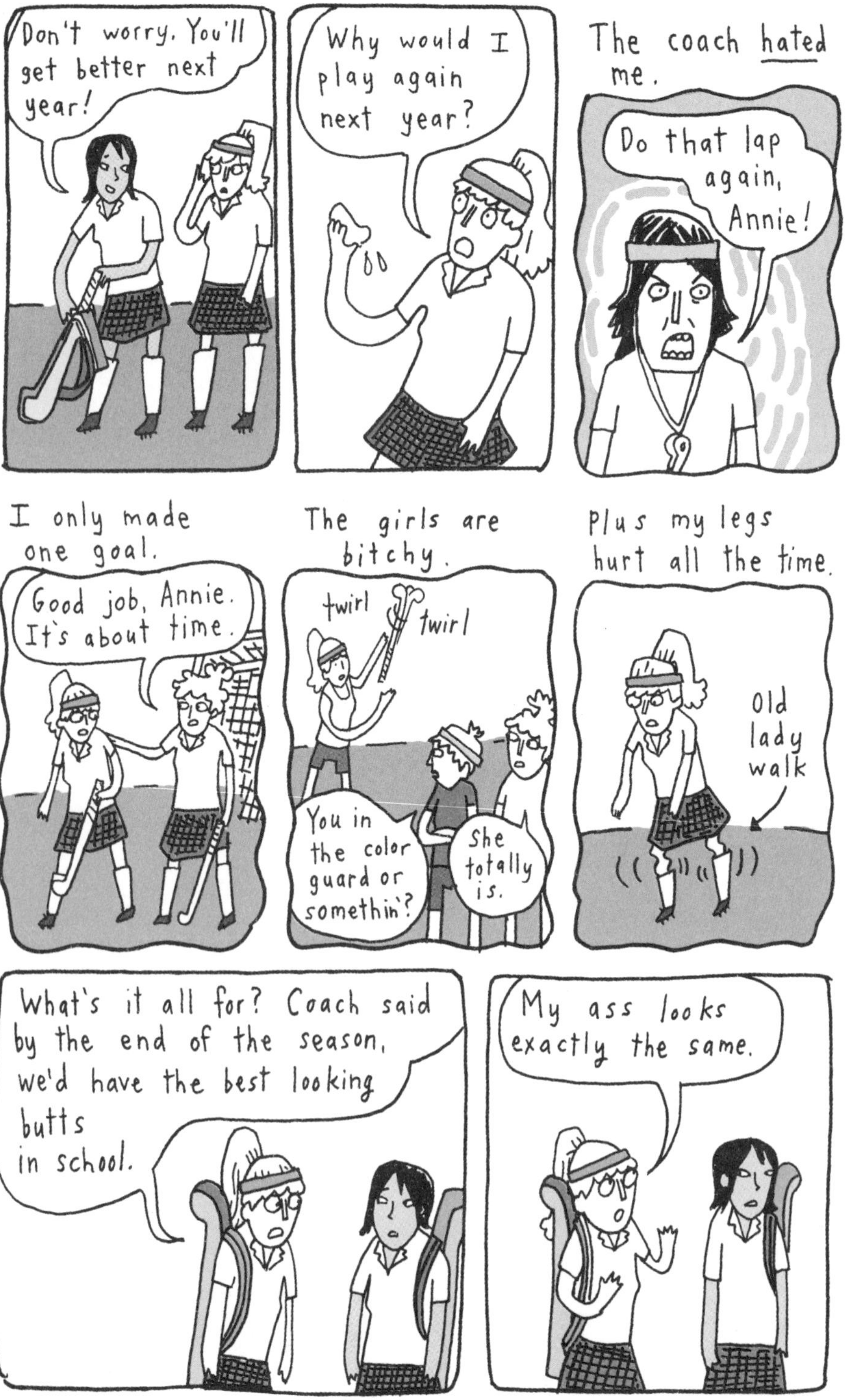
Don't worry. You'll get better next year!
Why would I play again next year?
The coach hated me.
Do that lap again, Annie!
I only made one goal.
Good job, Annie. It's about time.
The girls are bitchy.
twirl
twirl
You in the color guard or somethin'?
She totally is.
Plus my legs hurt all the time.
Old lady walk
What's it all for? Coach said by the end of the season, we'd have the best looking butts in school.
My ass looks exactly the same.

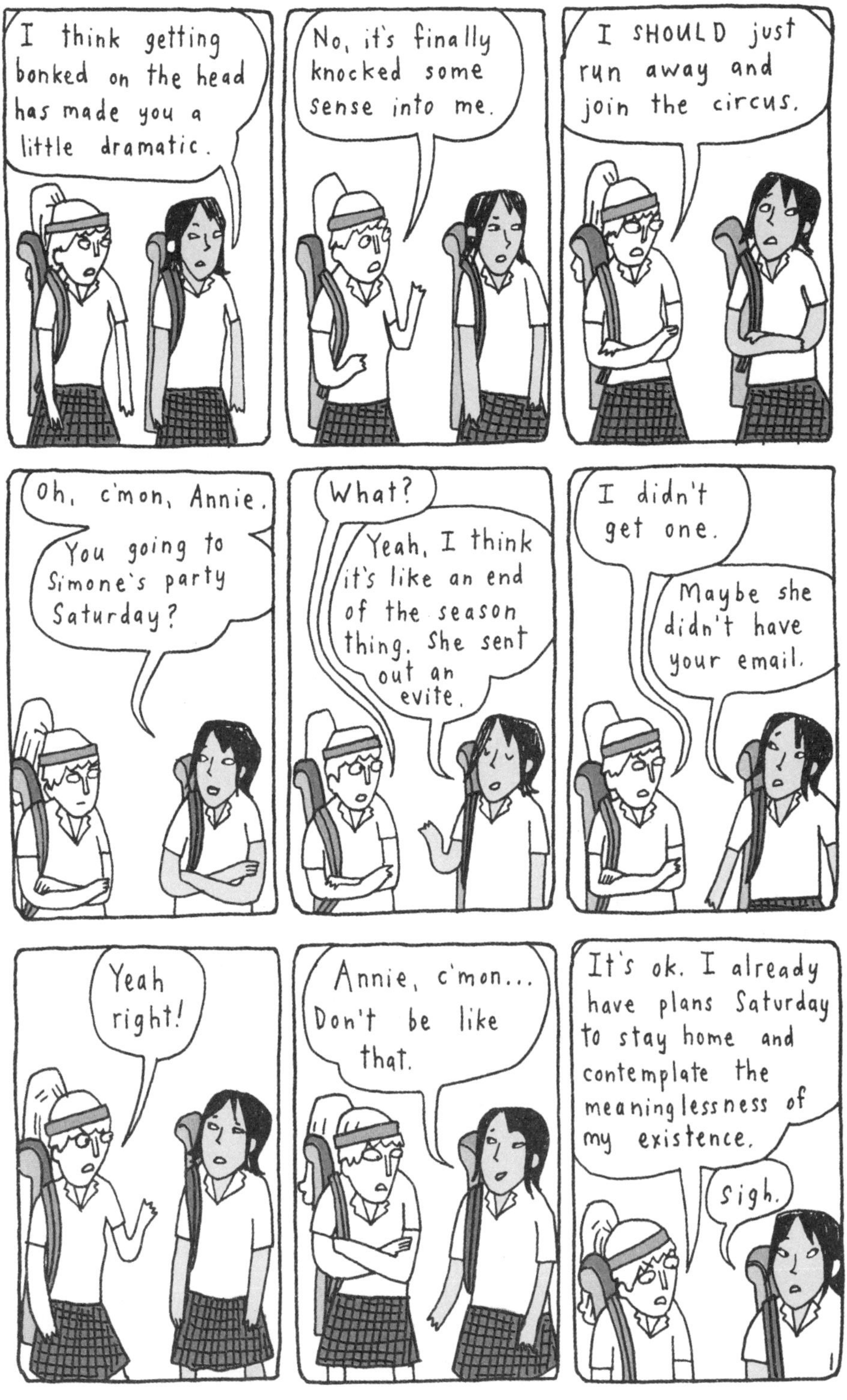

I think getting bonked on the head has made you a little dramatic.
No, it's finally knocked some sense into me.
I SHOULD just run away and join the circus.
Oh, c'mon, Annie.
You going to Simone's party Saturday?
What?
Yeah, I think it's like an end of the season thing. She sent out an evite.
I didn't get one.
Maybe she didn't have your email.
Yeah right!
Annie, c'mon... Don't be like that.
It's ok. I already have plans Saturday to stay home and contemplate the meaninglessness of my existence.
Sigh.

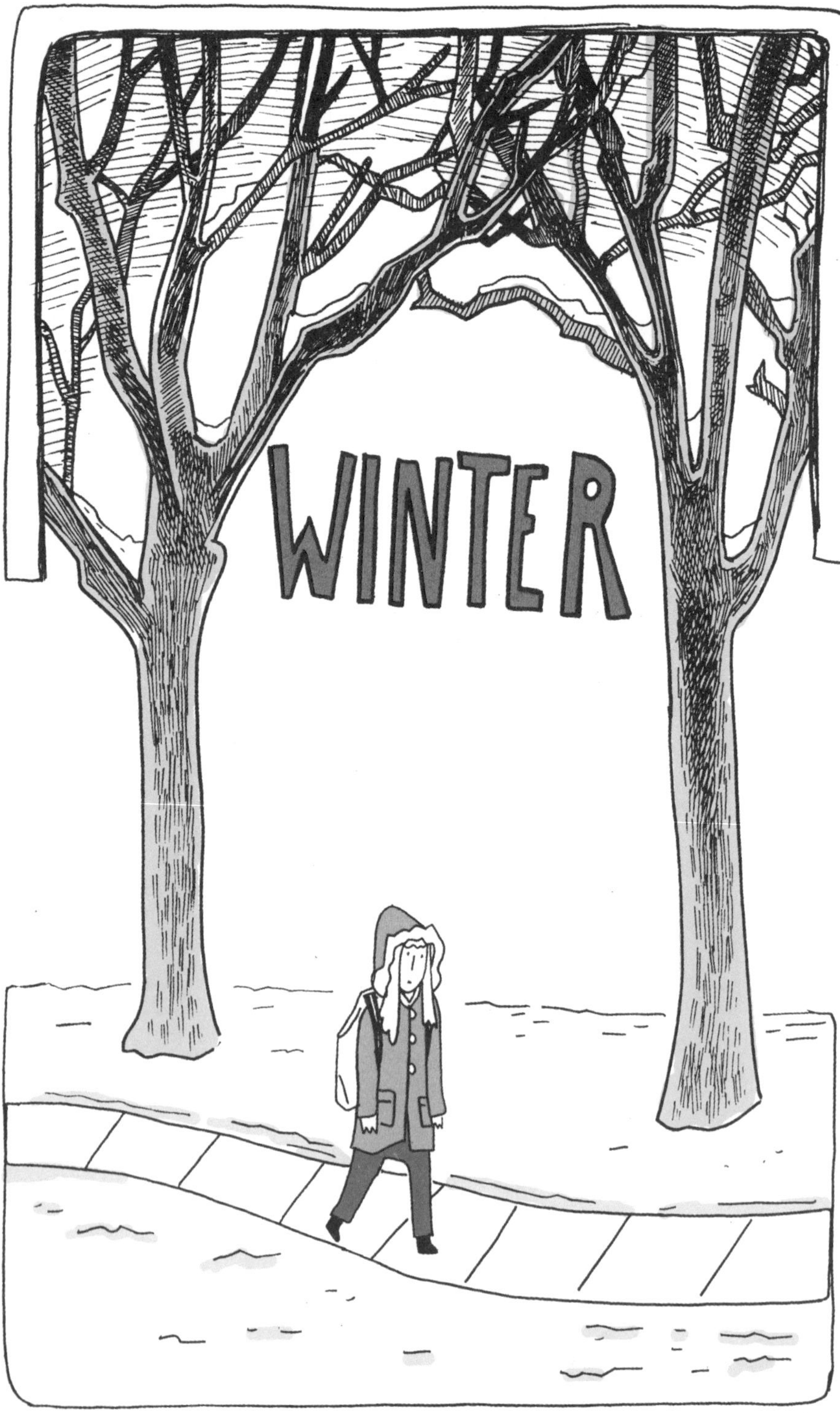
WINTER

SINGING a NEW SONG

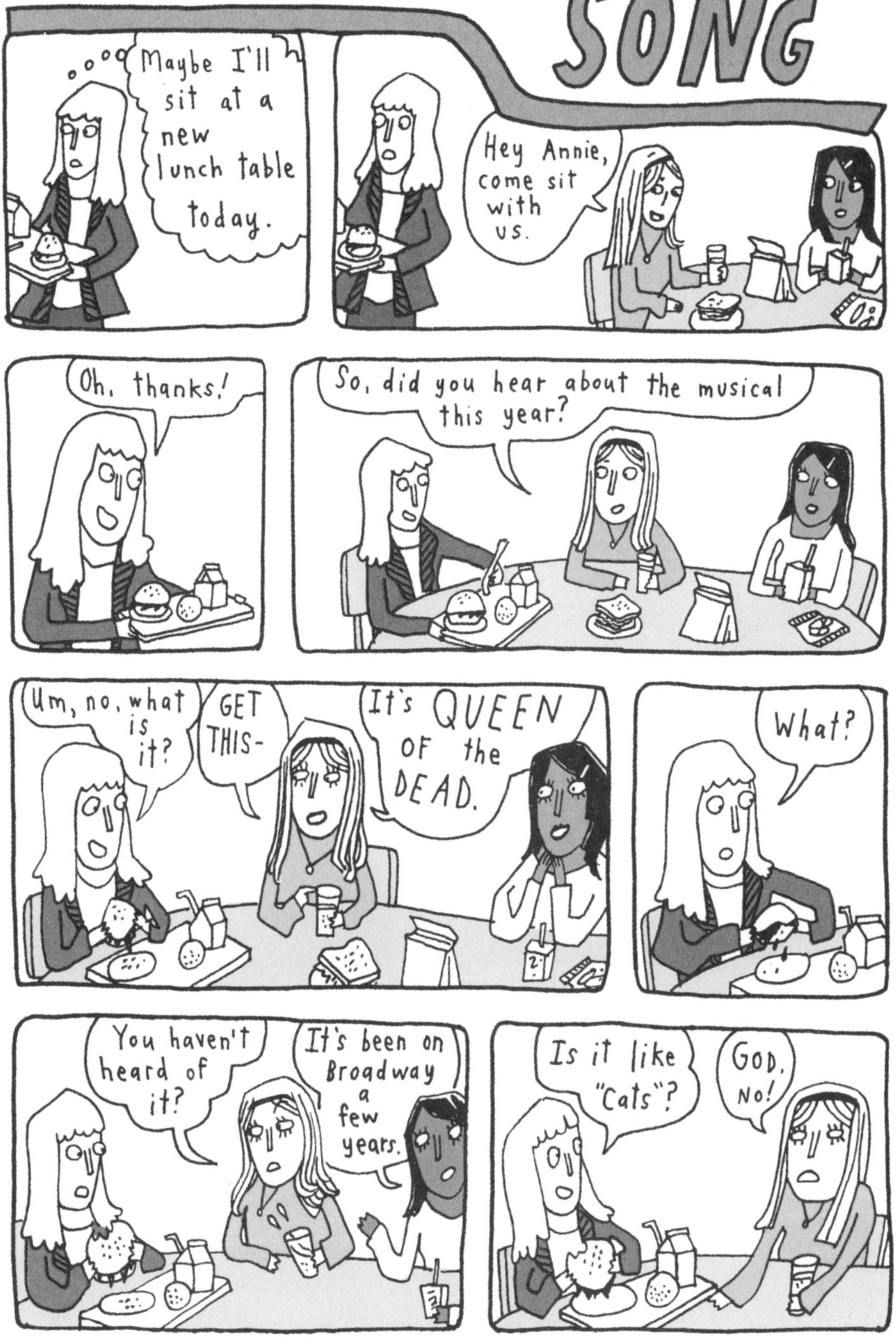

Maybe I'll sit at a new lunch table today.
Hey Annie, come sit with us.
Oh, thanks!
So, did you hear about the musical this year?
Um, no, what is it?
GET THIS-
It's QUEEN OF the DEAD.
What?
You haven't heard of it?
It's been on Broadway a few years.
Is it like "Cats"?
GOD, No!

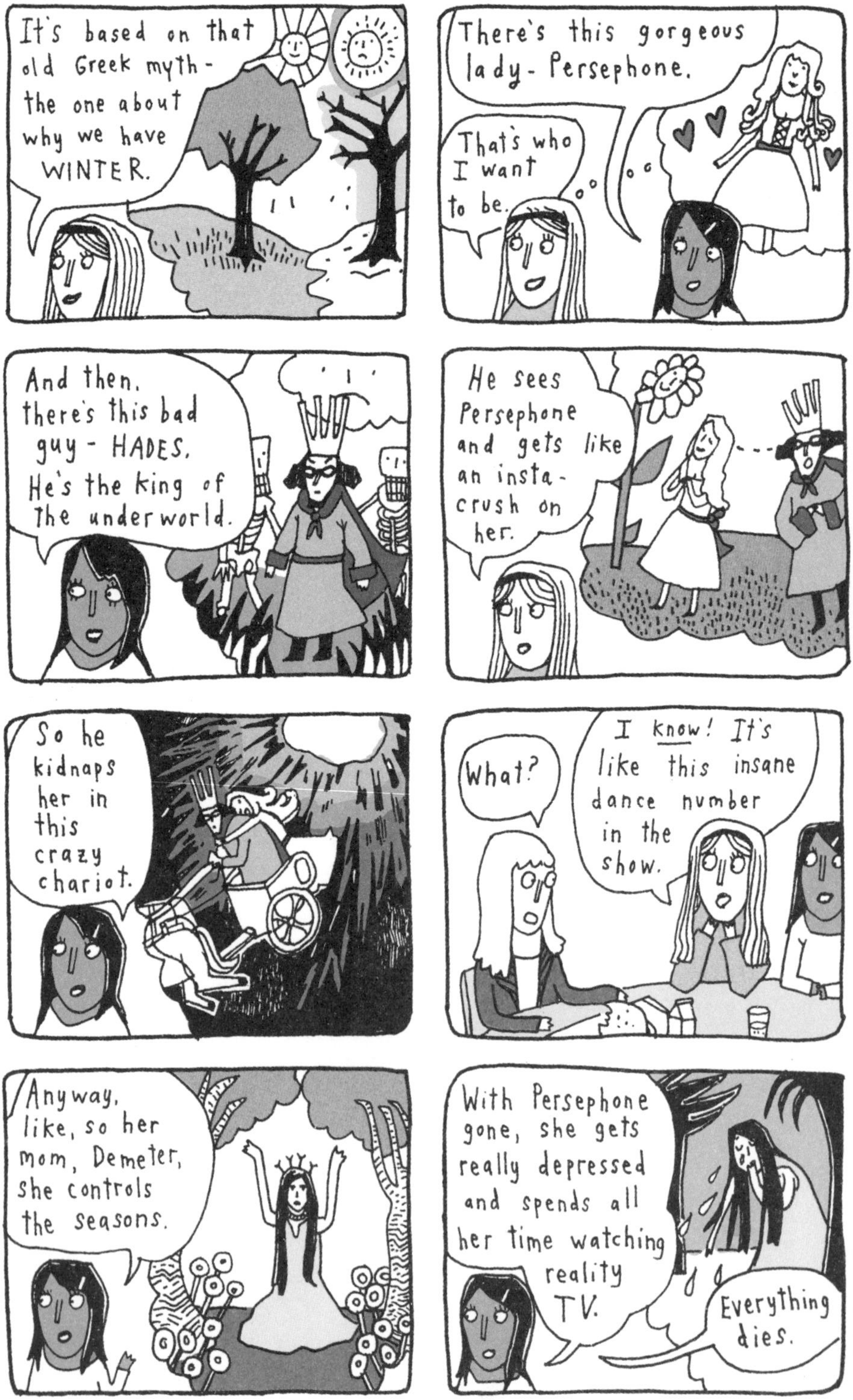
It's based on that old Greek myth - the one about why we have WINTER.
There's this gorgeous lady - Persephone.
That's who I want to be.
And then, there's this bad guy - HADES. He's the king of the underworld.
He sees Persephone and gets like an insta-crush on her.
So he kidnaps her in this crazy chariot.
What?
I know! It's like this insane dance number in the show.
Anyway, like, so her mom, Demeter, she controls the seasons.
With Persephone gone, she gets really depressed and spends all her time watching reality TV.
Everything dies.

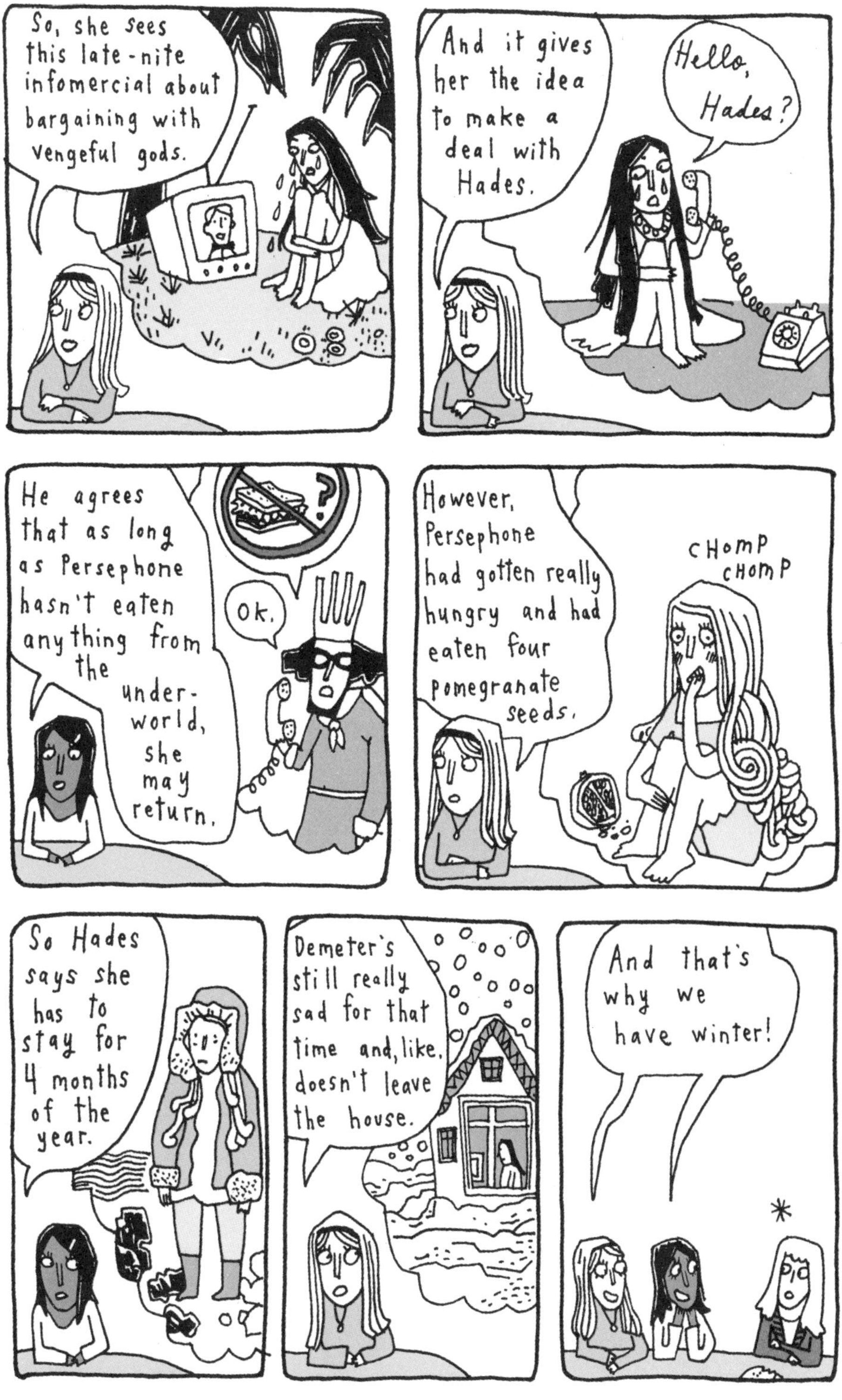
So, she sees this late-nite infomercial about bargaining with vengeful gods.
And it gives her the idea to make a deal with Hades.
Hello, Hades?
He agrees that as long as Persephone hasn't eaten anything from the under-world, she may return.
Ok.
However, Persephone had gotten really hungry and had eaten four pomegranate seeds.
CHOMP CHOMP
So Hades says she has to stay for 4 months of the year.
Demeter's still really sad for that time and, like, doesn't leave the house.
And that's why we have winter!

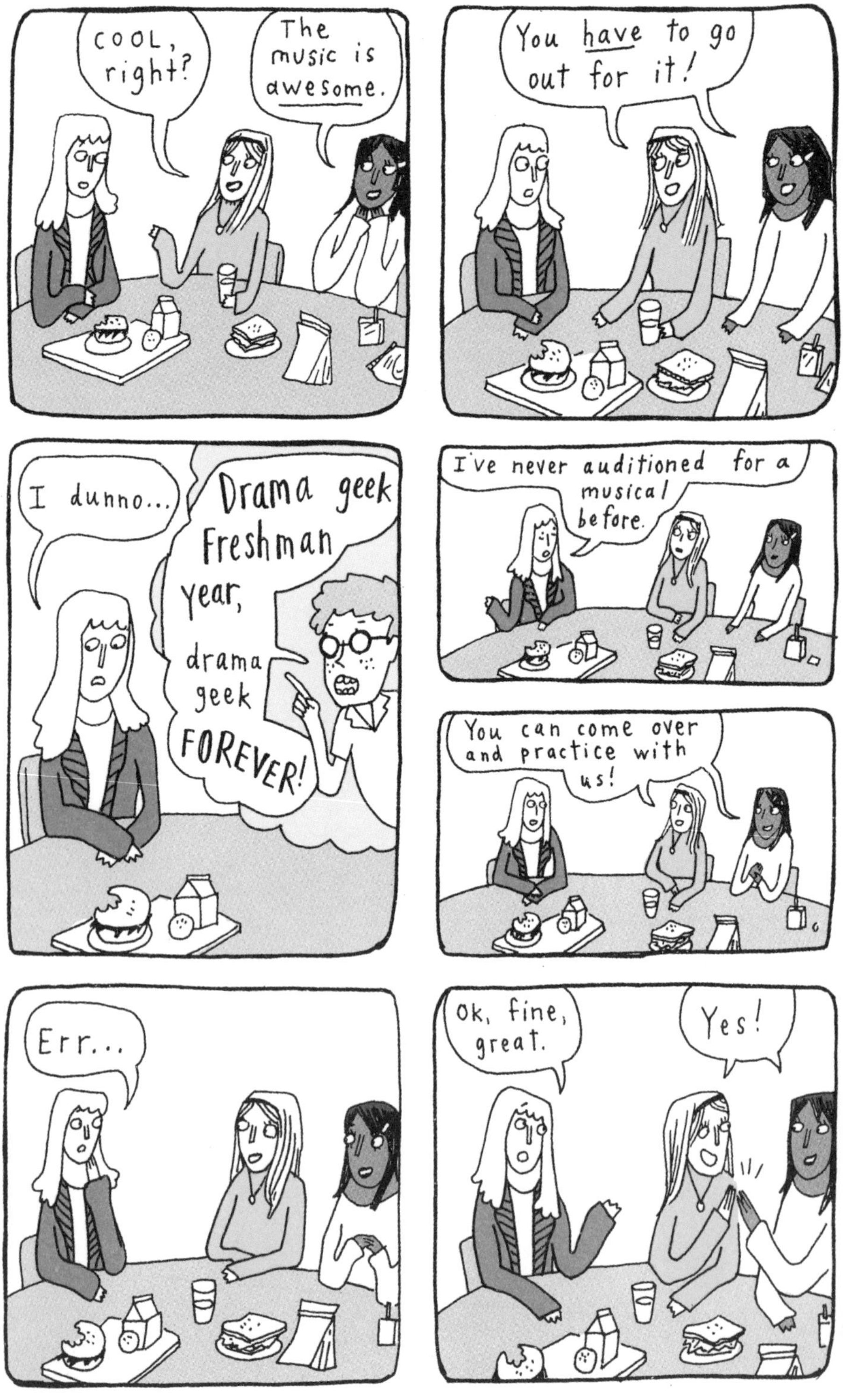
COOL, right?
The music is awesome.
You have to go out for it!
I dunno...
Drama geek Freshman year, drama geek FOREVER!
I've never auditioned for a musical before.
You can come over and practice with us!
Err...
Ok, fine, great.
Yes!

AUDACIOUS ANNIE

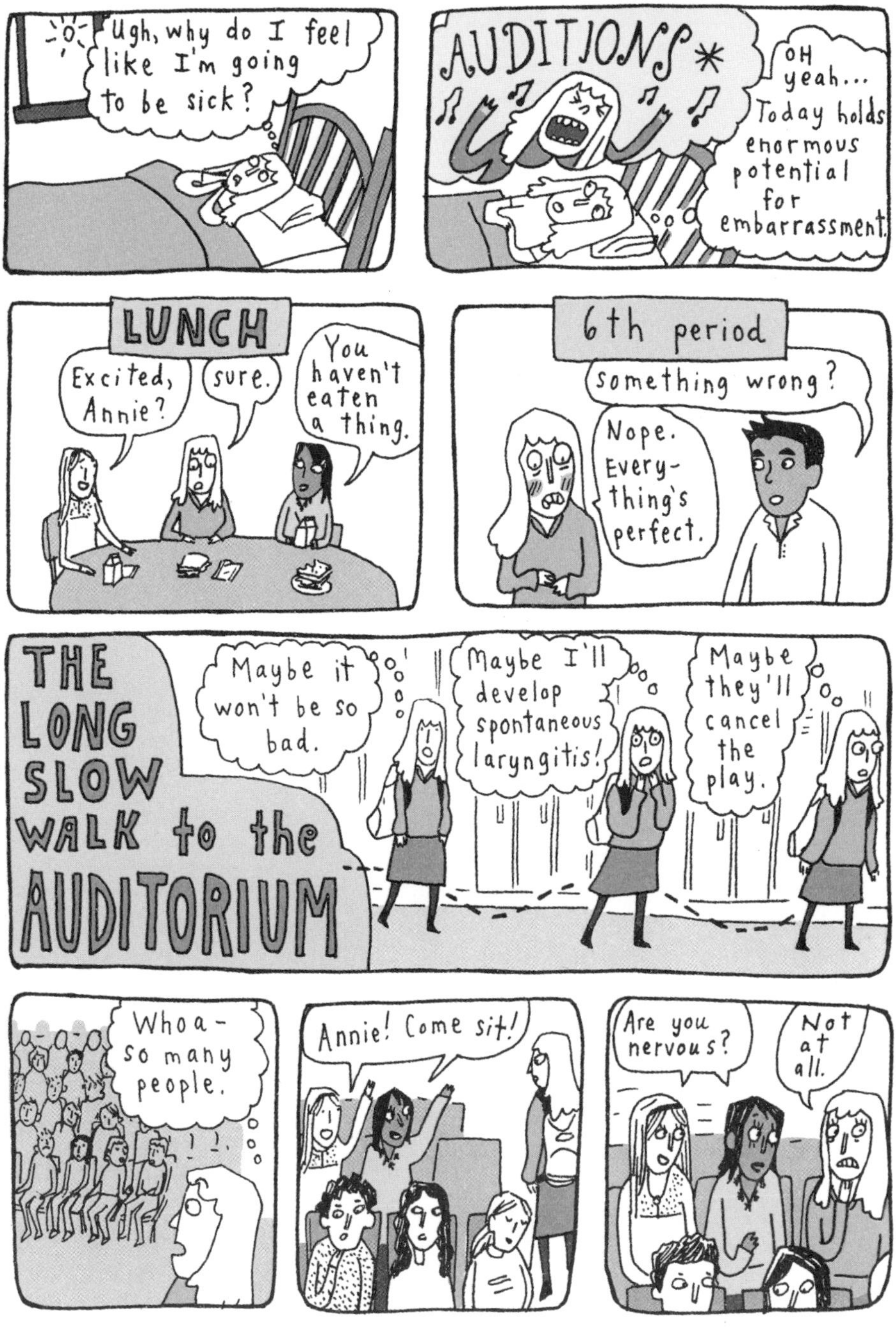
Ugh, why do I feel like I'm going to be sick?
AUDITIONS*
OH yeah... Today holds enormous potential for embarrassment.
LUNCH
Excited, Annie?
sure.
You haven't eaten a thing.
6th period
something wrong?
Nope. Everything's perfect.
THE LONG SLOW WALK to the AUDITORIUM
Maybe it won't be so bad.
Maybe I'll develop spontaneous laryngitis!
Maybe they'll cancel the play.
Whoa - so many people.
!!
Annie! Come sit!
Are you nervous?
Not at all.

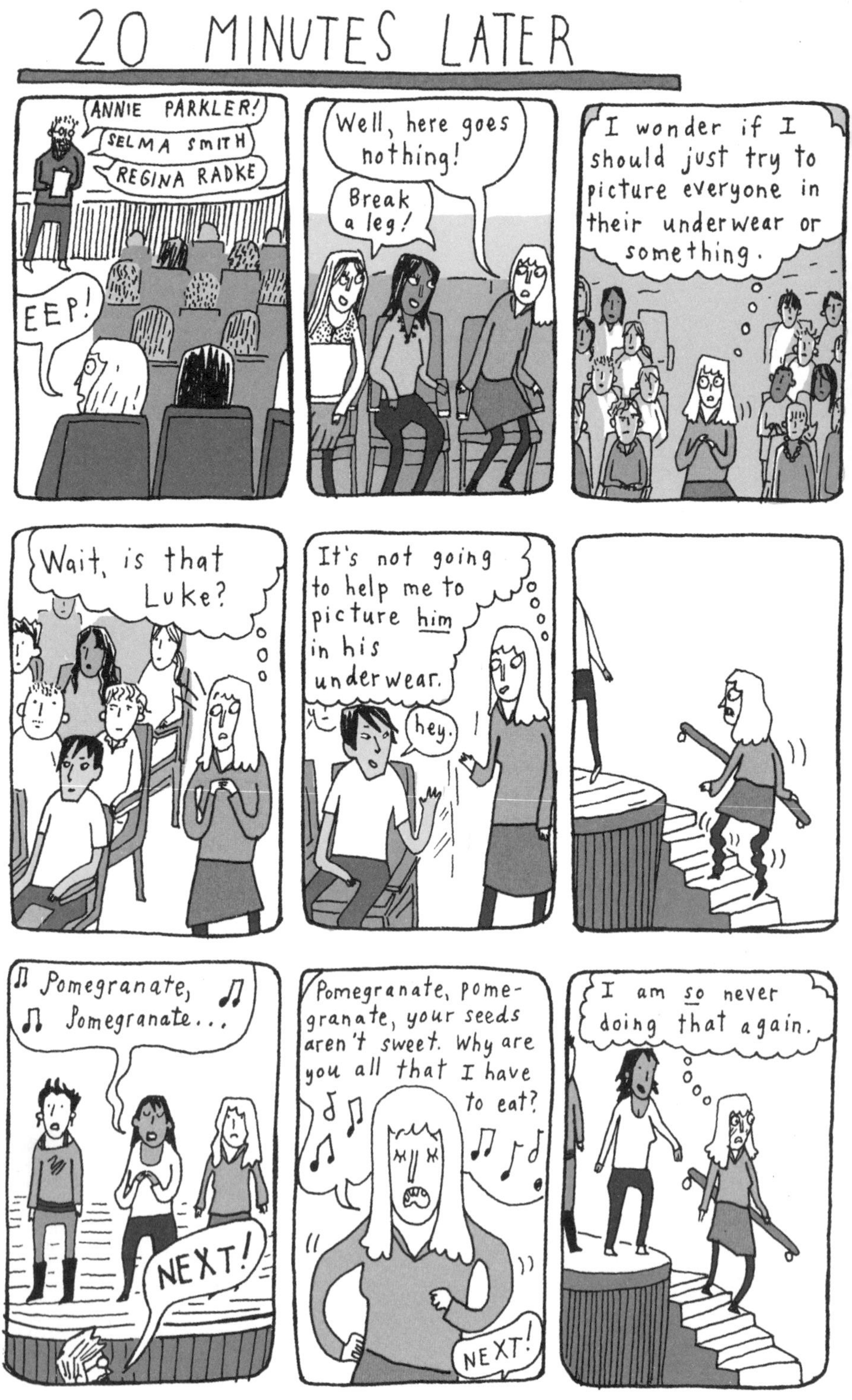
20 MINUTES LATER
ANNIE PARKLER!
SELMA SMITH
REGINA RADKE
EEP!
Well, here goes nothing!
Break a leg!
I wonder if I should just try to picture everyone in their underwear or something.
Wait, is that Luke?
It's not going to help me to picture him in his underwear.
hey.
Pomegranate, Pomegranate...
NEXT!
Pomegranate, pomegranate, your seeds aren't sweet. Why are you all that I have to eat?
NEXT!
I am so never doing that again.

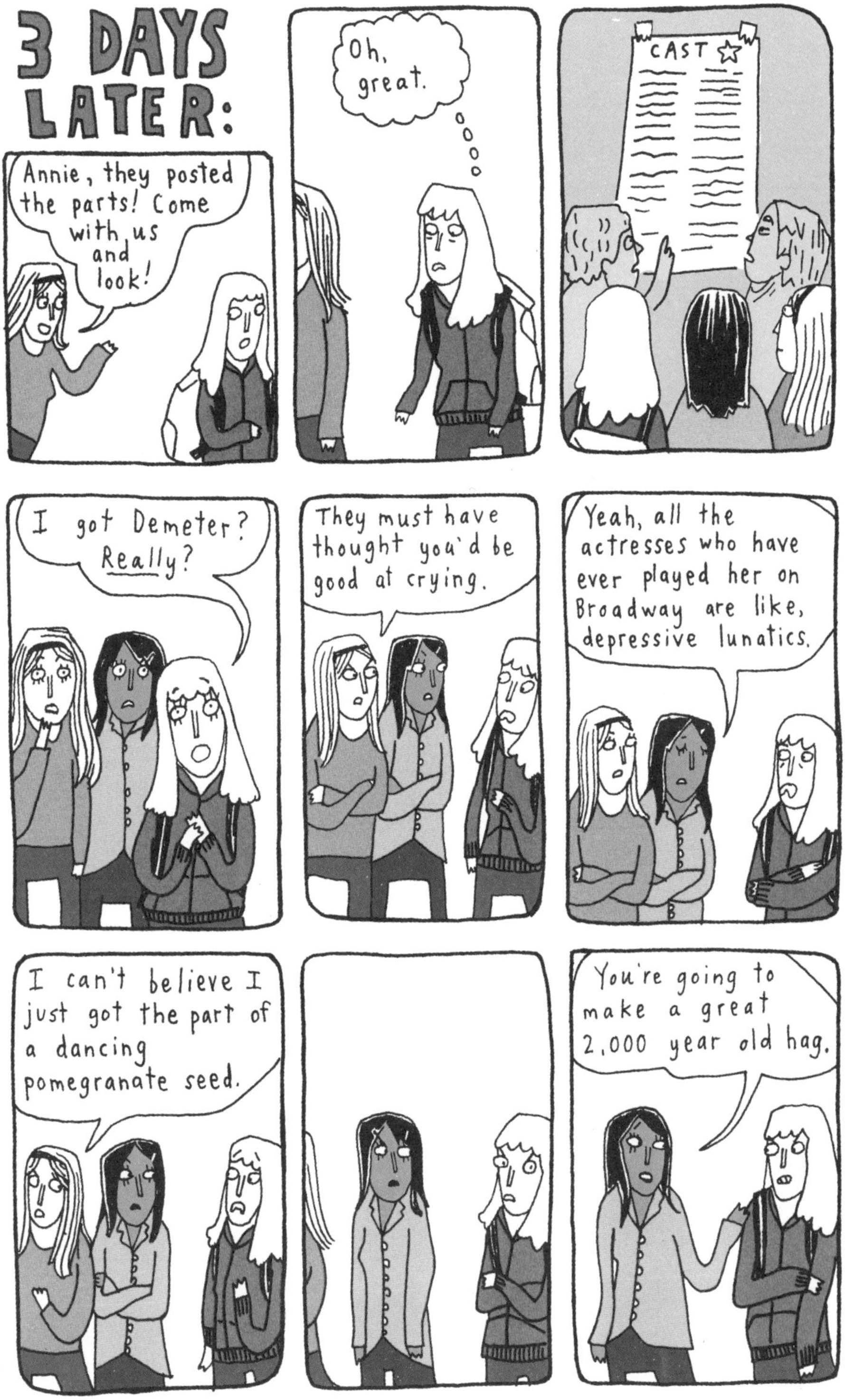
3 DAYS LATER:
Annie, they posted the parts! Come with us and look!
Oh, great.
CAST
I got Demeter? Really?
They must have thought you'd be good at crying.
Yeah, all the actresses who have ever played her on Broadway are like, depressive lunatics.
I can't believe I just got the part of a dancing pomegranate seed.
You're going to make a great 2,000 year old hag.

FIRST REHEARSAL: MEET YOUR NEMESIS

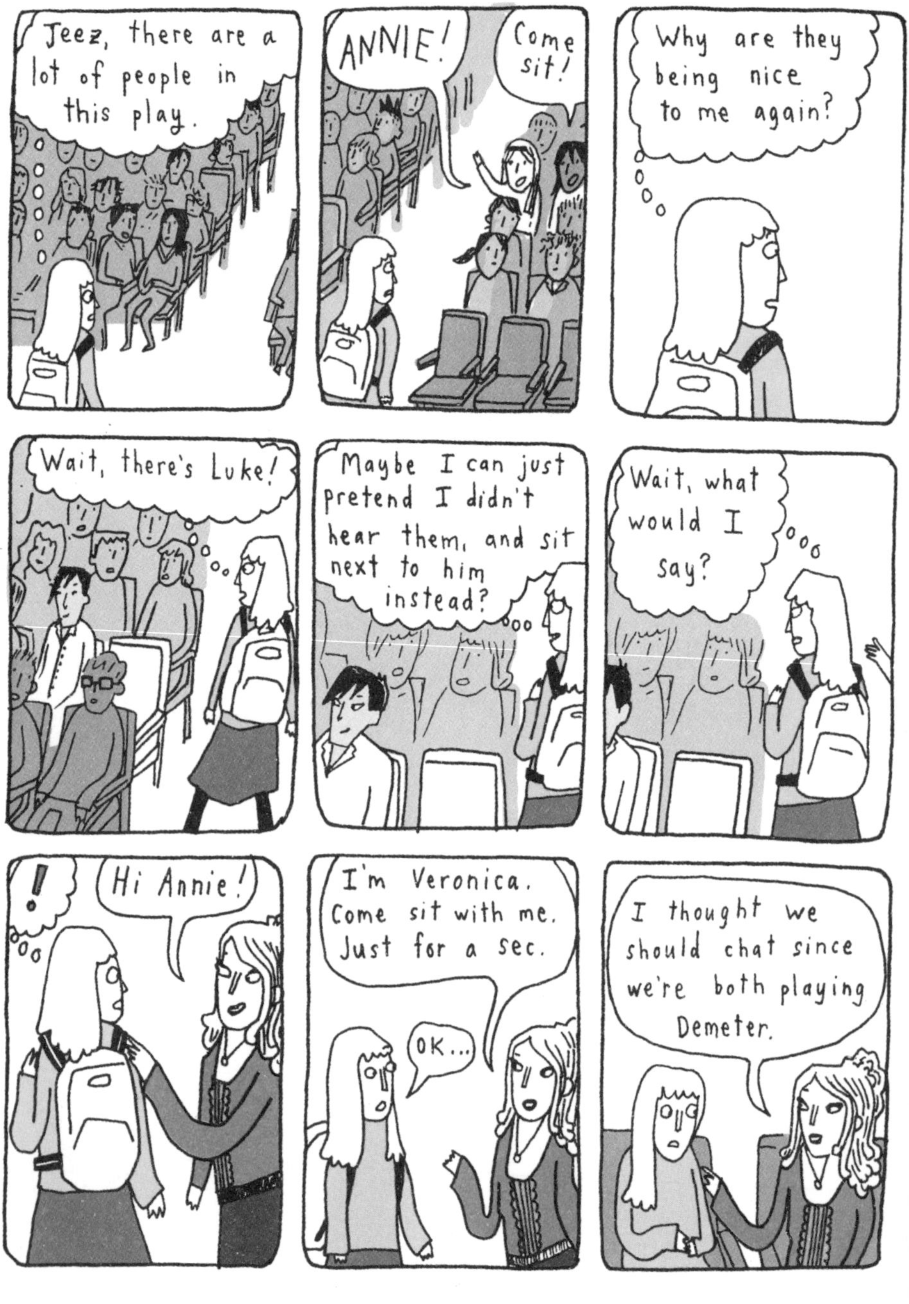
Jeez, there are a lot of people in this play.
ANNIE!
Come sit!
Why are they being nice to me again?
Wait, there's Luke!
Maybe I can just pretend I didn't hear them, and sit next to him instead?
Wait, what would I say?
!
Hi Annie!
I'm Veronica. Come sit with me. Just for a sec.
OK...
I thought we should chat since we're both playing Demeter.

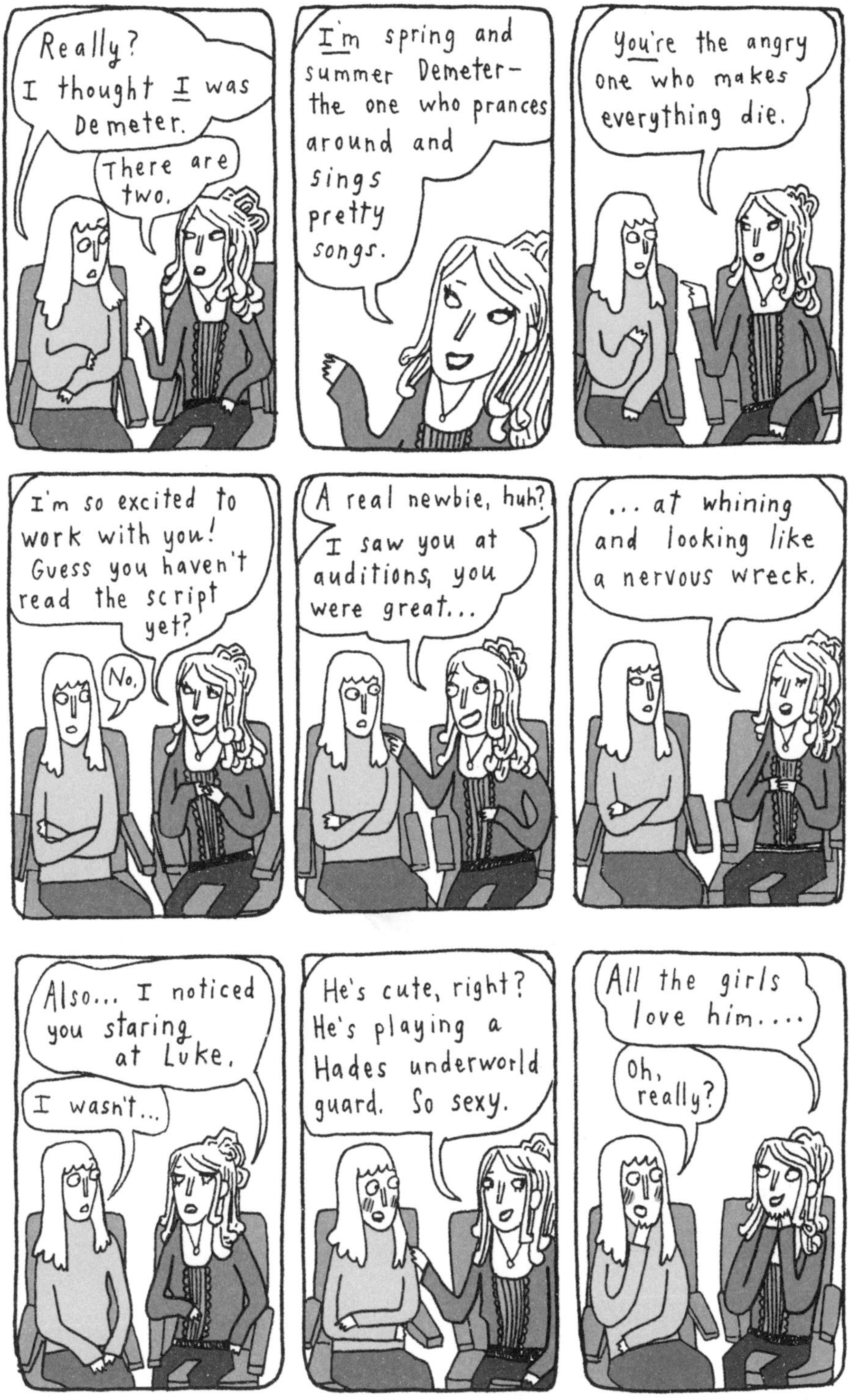

Really? I thought I was Demeter.
There are two.
I'm spring and summer Demeter- the one who prances around and sings pretty songs.
You're the angry one who makes everything die.
I'm so excited to work with you! Guess you haven't read the script yet?
No.
A real newbie, huh?
I saw you at auditions, you were great...
... at whining and looking like a nervous wreck.
Also... I noticed you staring at Luke.
I wasn't...
He's cute, right? He's playing a Hades underworld guard. So sexy.
All the girls love him....
Oh, really?

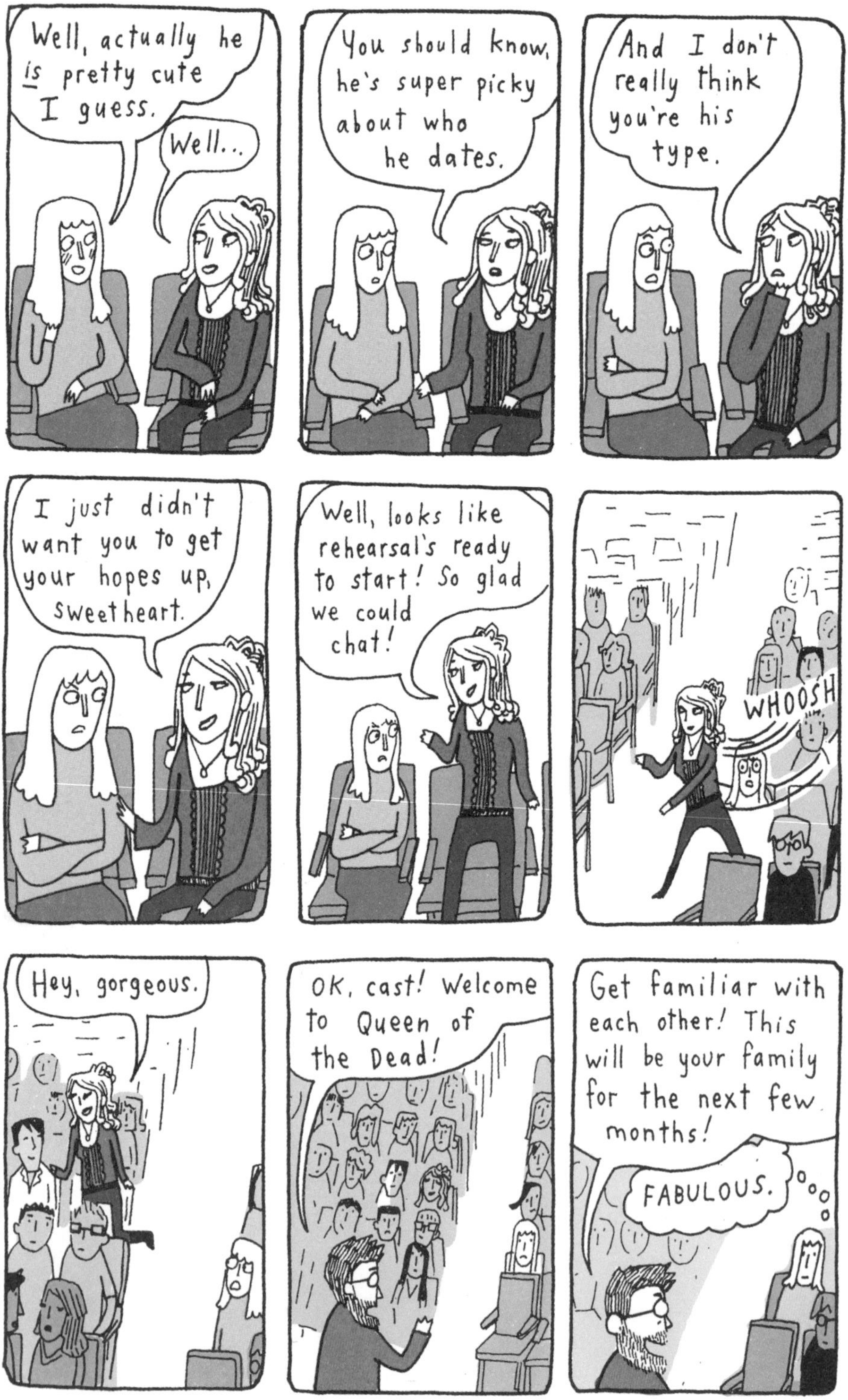
Well, actually he is pretty cute I guess.
Well...
You should know, he's super picky about who he dates.
And I don't really think you're his type.
I just didn't want you to get your hopes up, sweetheart.
Well, looks like rehearsal's ready to start! So glad we could chat!
WHOOSH
Hey, gorgeous.
OK, cast! Welcome to Queen of the Dead!
Get familiar with each other! This will be your family for the next few months!
FABULOUS.

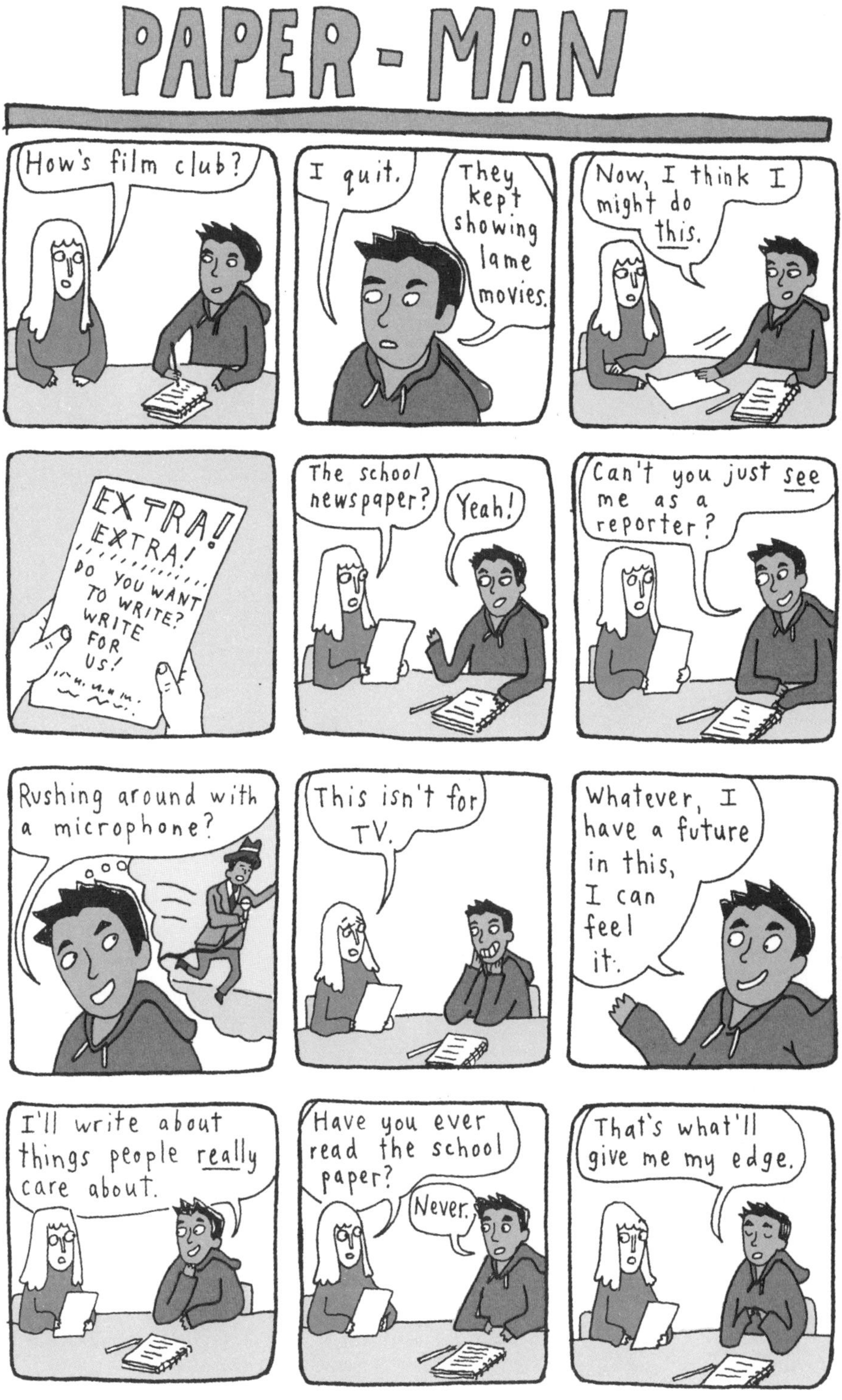
PAPER-MAN
How's film club?
I quit.
They kept showing lame movies.
Now, I think I might do this.
EXTRA! EXTRA! DO YOU WANT TO WRITE? WRITE FOR US!
The school newspaper?
Yeah!
Can't you just see me as a reporter?
Rushing around with a microphone?
This isn't for TV.
Whatever, I have a future in this, I can feel it.
I'll write about things people really care about.
Have you ever read the school paper?
Never.
That's what'll give me my edge.

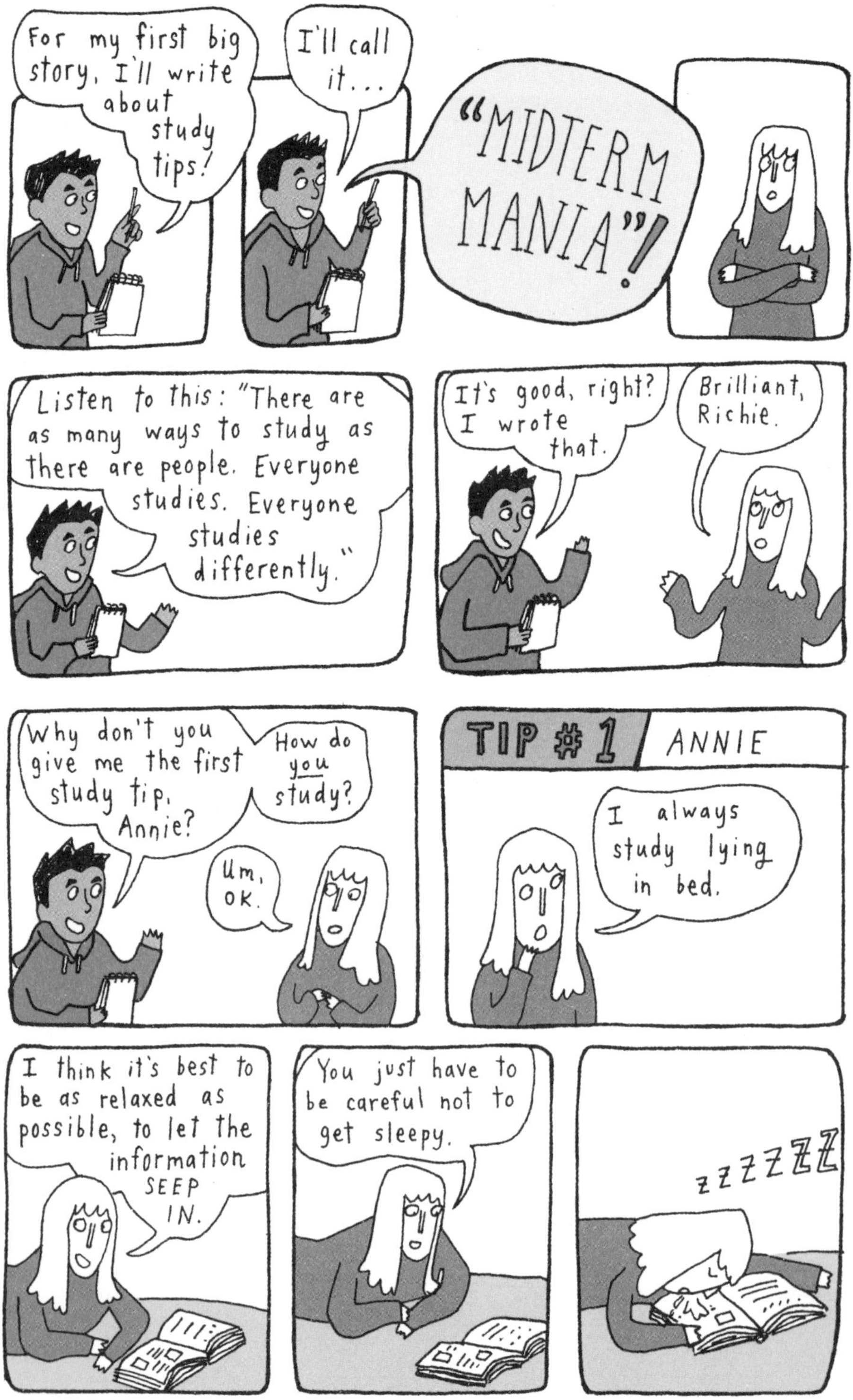
For my first big story, I'll write about study tips!
I'll call it...
"MIDTERM MANIA"!
Listen to this: "There are as many ways to study as there are people. Everyone studies. Everyone studies differently."
It's good, right? I wrote that.
Brilliant, Richie.
Why don't you give me the first study tip, Annie?
How do you study?
Um, OK.
TIP #1 ANNIE
I always study lying in bed.
I think it's best to be as relaxed as possible, to let the information SEEP IN.
You just have to be careful not to get sleepy.
zzzzzz

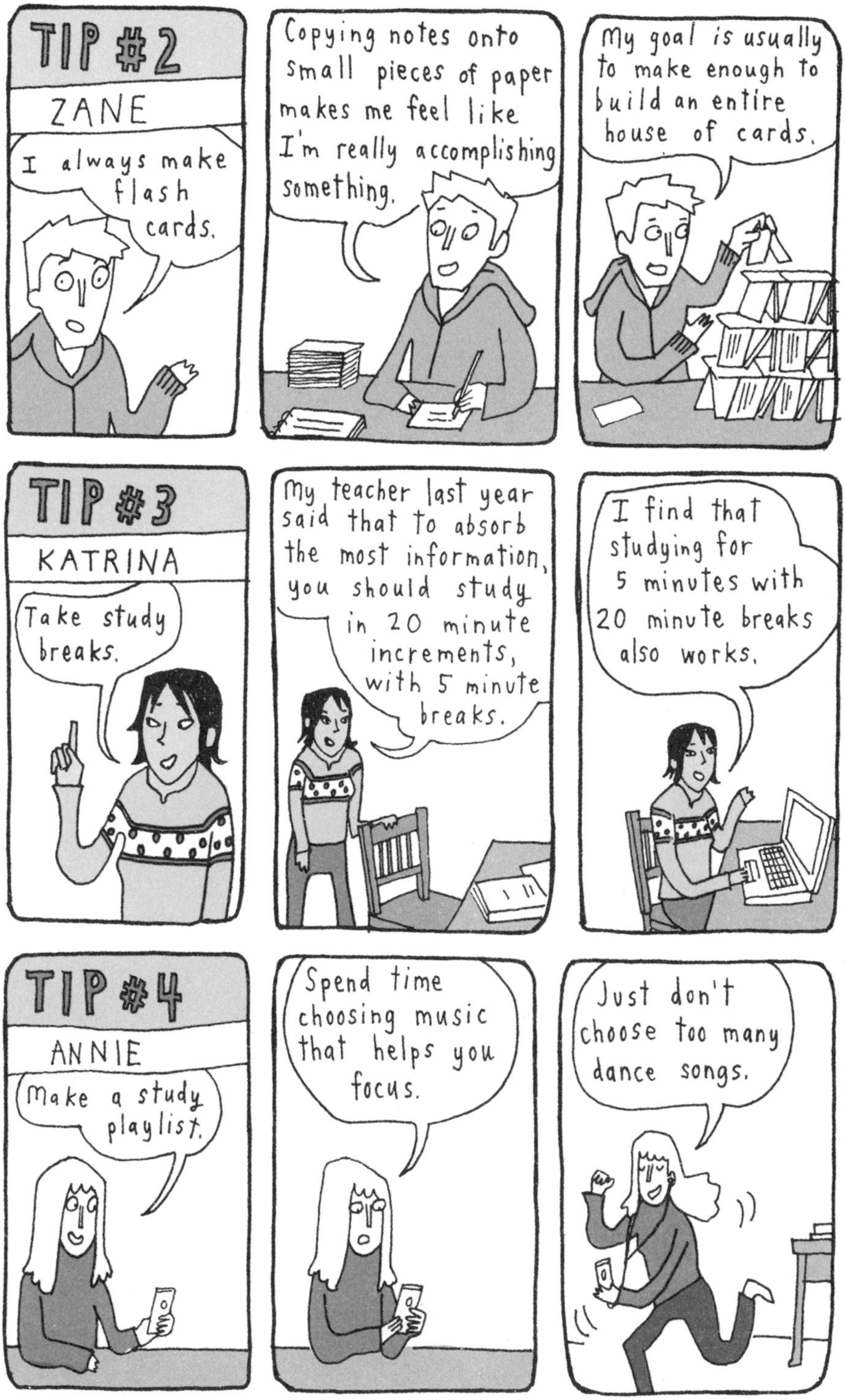
TIP #2
ZANE
I always make flash cards.
Copying notes onto small pieces of paper makes me feel like I'm really accomplishing something.
My goal is usually to make enough to build an entire house of cards.
TIP #3
KATRINA
Take study breaks.
My teacher last year said that to absorb the most information, you should study in 20 minute increments, with 5 minute breaks.
I find that studying for 5 minutes with 20 minute breaks also works.
TIP #4
ANNIE
Make a study playlist.
Spend time choosing music that helps you focus.
Just don't choose too many dance songs.

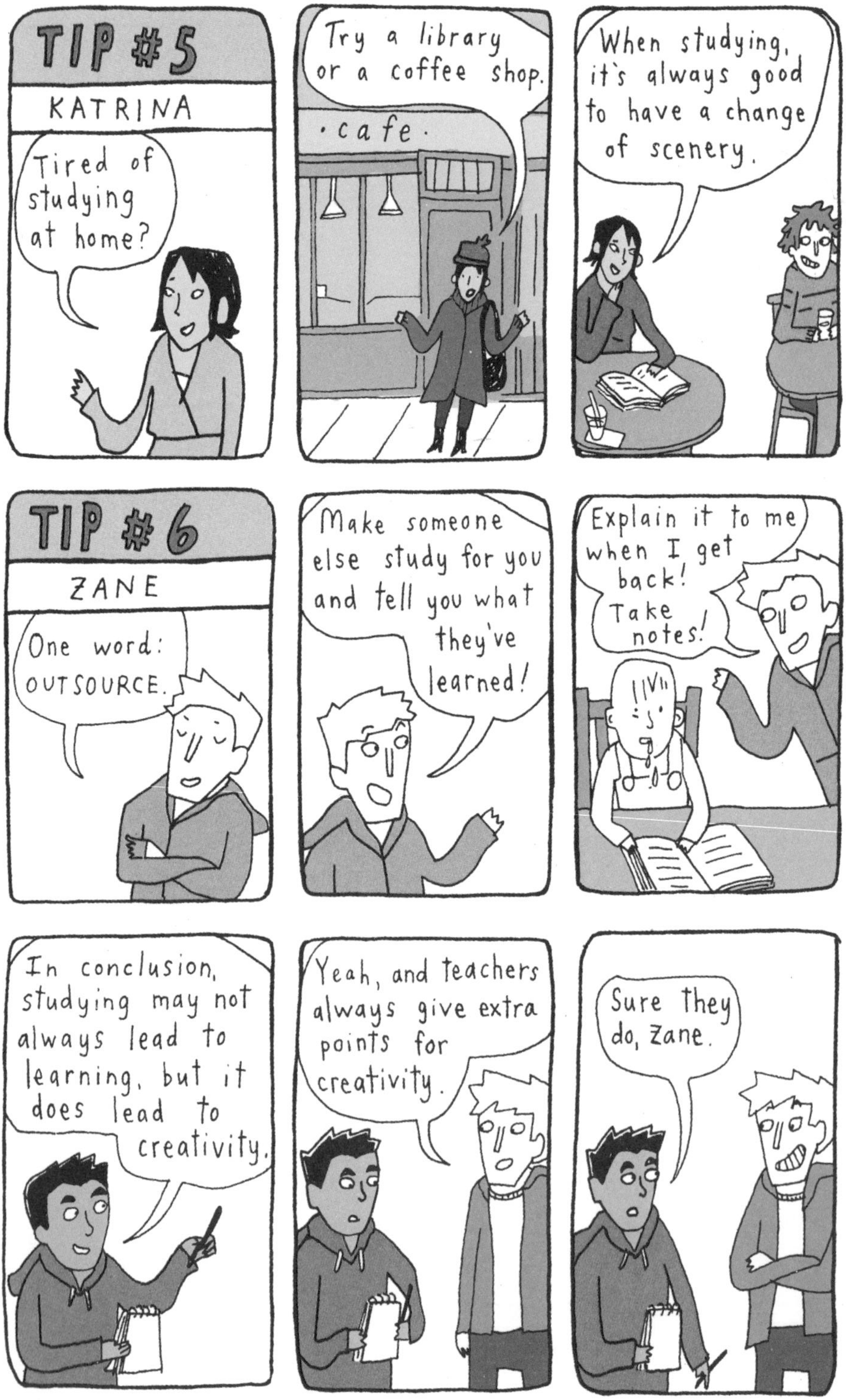
TIP #5
KATRINA
Tired of studying at home?
Try a library or a coffee shop.
·cafe·
When studying, it's always good to have a change of scenery.
TIP #6
ZANE
One word: OUTSOURCE.
Make someone else study for you and tell you what they've learned!
Explain it to me when I get back!
Take notes!
In conclusion, studying may not always lead to learning, but it does lead to creativity.
Yeah, and teachers always give extra points for creativity.
Sure they do, Zane.

REHEARSAL TIME
PRACTICE YOUR WHINE

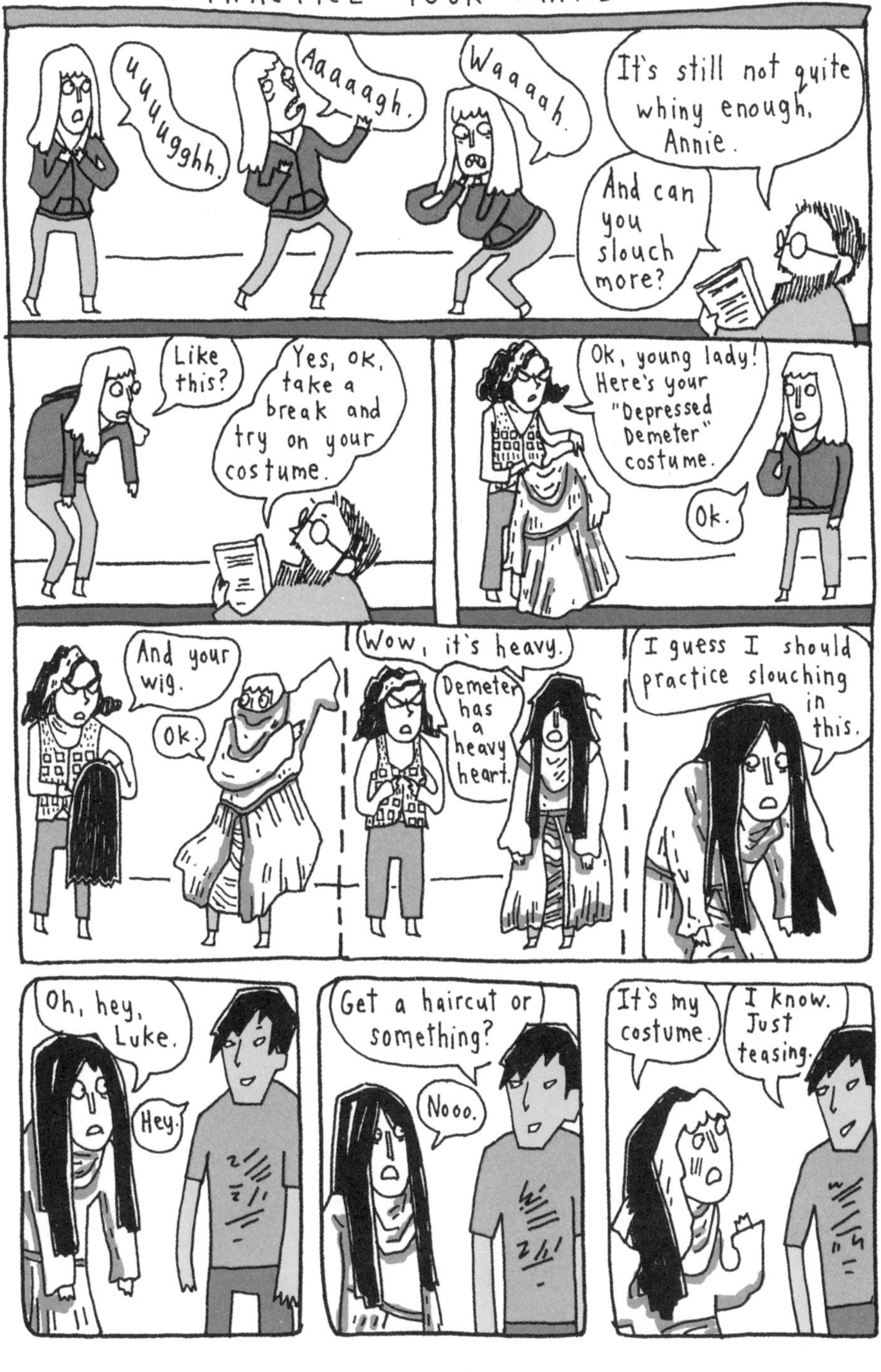

Uuuugghh.
Aaaaaagh.
Waaaaah.
It's still not quite whiny enough, Annie.
And can you slouch more?
Like this?
Yes, ok, take a break and try on your costume.
Ok, young lady! Here's your "Depressed Demeter" costume.
Ok.
And your wig.
Ok.
Wow, it's heavy.
Demeter has a heavy heart.
I guess I should practice slouching in this.
Oh, hey, Luke.
Hey.
Get a haircut or something?
Nooo.
It's my costume.
I know. Just teasing.

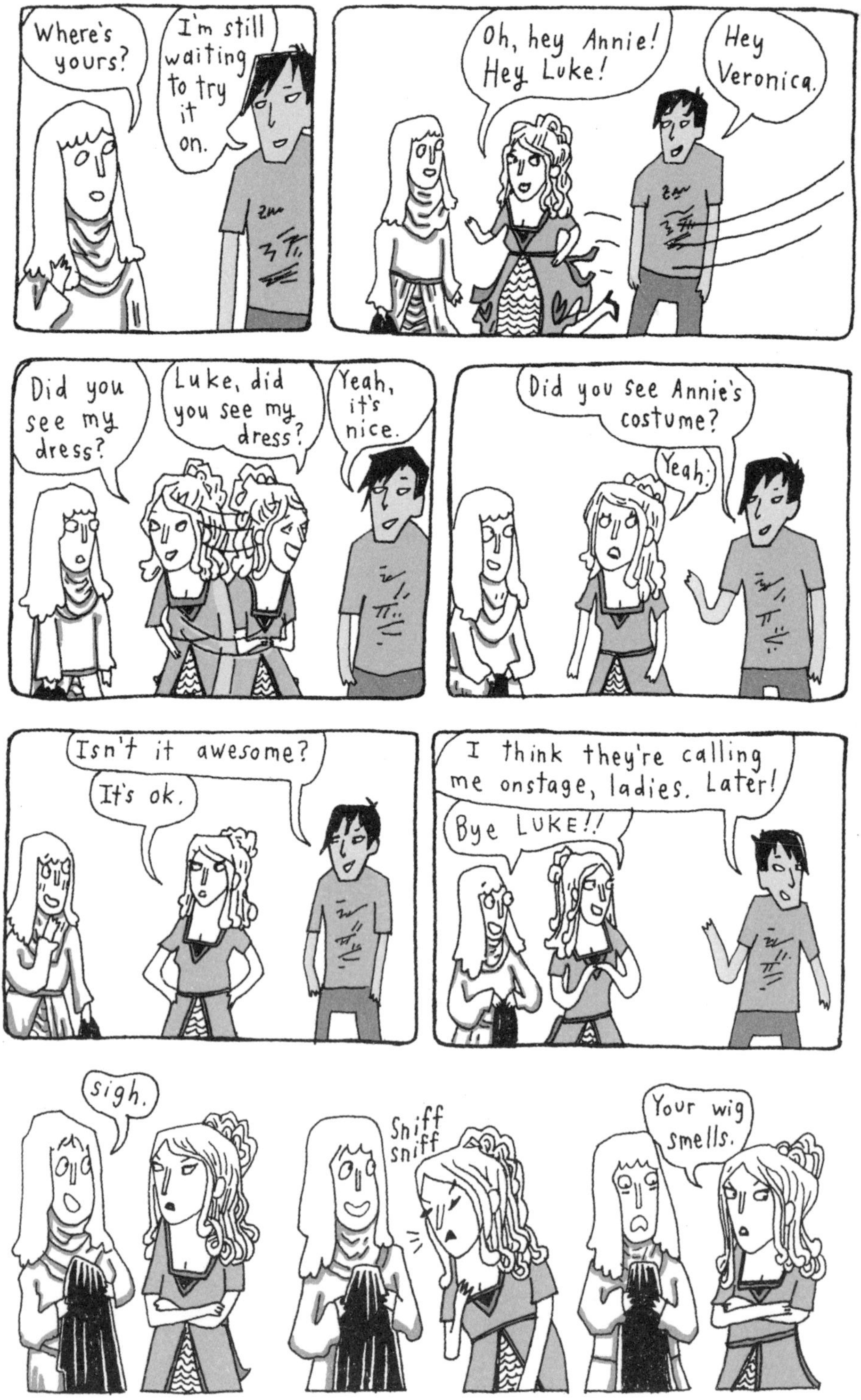

Where's yours?
I'm still waiting to try it on.
Oh, hey Annie! Hey Luke!
Hey Veronica.
Did you see my dress?
Luke, did you see my dress?
Yeah, it's nice.
Did you see Annie's costume?
Yeah.
Isn't it awesome?
It's ok.
I think they're calling me onstage, ladies. Later!
Bye LUKE!!
sigh.
Sniff sniff
Your wig smells.

PHONE-IN FRIENDSHIP

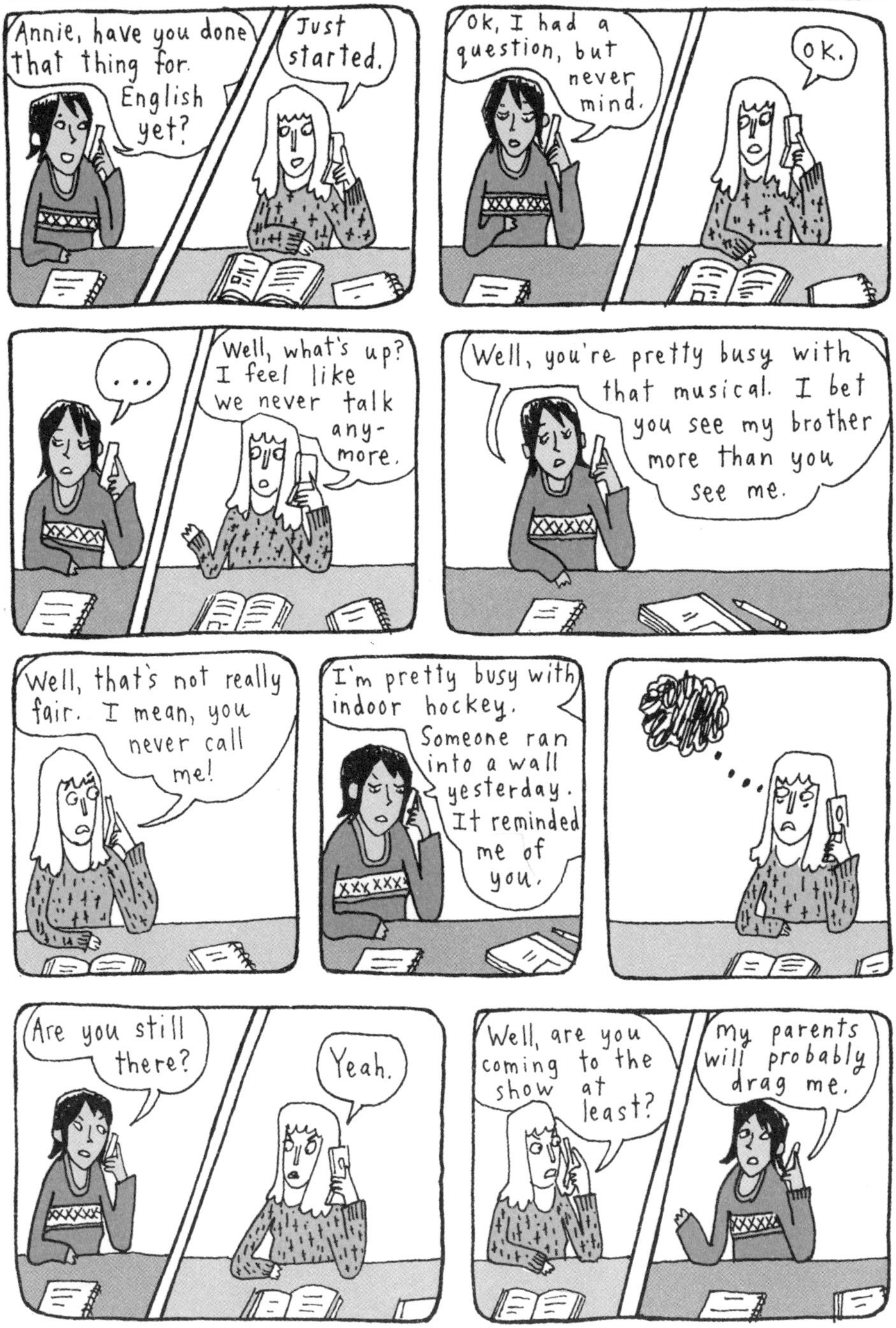
Annie, have you done that thing for English yet?
Just started.
Ok, I had a question, but never mind.
Ok.
...
Well, what's up? I feel like we never talk anymore.
Well, you're pretty busy with that musical. I bet you see my brother more than you see me.
Well, that's not really fair. I mean, you never call me!
I'm pretty busy with indoor hockey.
Someone ran into a wall yesterday. It reminded me of you.
Are you still there?
Yeah.
Well, are you coming to the show at least?
my parents will probably drag me.

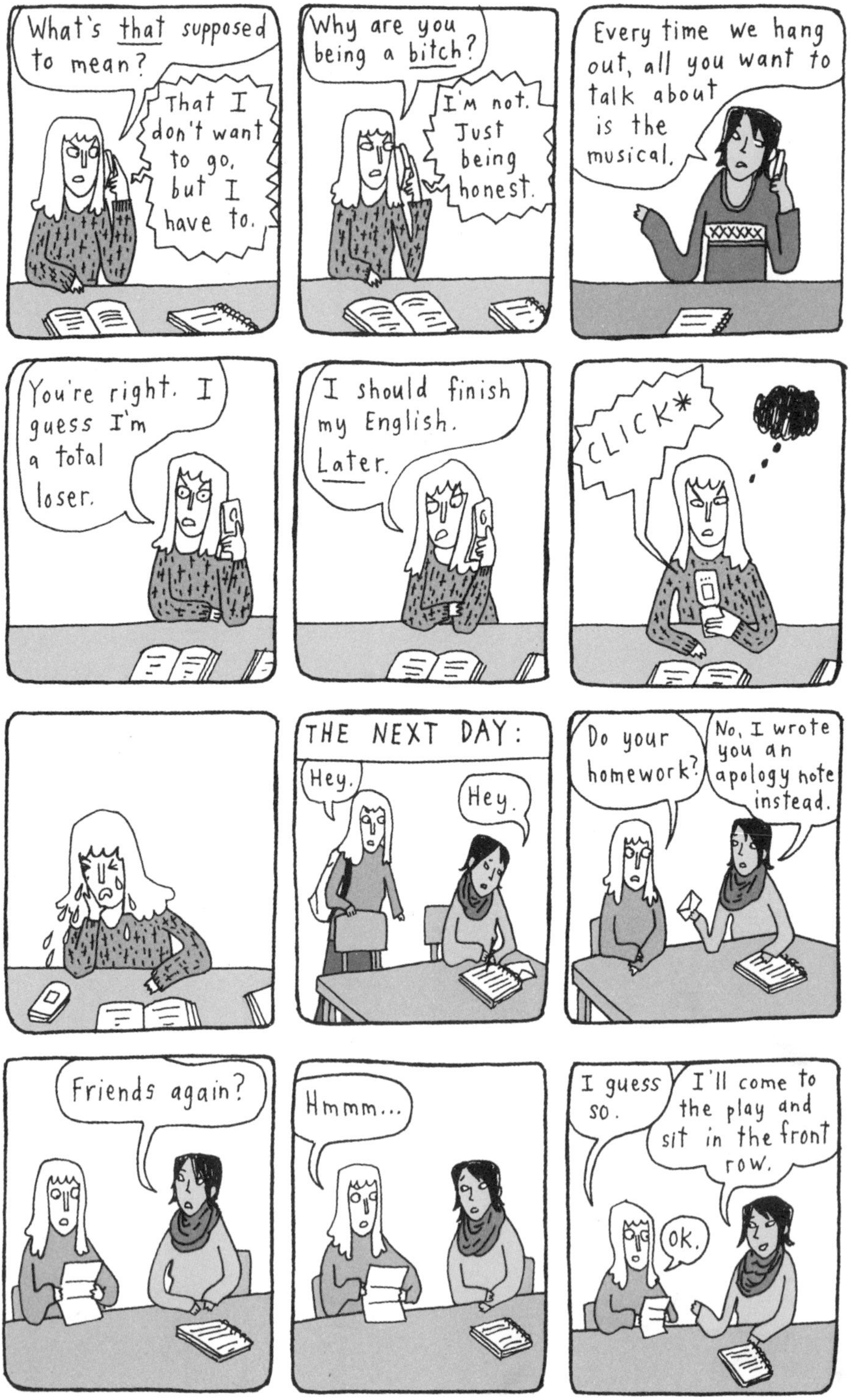
What's that supposed to mean?
That I don't want to go, but I have to.
Why are you being a bitch?
I'm not. Just being honest.
Every time we hang out, all you want to talk about is the musical.
You're right. I guess I'm a total loser.
I should finish my English. Later.
CLICK*
THE NEXT DAY:
Hey.
Hey.
Do your homework?
No, I wrote you an apology note instead.
Friends again?
Hmmm...
I guess so.
I'll come to the play and sit in the front row.
OK.

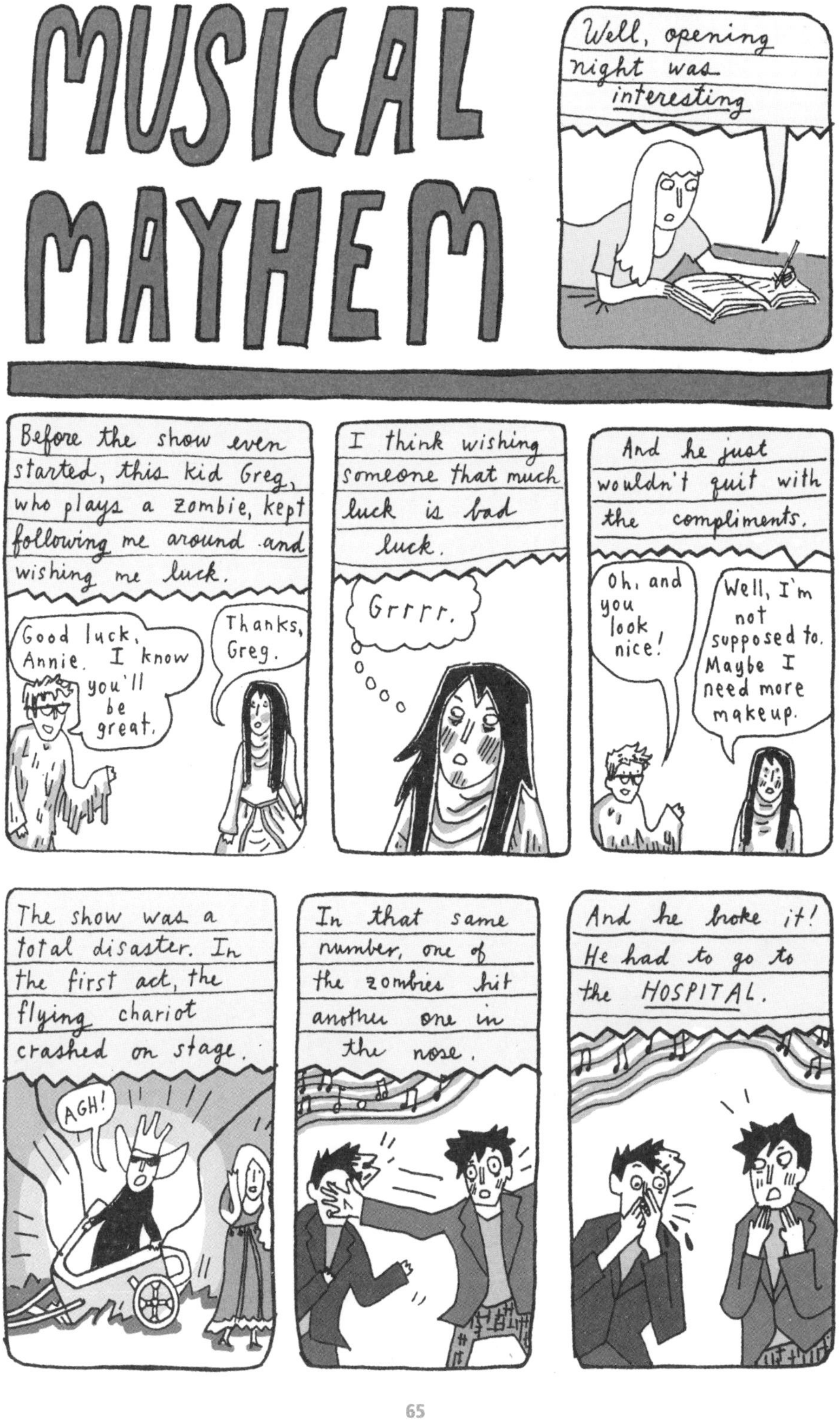
MUSICAL MAYHEM
Well, opening night was interesting
Before the show even started, this kid Greg, who plays a zombie, kept following me around and wishing me luck.
Good luck, Annie. I know you'll be great.
Thanks, Greg.
I think wishing someone that much luck is bad luck.
Grrrr.
And he just wouldn't quit with the compliments.
Oh, and you look nice!
Well, I'm not supposed to. Maybe I need more makeup.
The show was a total disaster. In the first act, the flying chariot crashed on stage.
AGH!
In that same number, one of the zombies hit another one in the nose.
And he broke it! He had to go to the HOSPITAL.

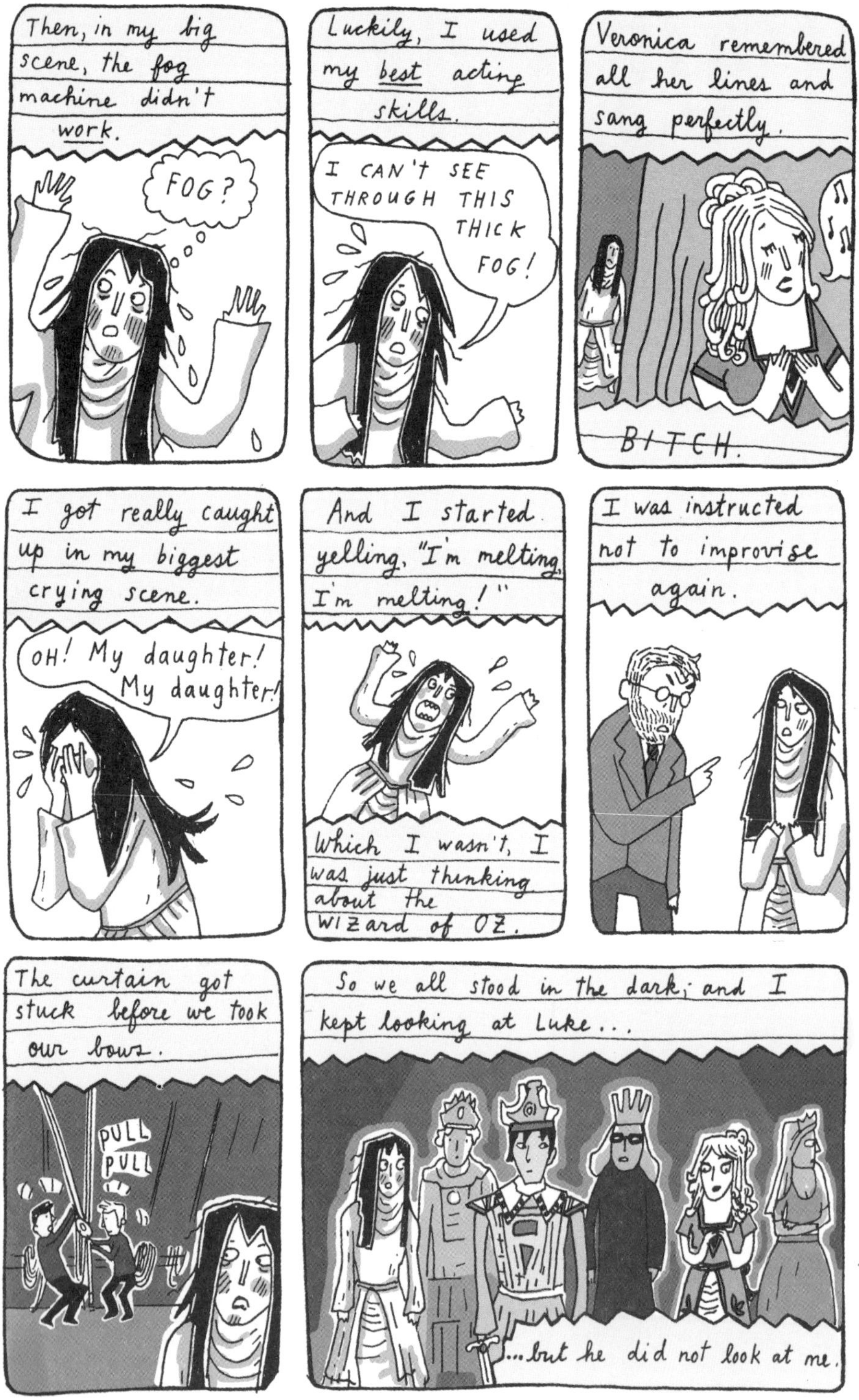
Then, in my big scene, the fog machine didn't work.
FOG?
Luckily, I used my best acting skills.
I CAN'T SEE THROUGH THIS THICK FOG!
Veronica remembered all her lines and sang perfectly.
BITCH.
I got really caught up in my biggest crying scene.
OH! My daughter! My daughter!
And I started yelling, "I'm melting, I'm melting!"
Which I wasn't, I was just thinking about the WIZard of OZ.
I was instructed not to improvise again.
The curtain got stuck before we took our bows.
PULL
PULL
So we all stood in the dark; and I kept looking at Luke...
...but he did not look at me.

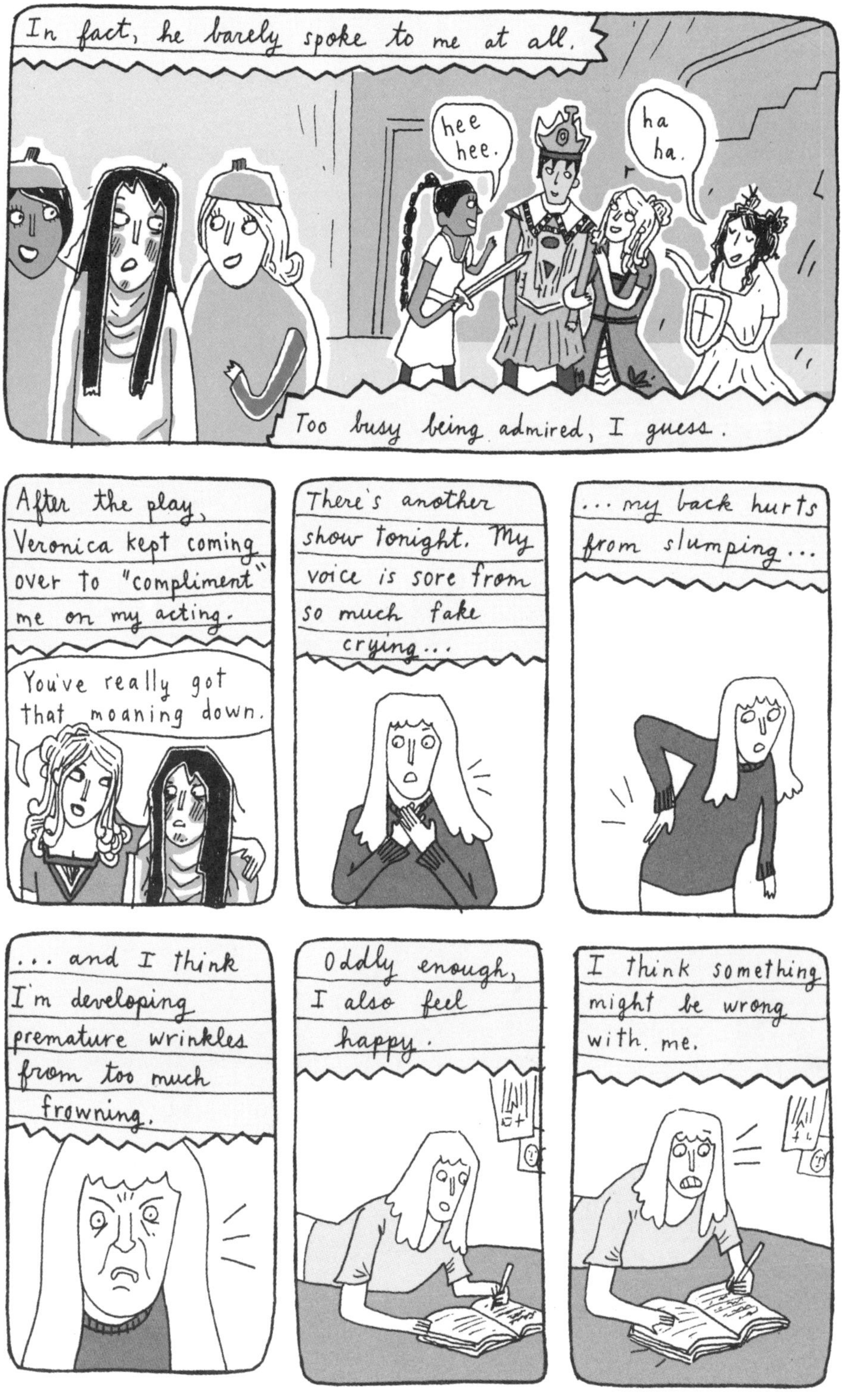
In fact, he barely spoke to me at all.
hee hee.
ha ha.
Too busy being admired, I guess.
After the play, Veronica kept coming over to "compliment" me on my acting.
You've really got that moaning down.
There's another show tonight. My voice is sore from so much fake crying...
... my back hurts from slumping...
... and I think I'm developing premature wrinkles from too much frowning.
Oddly enough, I also feel happy.
I think something might be wrong with me.

CLOSING NIGHT CAST PARTY: I'D LIKE A DIFFERENT ROLE

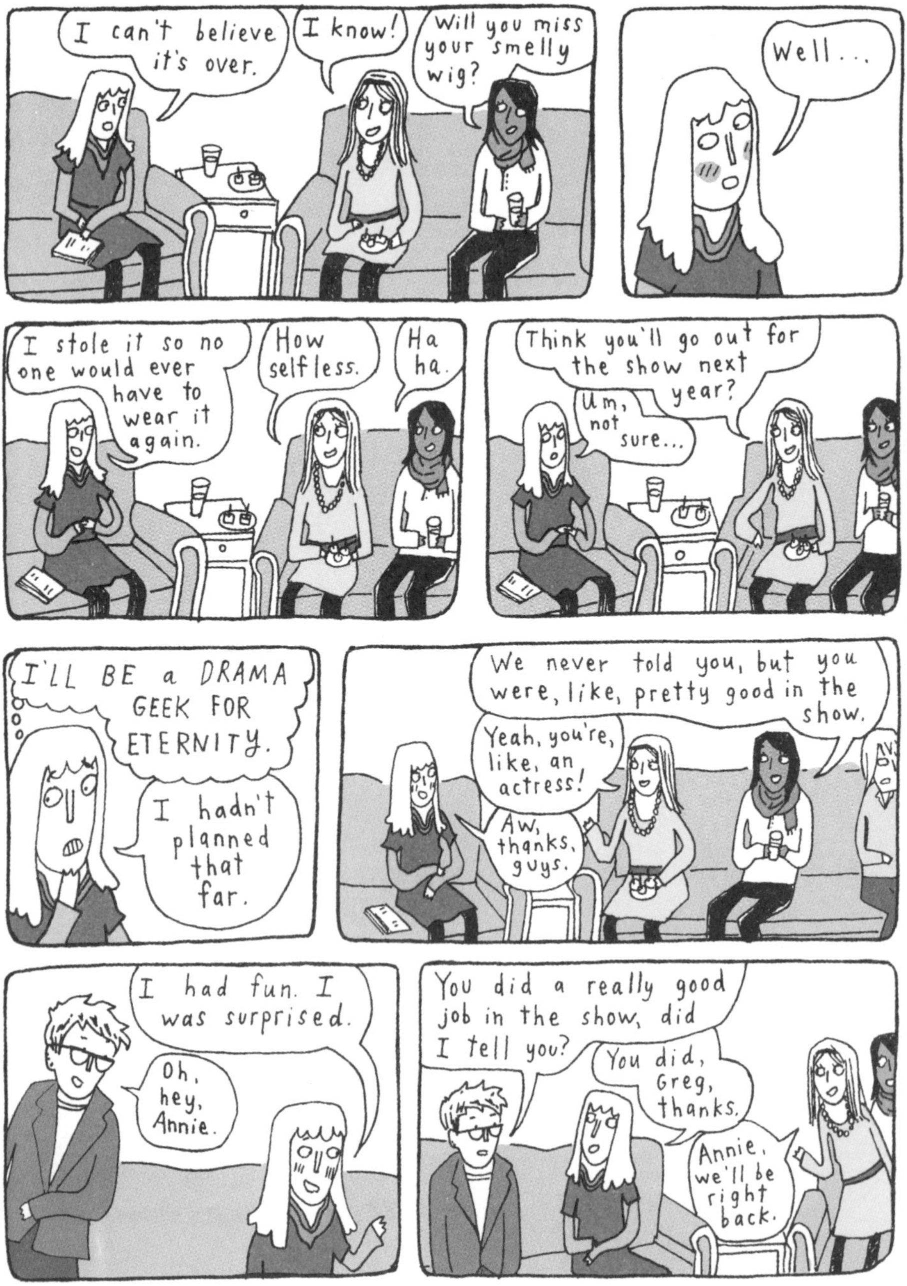
I can't believe it's over.
I know!
Will you miss your smelly wig?
Well...
I stole it so no one would ever have to wear it again.
How selfless.
Ha ha.
Think you'll go out for the show next year?
Um, not sure...
I'LL BE a DRAMA GEEK FOR ETERNITY.
I hadn't planned that far.
We never told you, but you were, like, pretty good in the show.
Yeah, you're, like, an actress!
Aw, thanks, guys.
I had fun. I was surprised.
Oh, hey, Annie.
You did a really good job in the show, did I tell you?
You did, Greg, thanks.
Annie, we'll be right back.

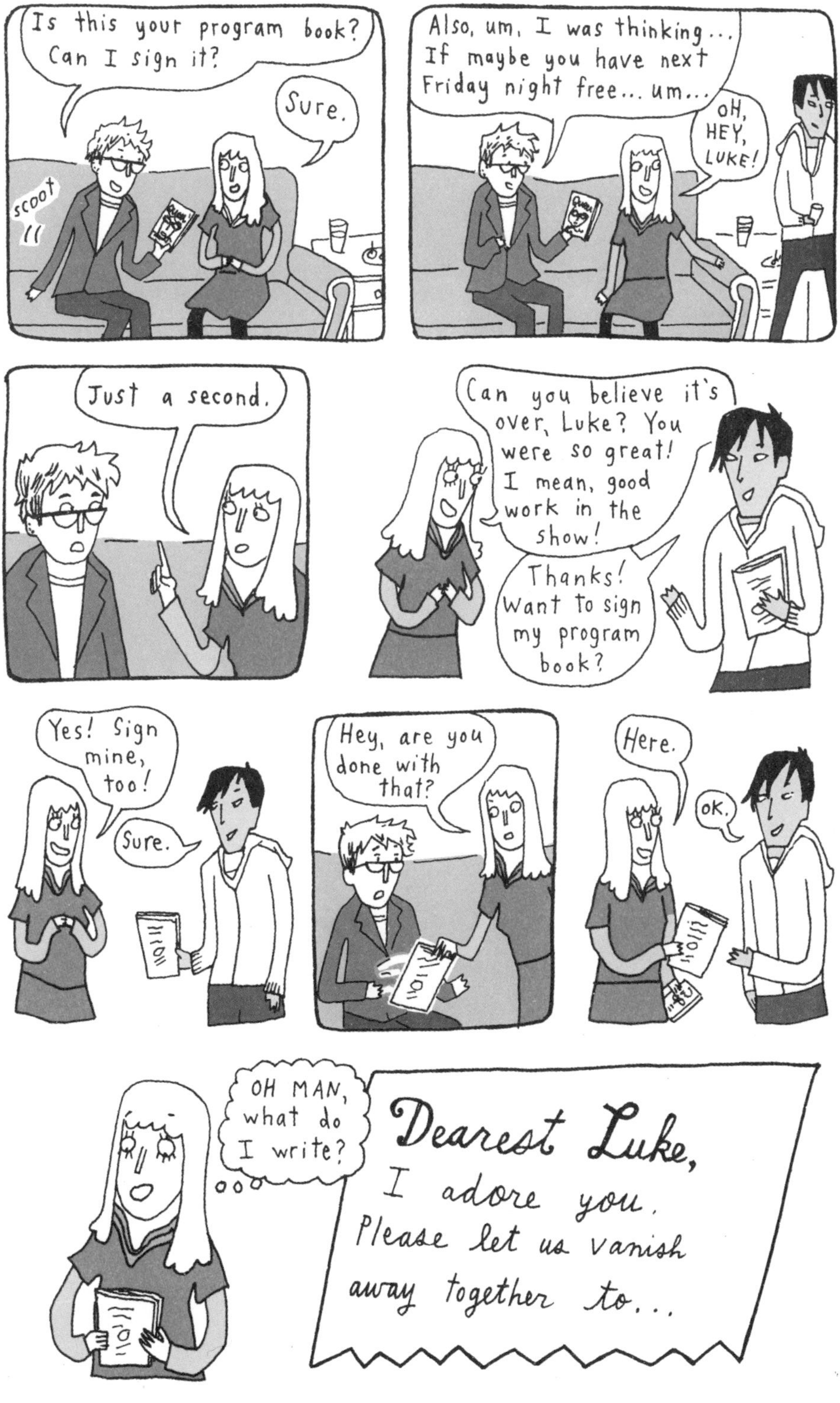

Is this your program book? Can I sign it?
Sure.
scoot
Also, um, I was thinking... If maybe you have next Friday night free... um...
OH, HEY, LUKE!
Just a second.
Can you believe it's over, Luke? You were so great! I mean, good work in the show!
Thanks! Want to sign my program book?
Yes! Sign mine, too!
Sure.
Hey, are you done with that?
Here.
OK.
OH MAN, what do I write?
Dearest Luke,
I adore you.
Please let us vanish away together to...

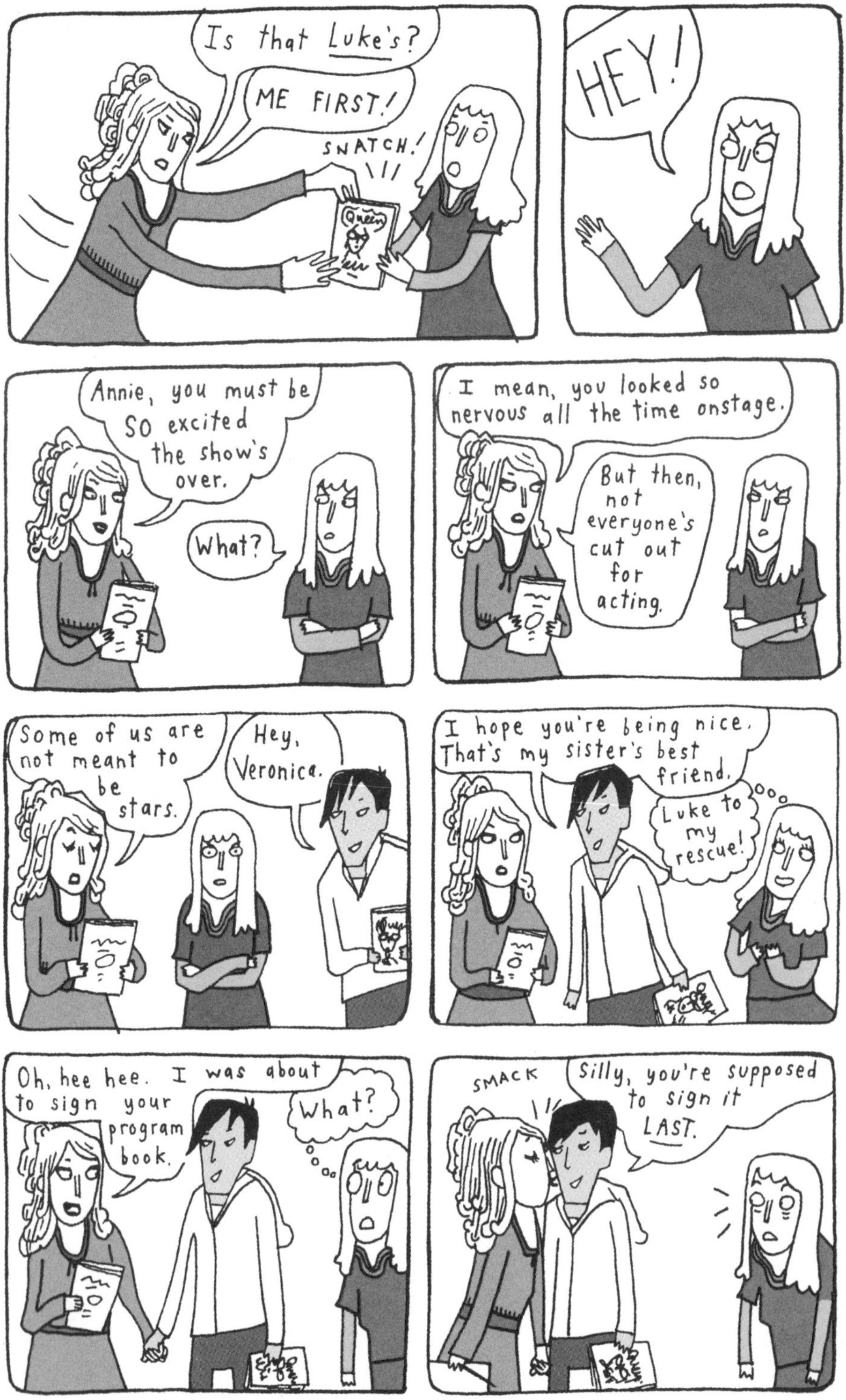
Is that Luke's?
ME FIRST!
SNATCH!
HEY!
Annie, you must be SO excited the show's over.
What?
I mean, you looked so nervous all the time onstage.
But then, not everyone's cut out for acting.
Some of us are not meant to be stars.
Hey, Veronica.
I hope you're being nice. That's my sister's best friend.
Luke to my rescue!
Oh, hee hee. I was about to sign your program book.
What?
SMACK
Silly, you're supposed to sign it LAST.

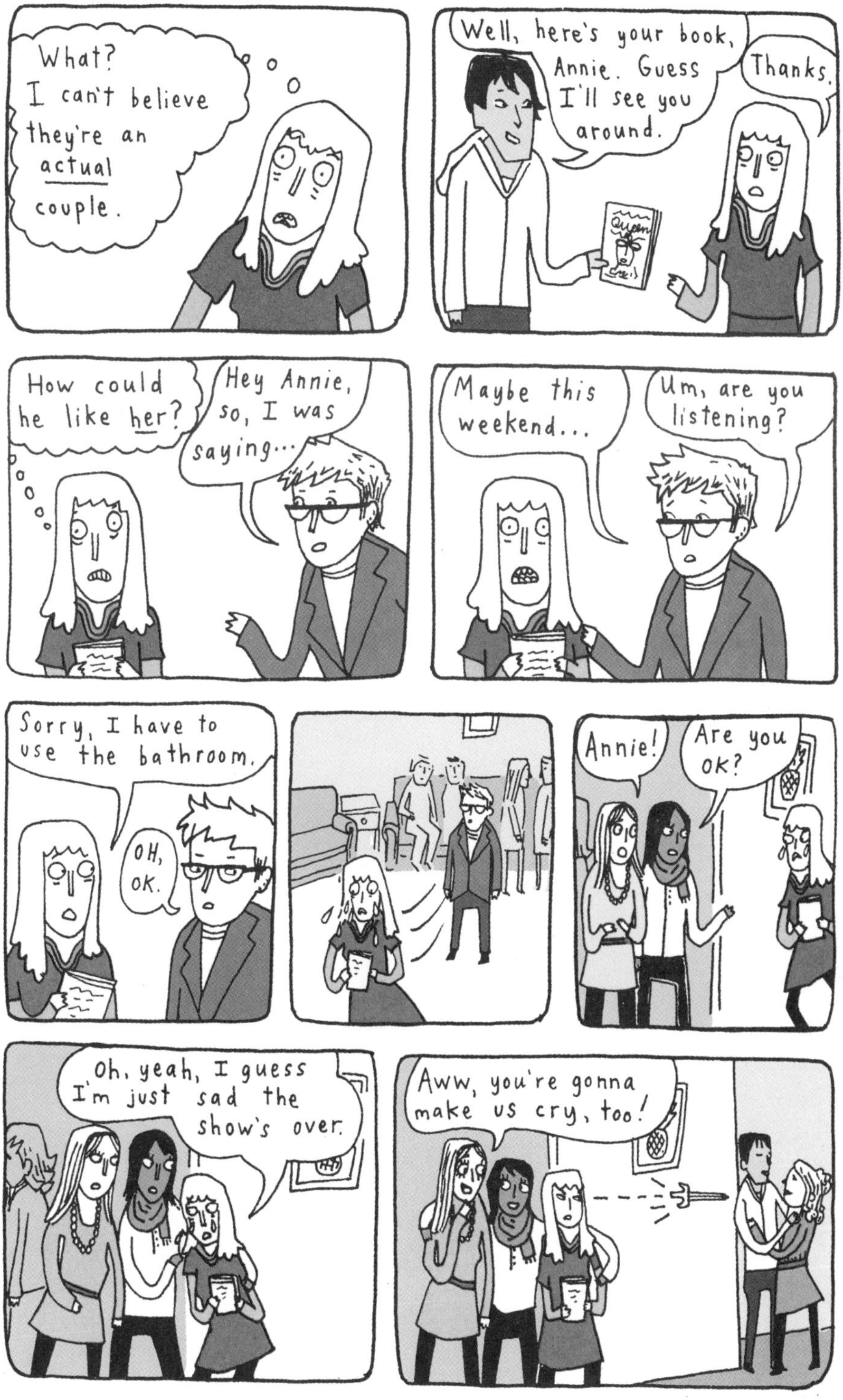
What? I can't believe they're an actual couple.
Well, here's your book, Annie. Guess I'll see you around.
Thanks.
Queen
How could he like her?
Hey Annie, so, I was saying...
Maybe this weekend...
Um, are you listening?
Sorry, I have to use the bathroom.
OH, OK.
Annie!
Are you OK?
Oh, yeah, I guess I'm just sad the show's over.
Aww, you're gonna make us cry, too!

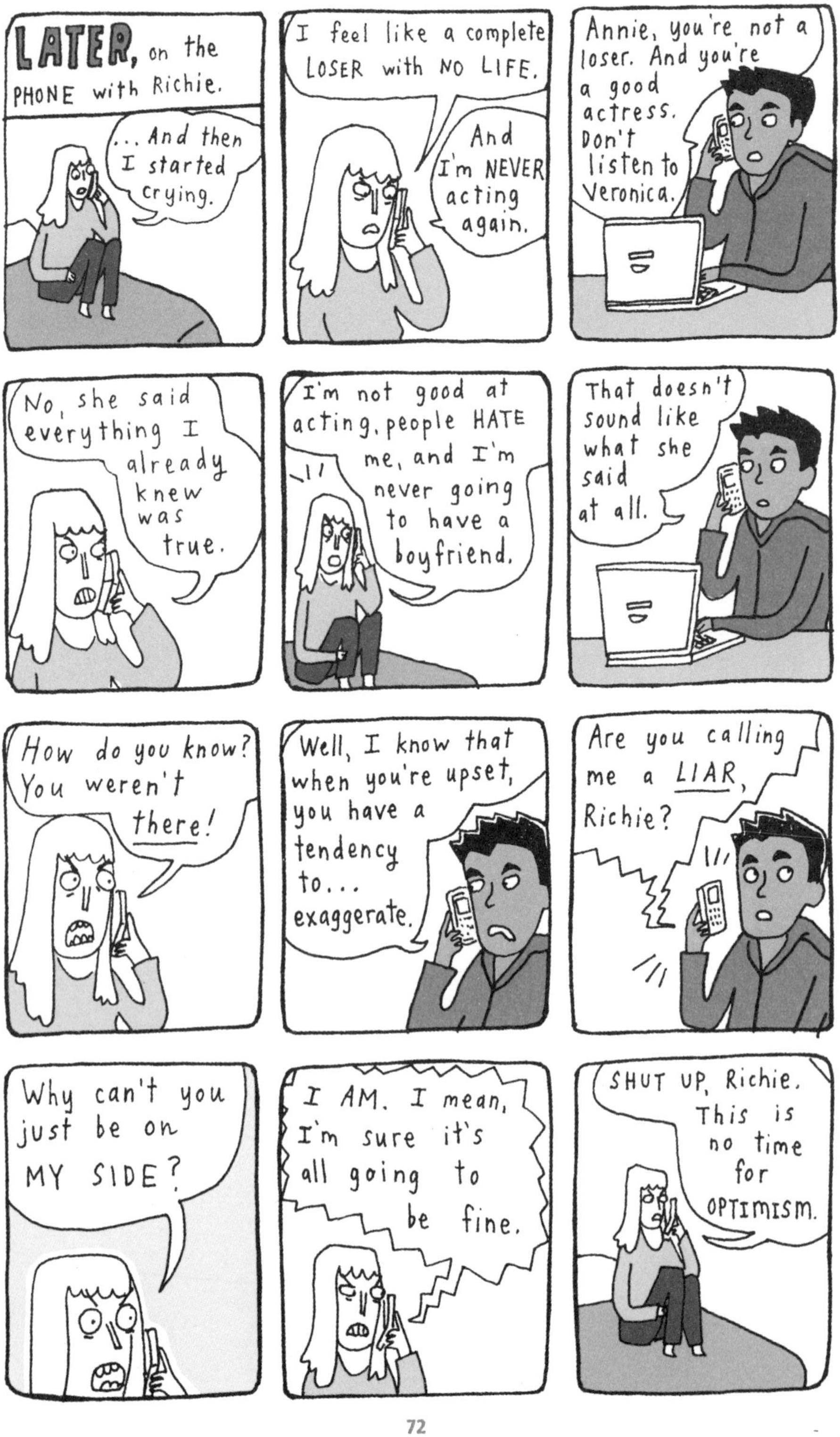

LATER, on the PHONE with Richie.
...And then I started crying.
I feel like a complete LOSER with NO LIFE.
And I'm NEVER acting again.
Annie, you're not a loser. And you're a good actress. Don't listen to Veronica.
No, she said everything I already knew was true.
I'm not good at acting, people HATE me, and I'm never going to have a boyfriend.
That doesn't sound like what she said at all.
How do you know? You weren't there!
Well, I know that when you're upset, you have a tendency to... exaggerate.
Are you calling me a LIAR, Richie?
Why can't you just be on MY SIDE?
I AM. I mean, I'm sure it's all going to be fine.
SHUT UP, Richie. This is no time for OPTIMISM.

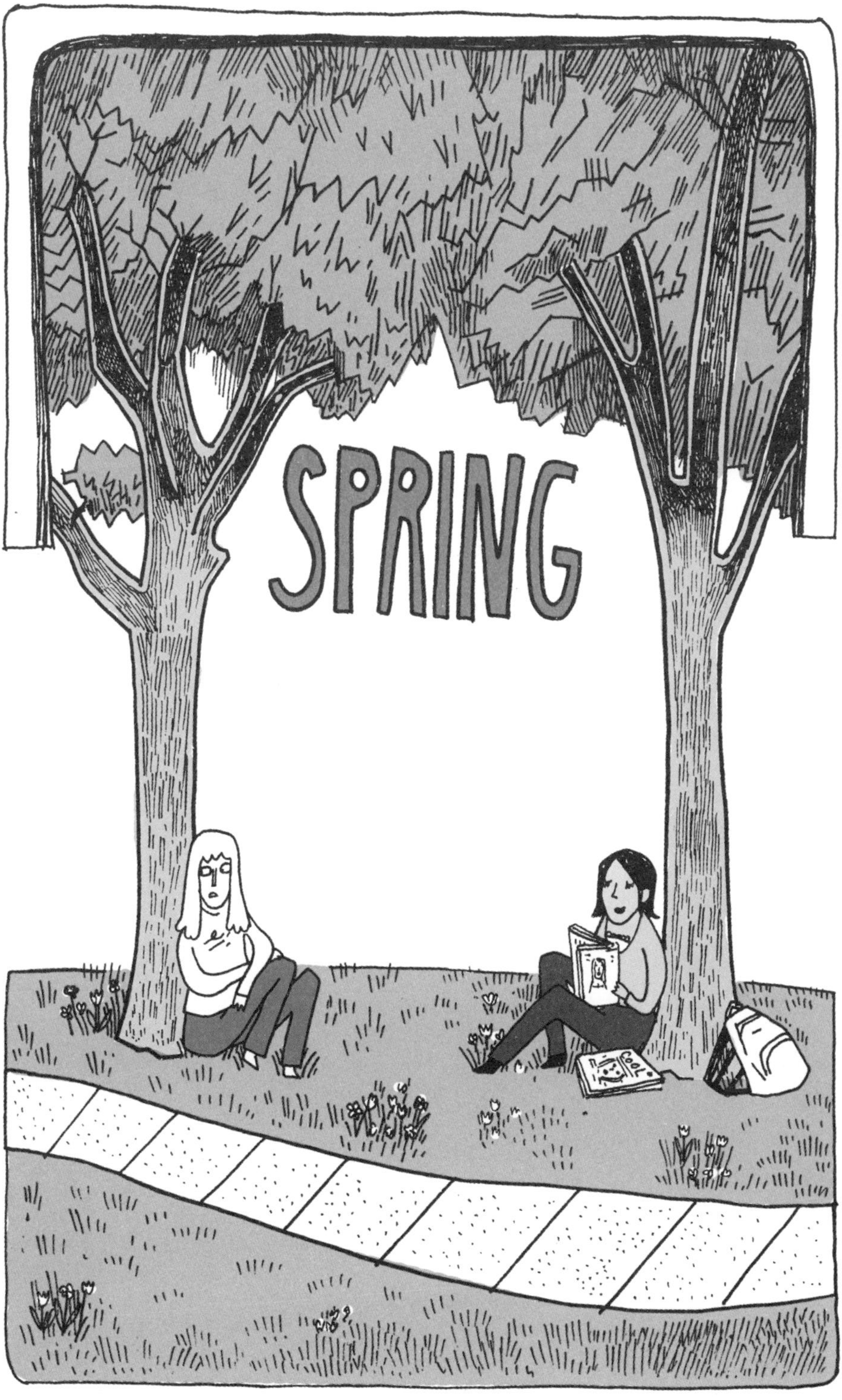
SPRING

UN-SEASONAL DEPRESSION

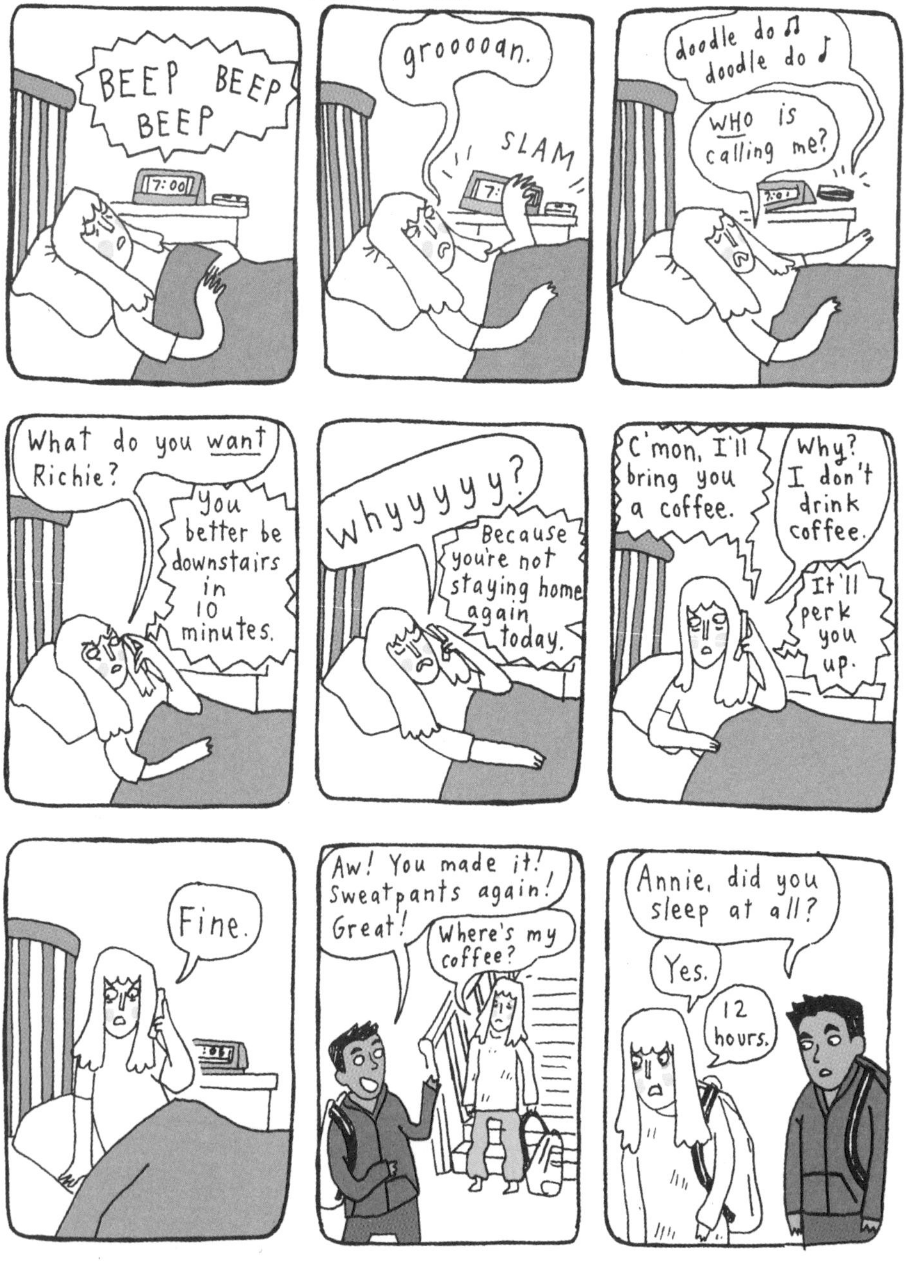
BEEP BEEP BEEP
7:00
groooooan.
SLAM
doodle do ♫ doodle do ♪
WHO is calling me?
What do you want Richie?
You better be downstairs in 10 minutes.
whyyyyy?
Because you're not staying home again today.
C'mon, I'll bring you a coffee.
Why? I don't drink coffee.
It'll perk you up.
Fine.
Aw! You made it! Sweatpants again! Great!
Where's my coffee?
Annie, did you sleep at all?
Yes.
12 hours.

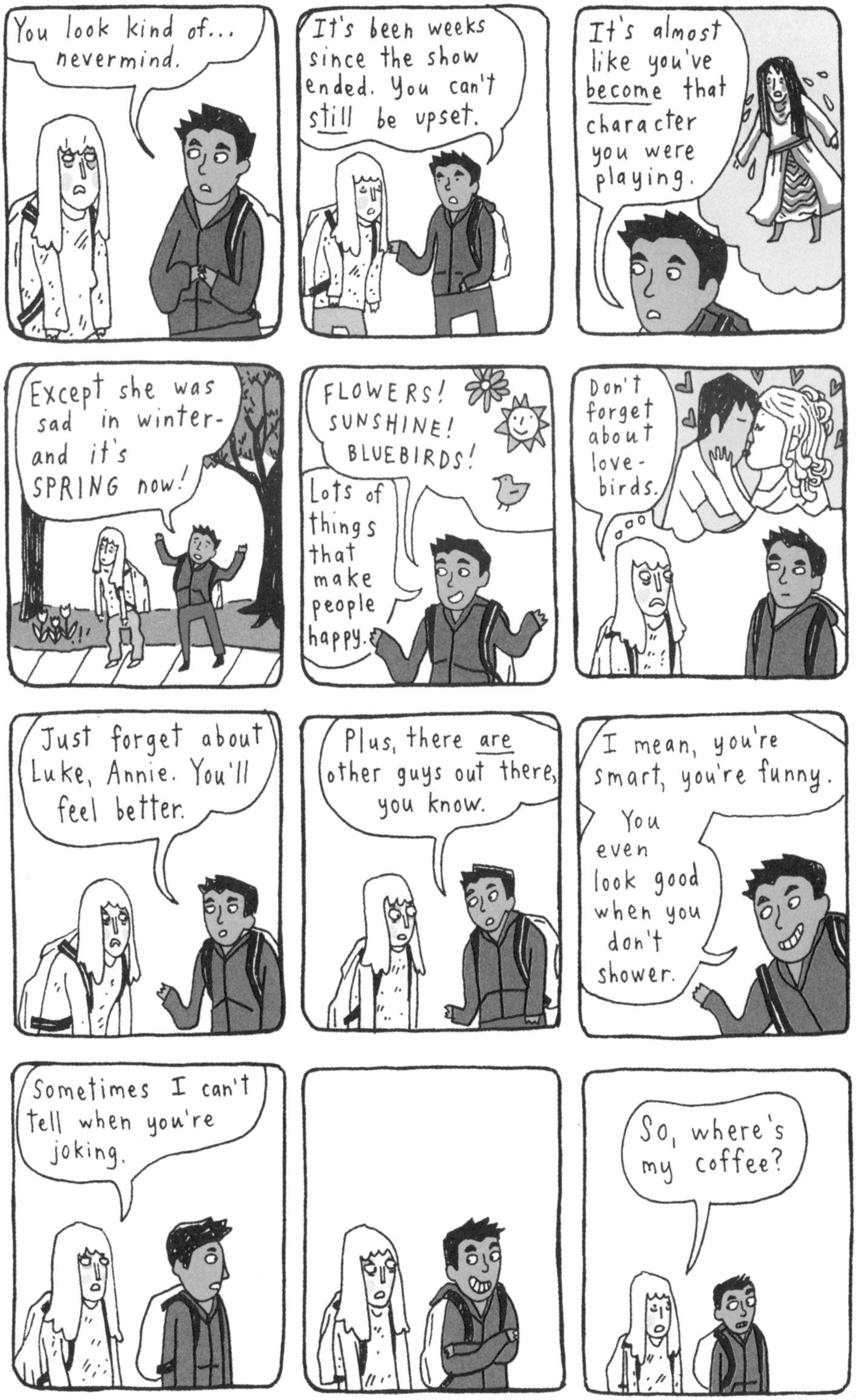
You look kind of... nevermind.
It's been weeks since the show ended. You can't still be upset.
It's almost like you've become that character you were playing.
Except she was sad in winter- and it's SPRING now!
FLOWERS! SUNSHINE! BLUEBIRDS!
Lots of things that make people happy.
Don't forget about love-birds.
Just forget about Luke, Annie. You'll feel better.
Plus, there are other guys out there, you know.
I mean, you're smart, you're funny.
You even look good when you don't shower.
Sometimes I can't tell when you're joking.
So, where's my coffee?

JUST ANOTHER DAY

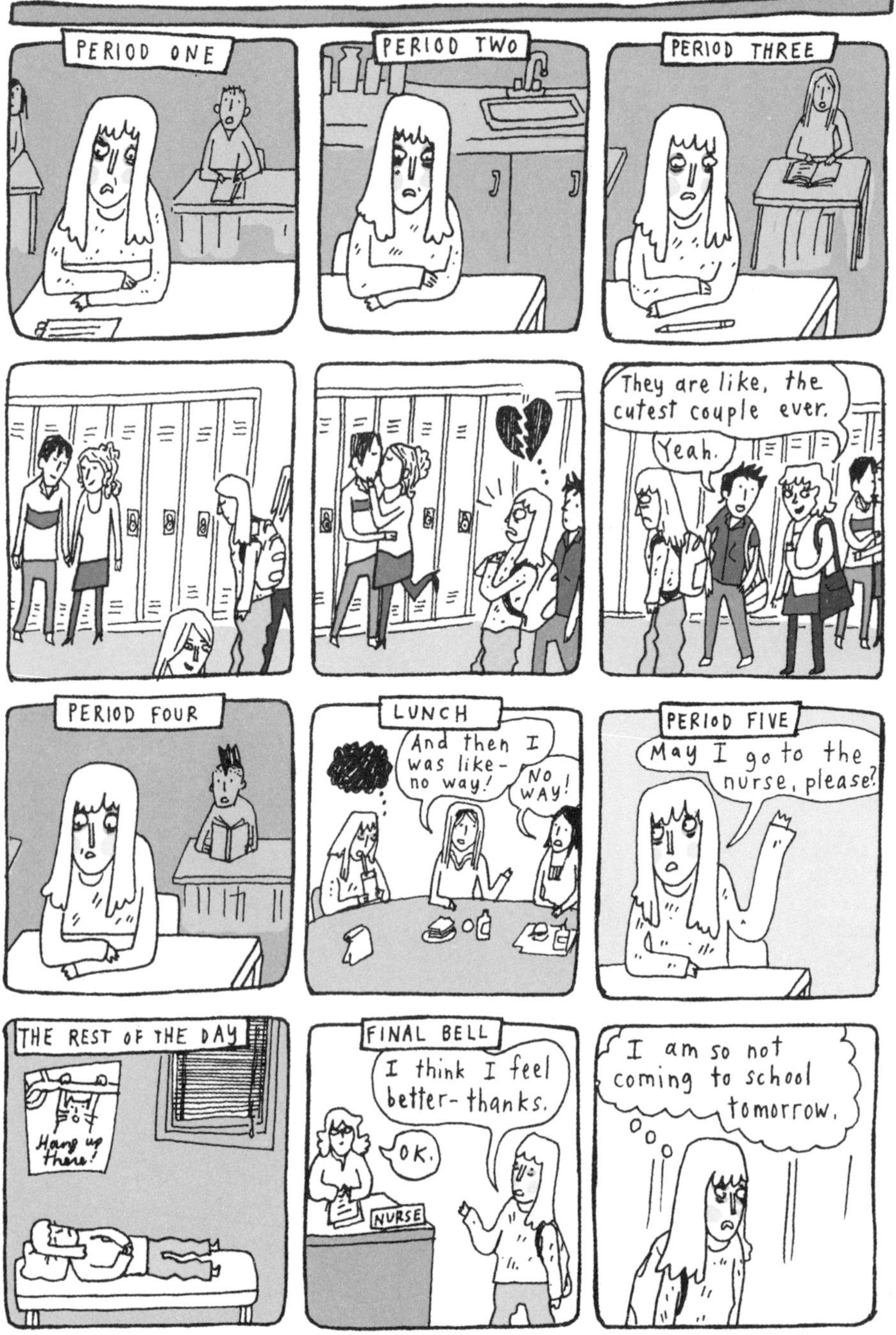
PERIOD ONE
PERIOD TWO
PERIOD THREE
They are like, the cutest couple ever.
Yeah.
PERIOD FOUR
LUNCH
And then I was like- no way!
NO WAY!
PERIOD FIVE
May I go to the nurse, please?
THE REST OF THE DAY
Hang up there!
FINAL BELL
I think I feel better- thanks.
OK.
NURSE
I am so not coming to school tomorrow.

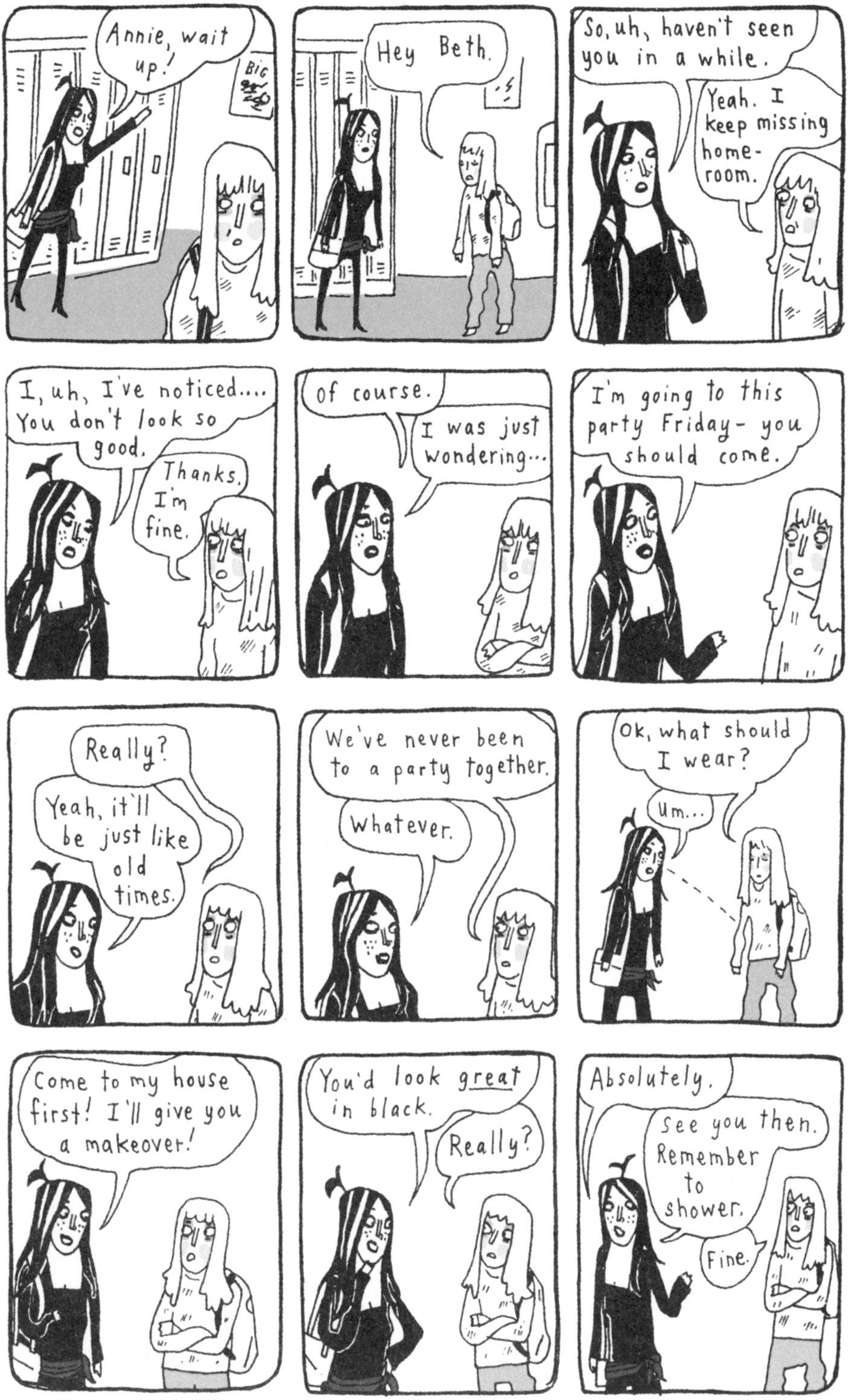
Annie, wait up!
Hey Beth.
So, uh, haven't seen you in a while.
Yeah. I keep missing home-room.
I, uh, I've noticed.... You don't look so good.
Thanks. I'm fine.
Of course.
I was just wondering...
I'm going to this party Friday- you should come.
Really?
Yeah, it'll be just like old times.
We've never been to a party together.
Whatever.
Ok, what should I wear?
Um...
Come to my house first! I'll give you a makeover!
You'd look great in black.
Really?
Absolutely.
See you then. Remember to shower.
Fine.

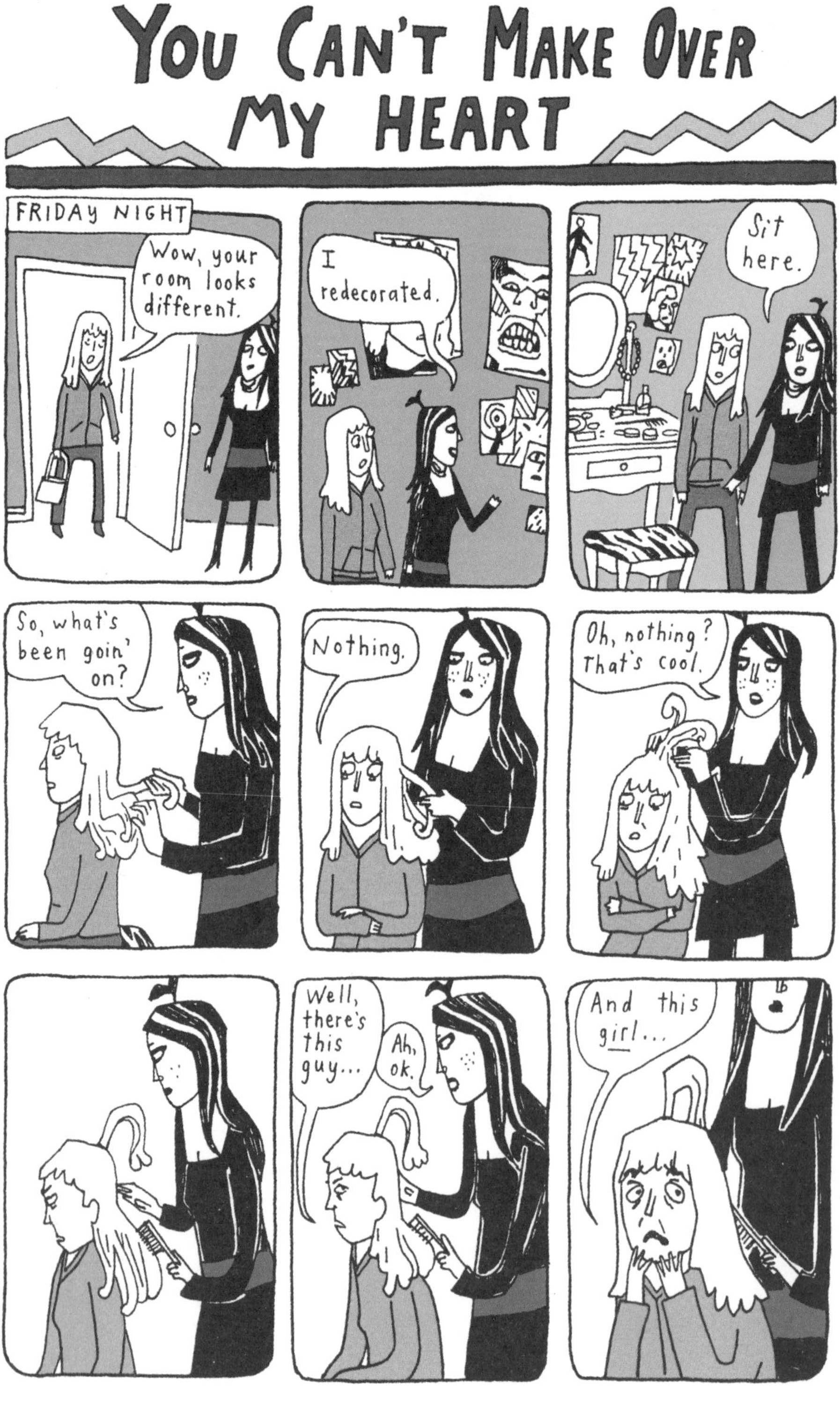
YOU CAN'T MAKE OVER MY HEART
FRIDAY NIGHT
Wow, your room looks different.
I redecorated.
Sit here.
So, what's been goin' on?
Nothing.
Oh, nothing? That's cool.
Well, there's this guy...
Ah, ok.
And this girl...

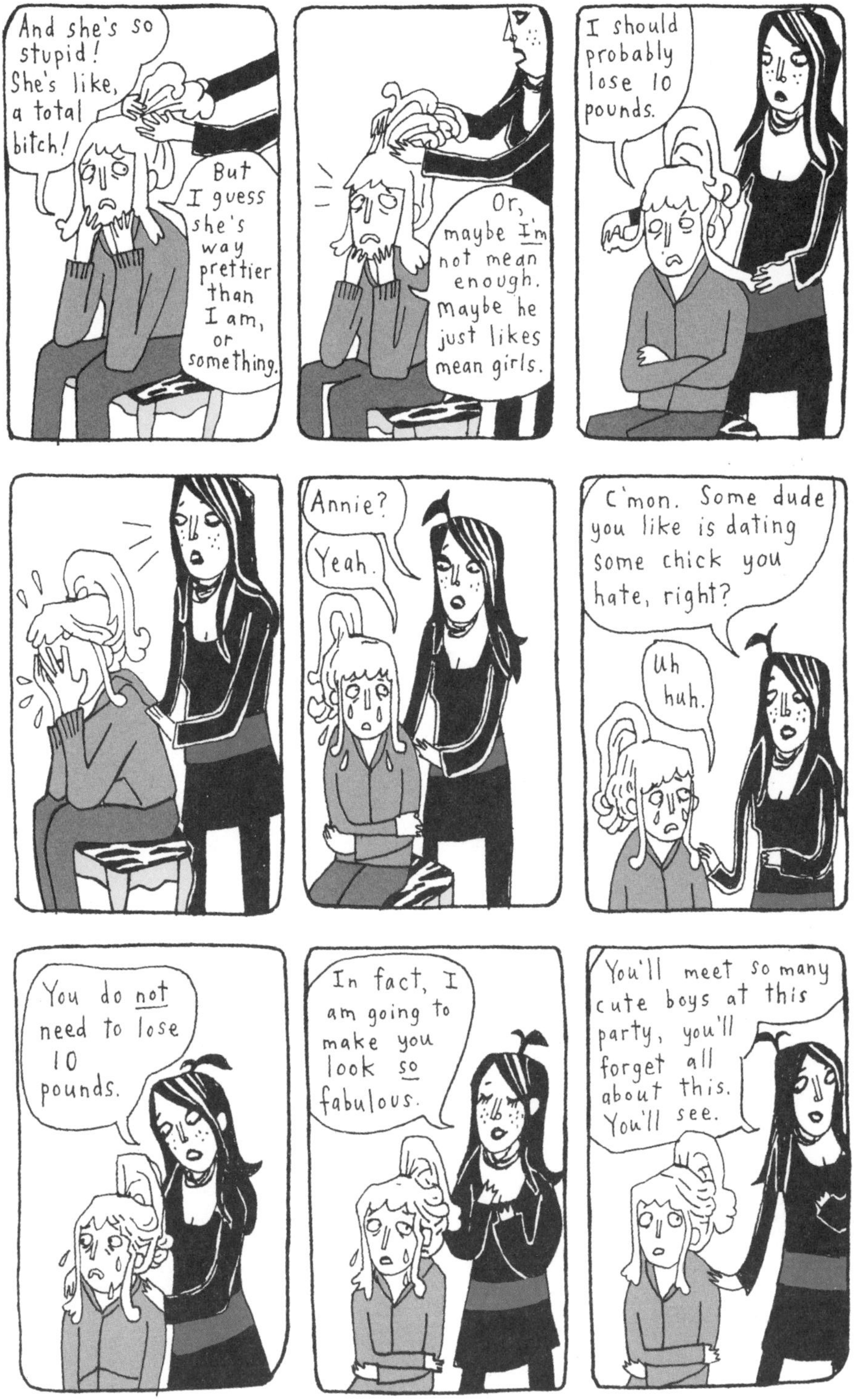
And she's so stupid! She's like, a total bitch!
But I guess she's way prettier than I am, or something.
Or, maybe I'm not mean enough. Maybe he just likes mean girls.
I should probably lose 10 pounds.
Annie?
Yeah.
C'mon. Some dude you like is dating some chick you hate, right?
Uh huh.
You do not need to lose 10 pounds.
In fact, I am going to make you look so fabulous.
You'll meet so many cute boys at this party, you'll forget all about this. You'll see.

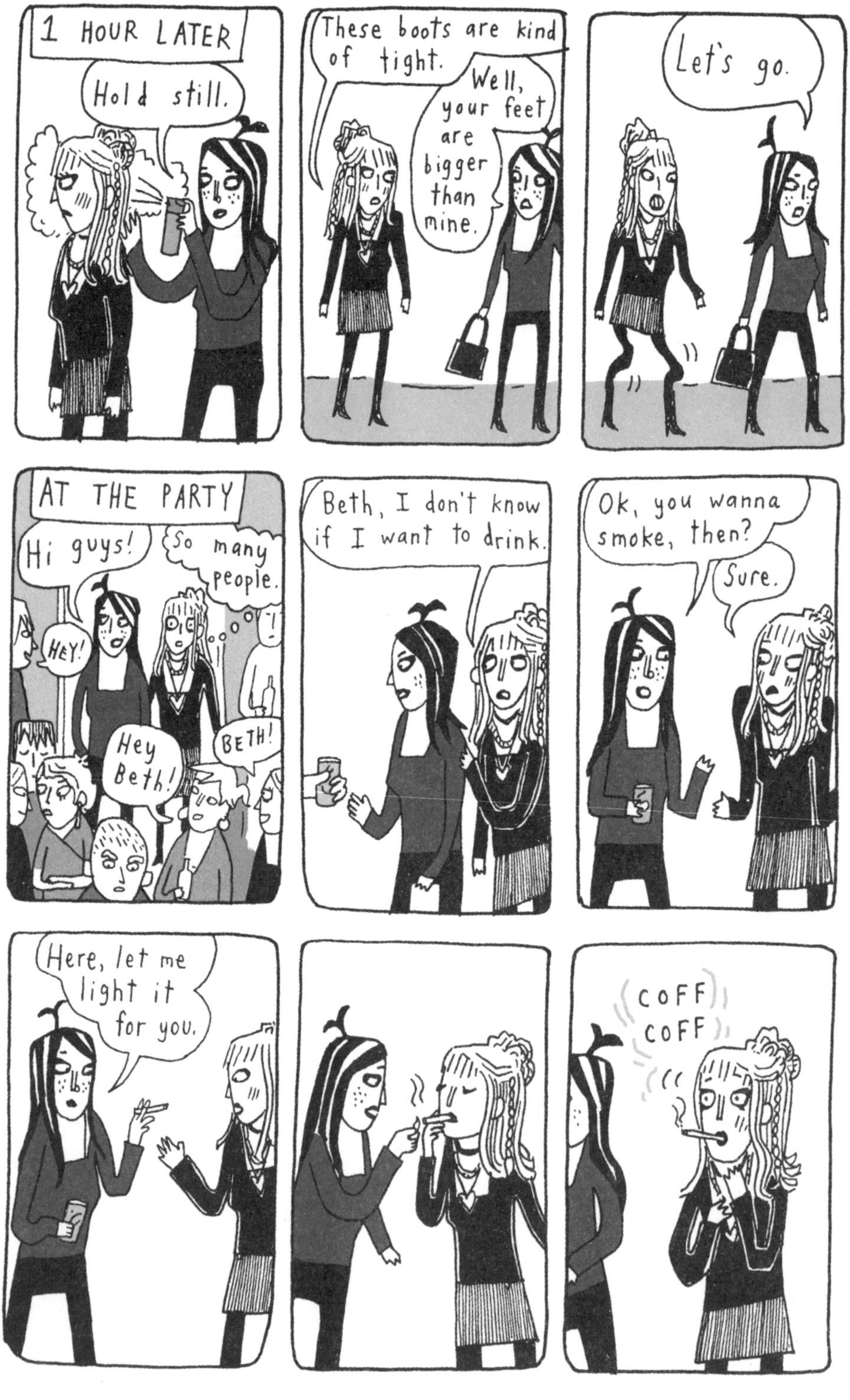
1 HOUR LATER
Hold still.
These boots are kind of tight.
Well, your feet are bigger than mine.
Let's go.
AT THE PARTY
Hi guys!
So many people.
HEY!
Hey Beth!
BETH!
Beth, I don't know if I want to drink.
Ok, you wanna smoke, then?
Sure.
Here, let me light it for you.
COFF
COFF

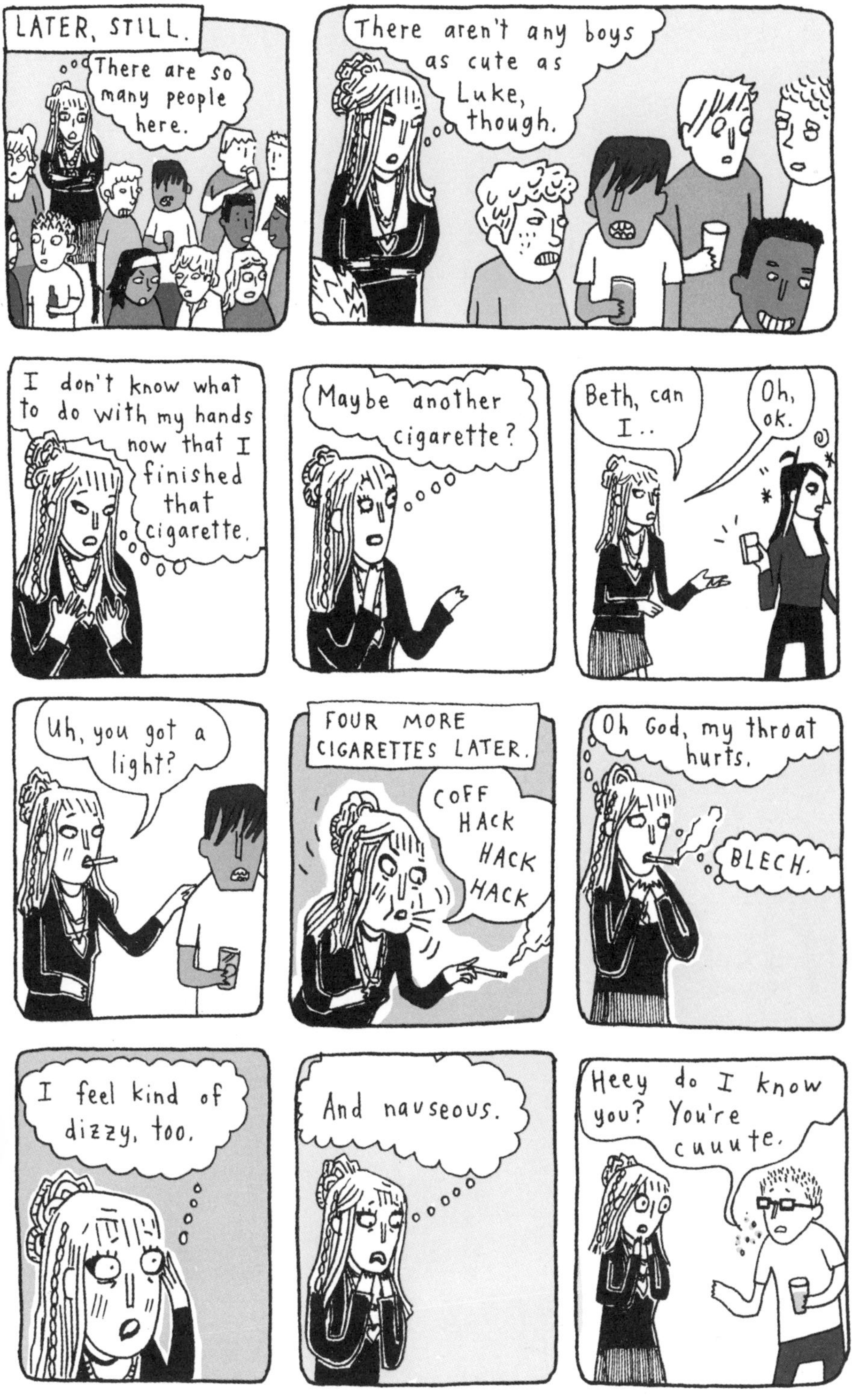
LATER, STILL.
There are so many people here.
There aren't any boys as cute as Luke, though.
I don't know what to do with my hands now that I finished that cigarette.
Maybe another cigarette?
Beth, can I..
Oh, ok.
Uh, you got a light?
FOUR MORE CIGARETTES LATER.
COFF HACK HACK HACK
Oh God, my throat hurts.
BLECH.
I feel kind of dizzy, too.
And nauseous.
Heey do I know you? You're cuuute.

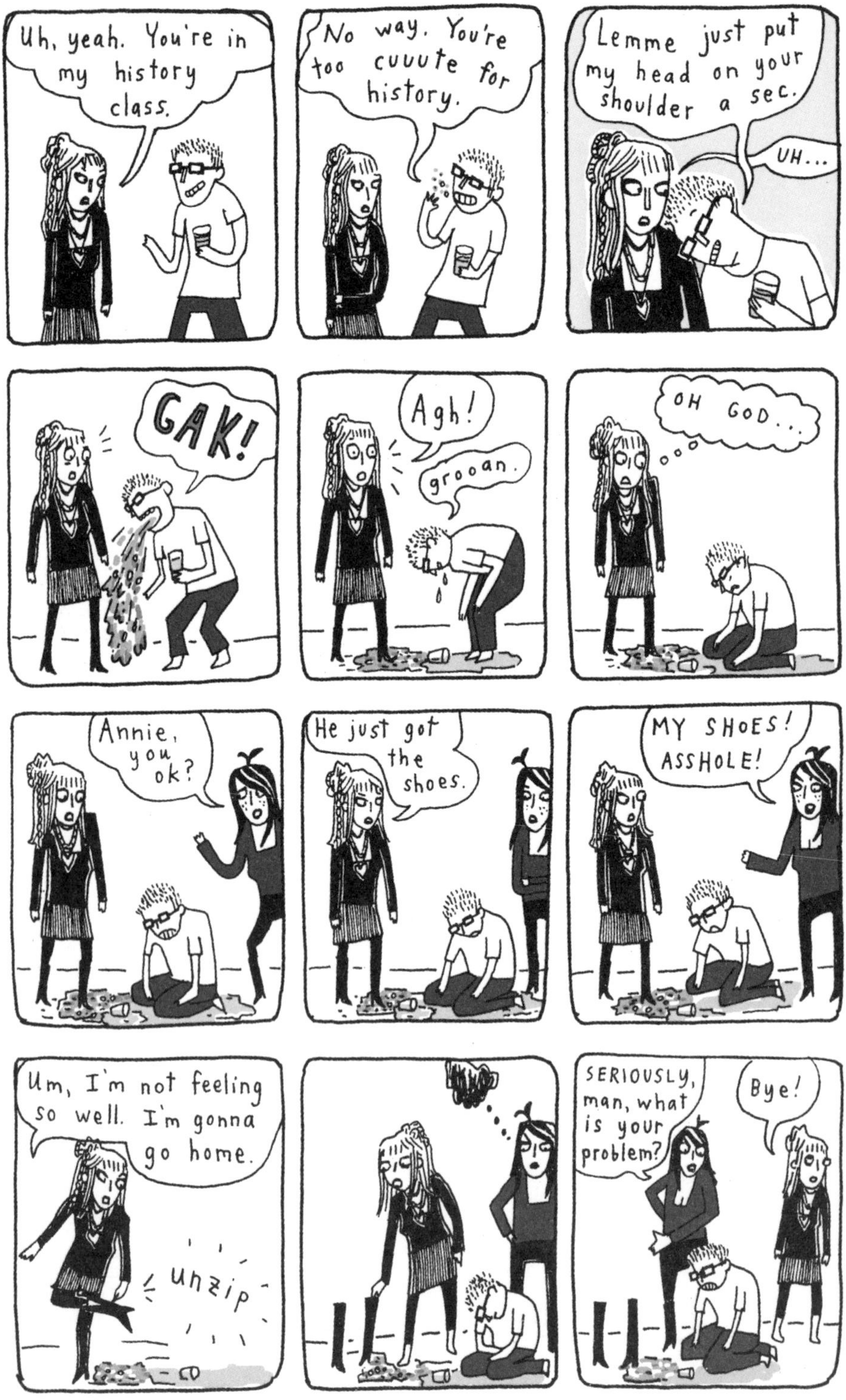

Uh, yeah. You're in my history class.
No way. You're too cuuute for history.
Lemme just put my head on your shoulder a sec.
UH...
GAK!
Agh!
grooan.
OH GOD...
Annie, you ok?
He just got the shoes.
MY SHOES! ASSHOLE!
Um, I'm not feeling so well. I'm gonna go home.
unzip
SERIOUSLY, man, what is your problem?
Bye!

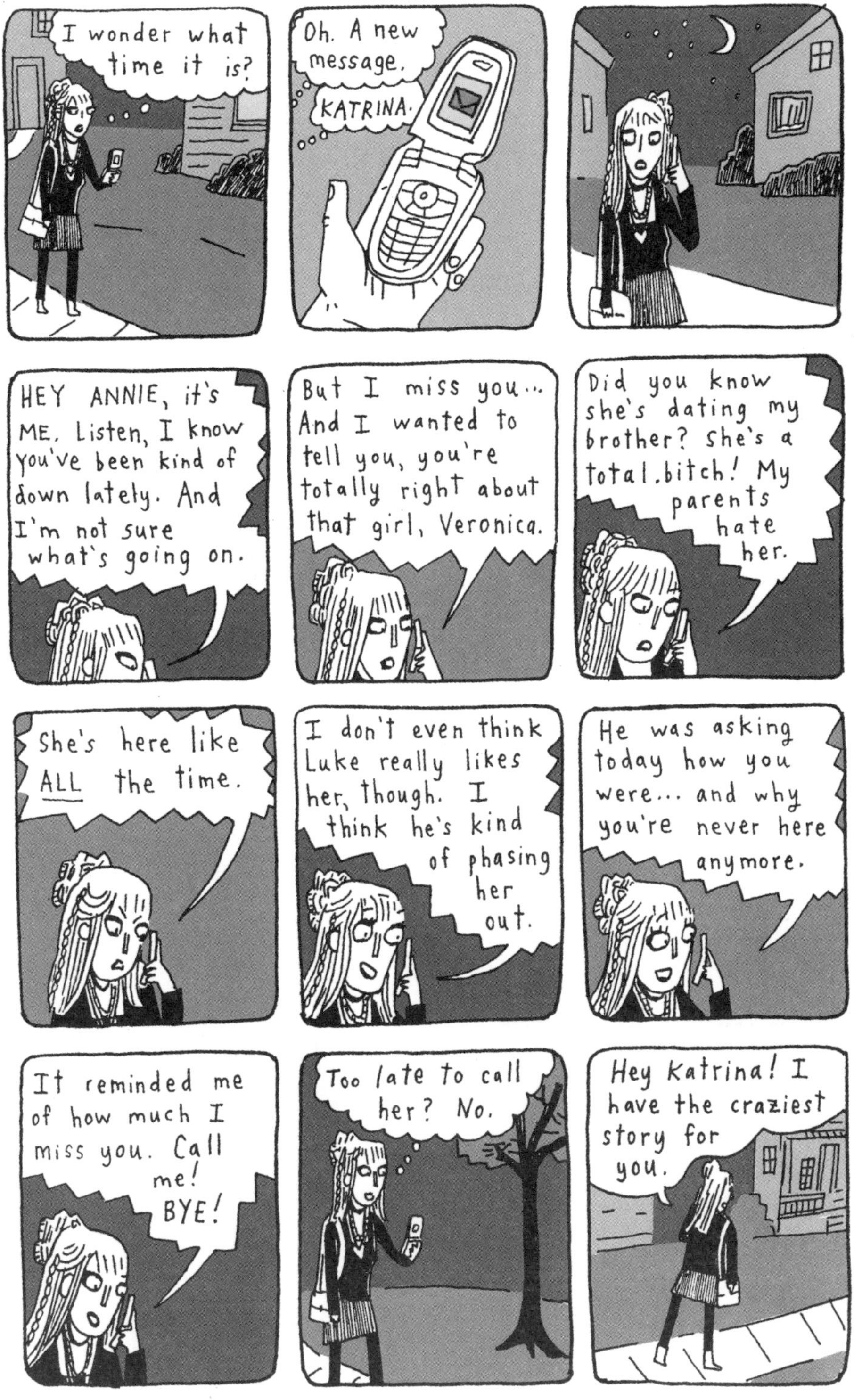
I wonder what time it is?
Oh. A new message.
KATRINA.
HEY ANNIE, it's ME. Listen, I know you've been kind of down lately. And I'm not sure what's going on.
But I miss you... And I wanted to tell you, you're totally right about that girl, Veronica.
Did you know she's dating my brother? She's a total bitch! My parents hate her.
She's here like ALL the time.
I don't even think Luke really likes her, though. I think he's kind of phasing her out.
He was asking today how you were... and why you're never here anymore.
It reminded me of how much I miss you. Call me! BYE!
Too late to call her? No.
Hey Katrina! I have the craziest story for you.

MY OWN BRAND of ROCK BAND

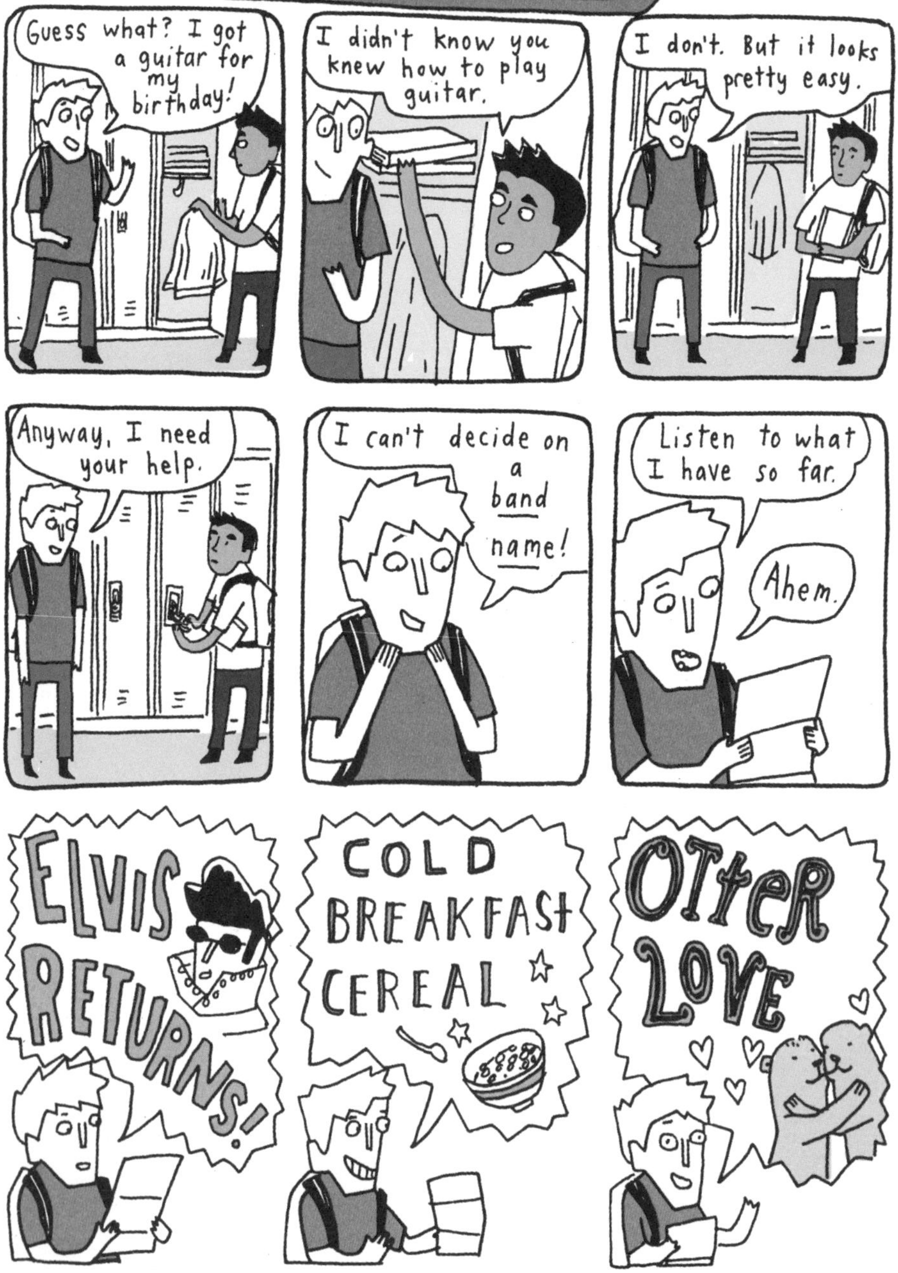
Guess what? I got a guitar for my birthday!
I didn't know you knew how to play guitar.
I don't. But it looks pretty easy.
Anyway, I need your help.
I can't decide on a band name!
Listen to what I have so far.
Ahem.
ELVIS RETURNS!
COLD BREAKFAST CEREAL
OTTER LOVE

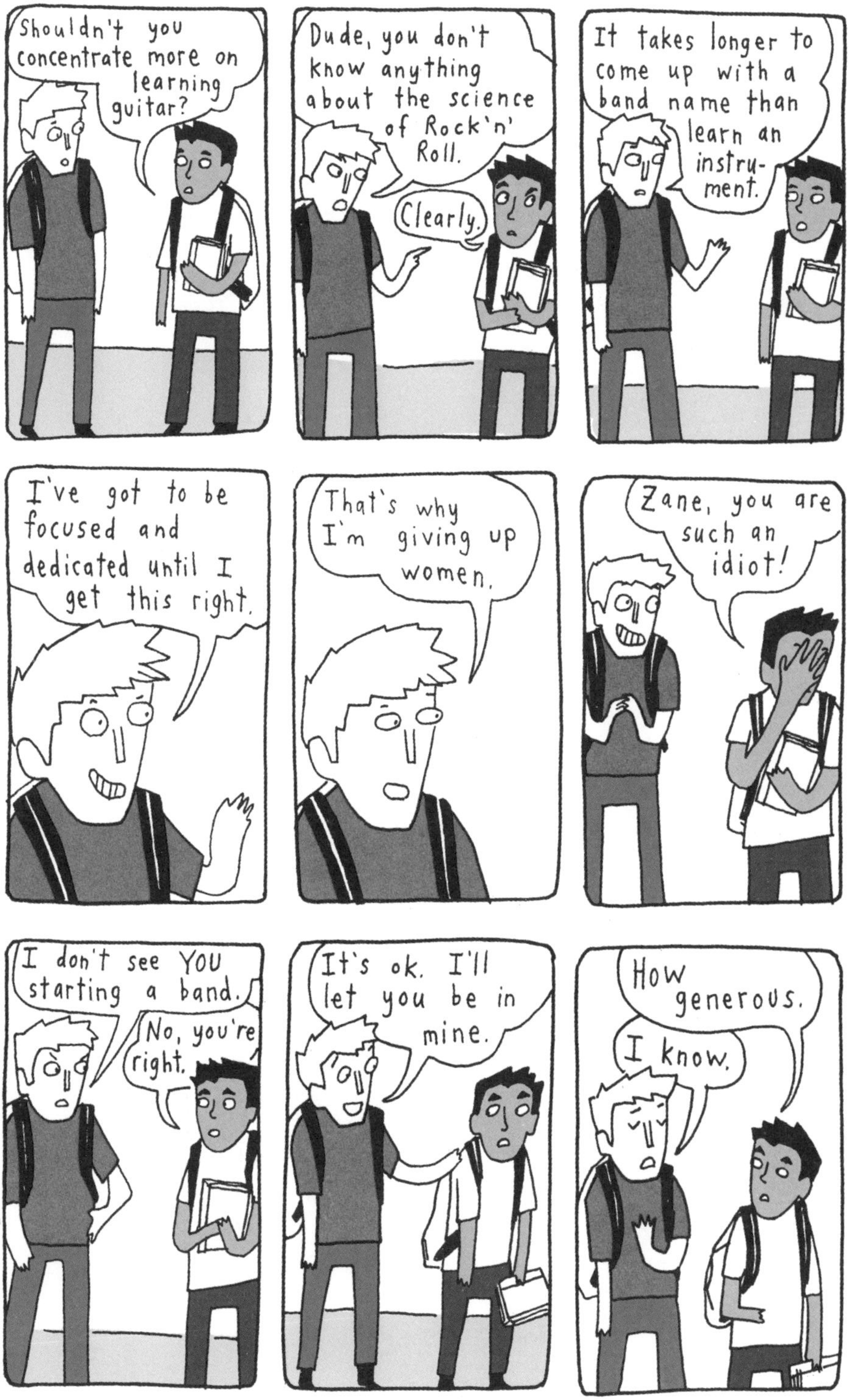
Shouldn't you concentrate more on learning guitar?
Dude, you don't know anything about the science of Rock 'n' Roll.
Clearly.
It takes longer to come up with a band name than learn an instrument.
I've got to be focused and dedicated until I get this right.
That's why I'm giving up women.
Zane, you are such an idiot!
I don't see YOU starting a band.
No, you're right.
It's ok. I'll let you be in mine.
How generous.
I know.

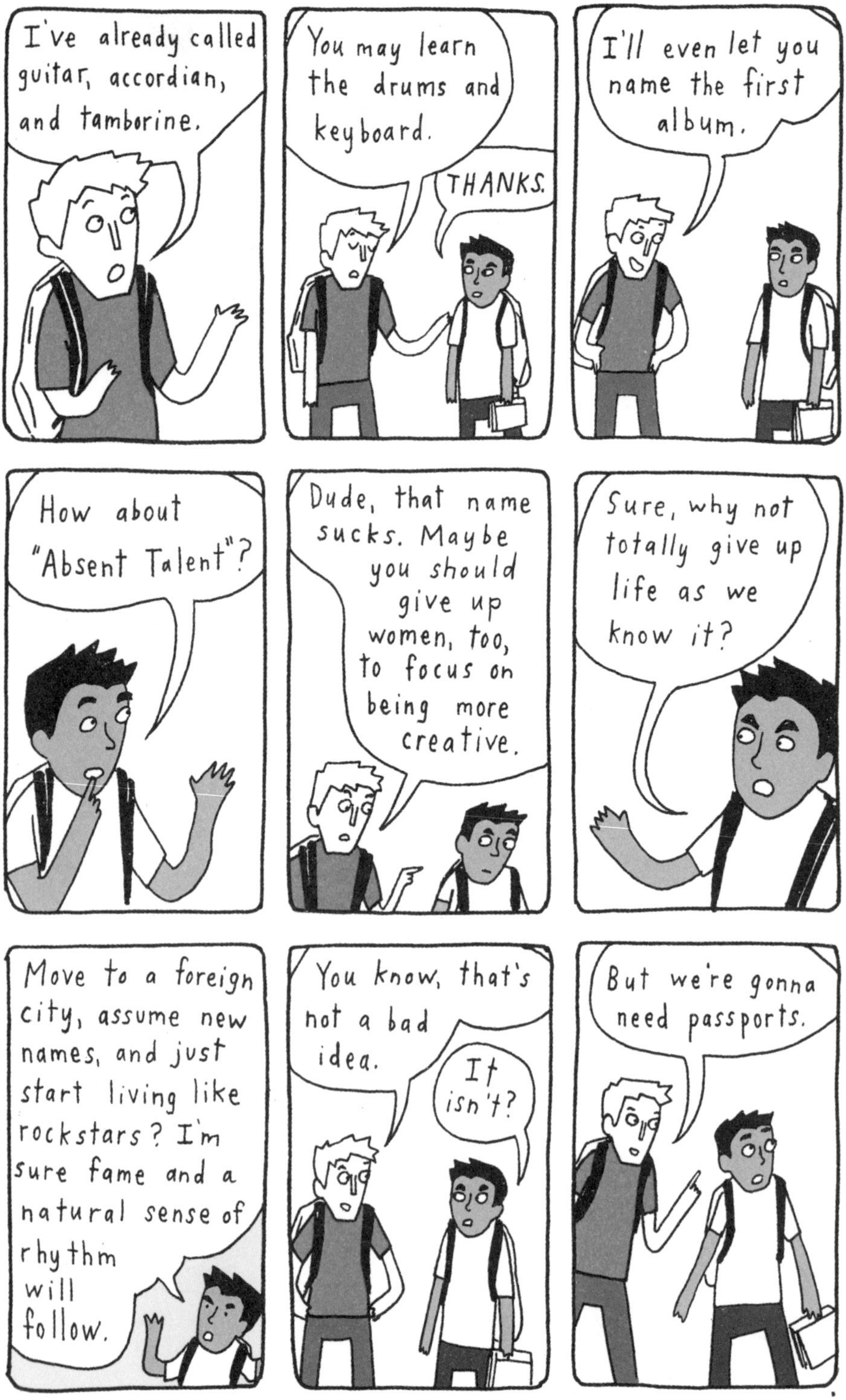
I've already called guitar, accordian, and tamborine.
You may learn the drums and keyboard.
THANKS.
I'll even let you name the first album.
How about "Absent Talent"?
Dude, that name sucks. Maybe you should give up women, too, to focus on being more creative.
Sure, why not totally give up life as we know it?
Move to a foreign city, assume new names, and just start living like rockstars? I'm sure fame and a natural sense of rhythm will follow.
You know, that's not a bad idea.
It isn't?
But we're gonna need passports.

BAND STAND

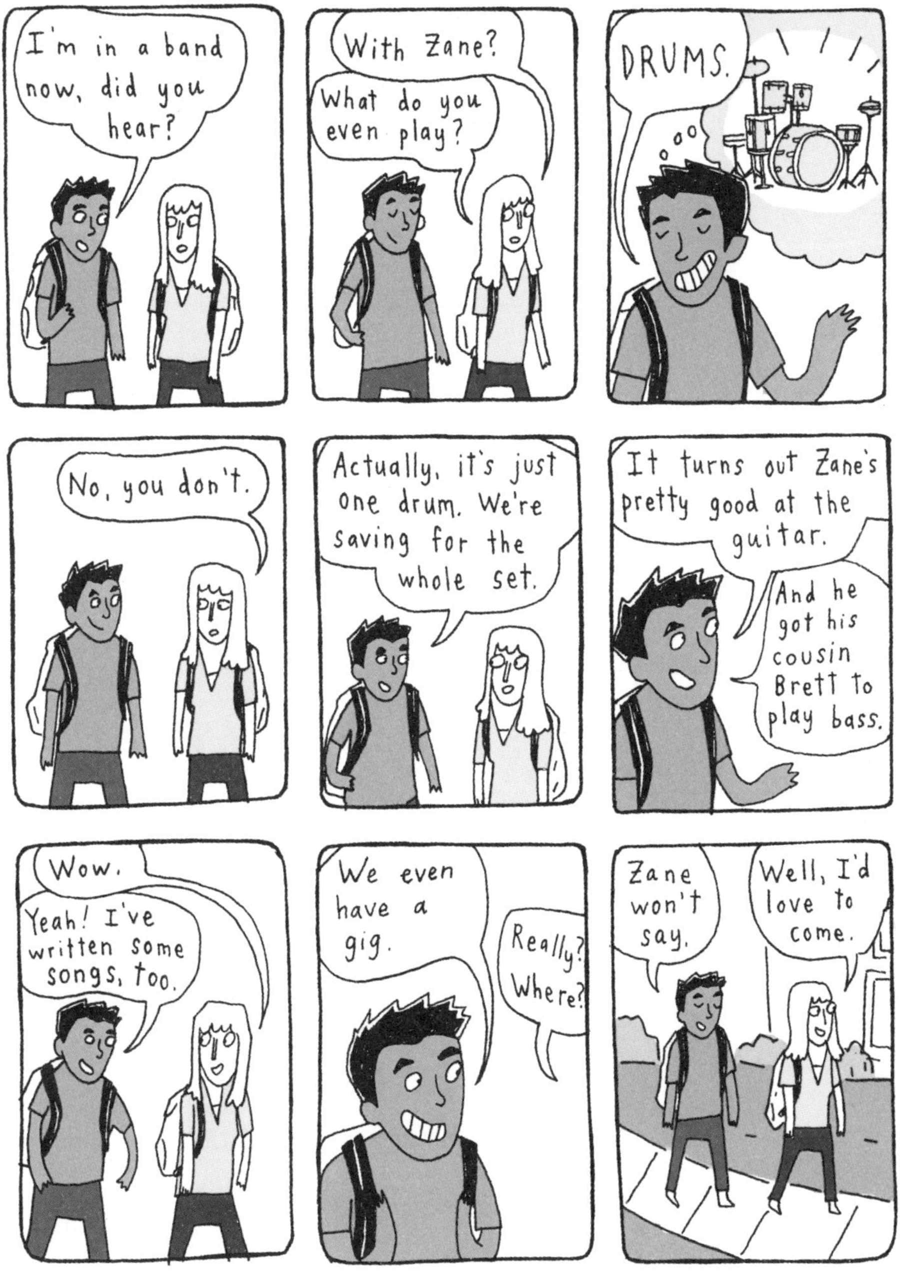
I'm in a band now, did you hear?
With Zane?
What do you even play?
DRUMS.
No, you don't.
Actually, it's just one drum. We're saving for the whole set.
It turns out Zane's pretty good at the guitar.
And he got his cousin Brett to play bass.
Wow.
Yeah! I've written some songs, too.
We even have a gig.
Really? Where?
Zane won't say.
Well, I'd love to come.

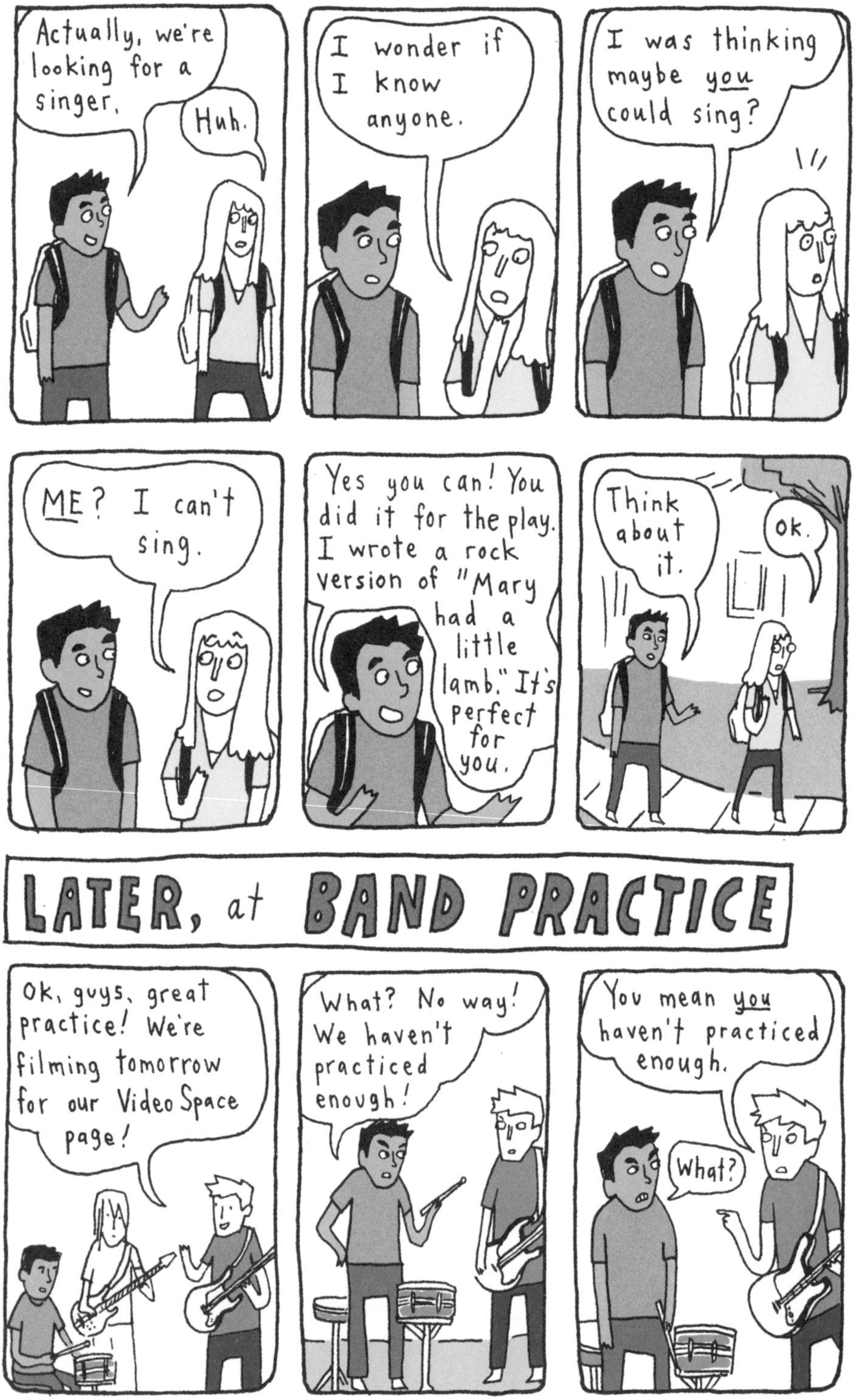
Actually, we're looking for a singer.
Huh.
I wonder if I know anyone.
I was thinking maybe you could sing?
ME? I can't sing.
Yes you can! You did it for the play. I wrote a rock version of "Mary had a little lamb." It's perfect for you.
Think about it.
Ok.
LATER, at BAND PRACTICE
Ok, guys, great practice! We're filming tomorrow for our Video Space page!
What? No way! We haven't practiced enough!
You mean you haven't practiced enough.
What?

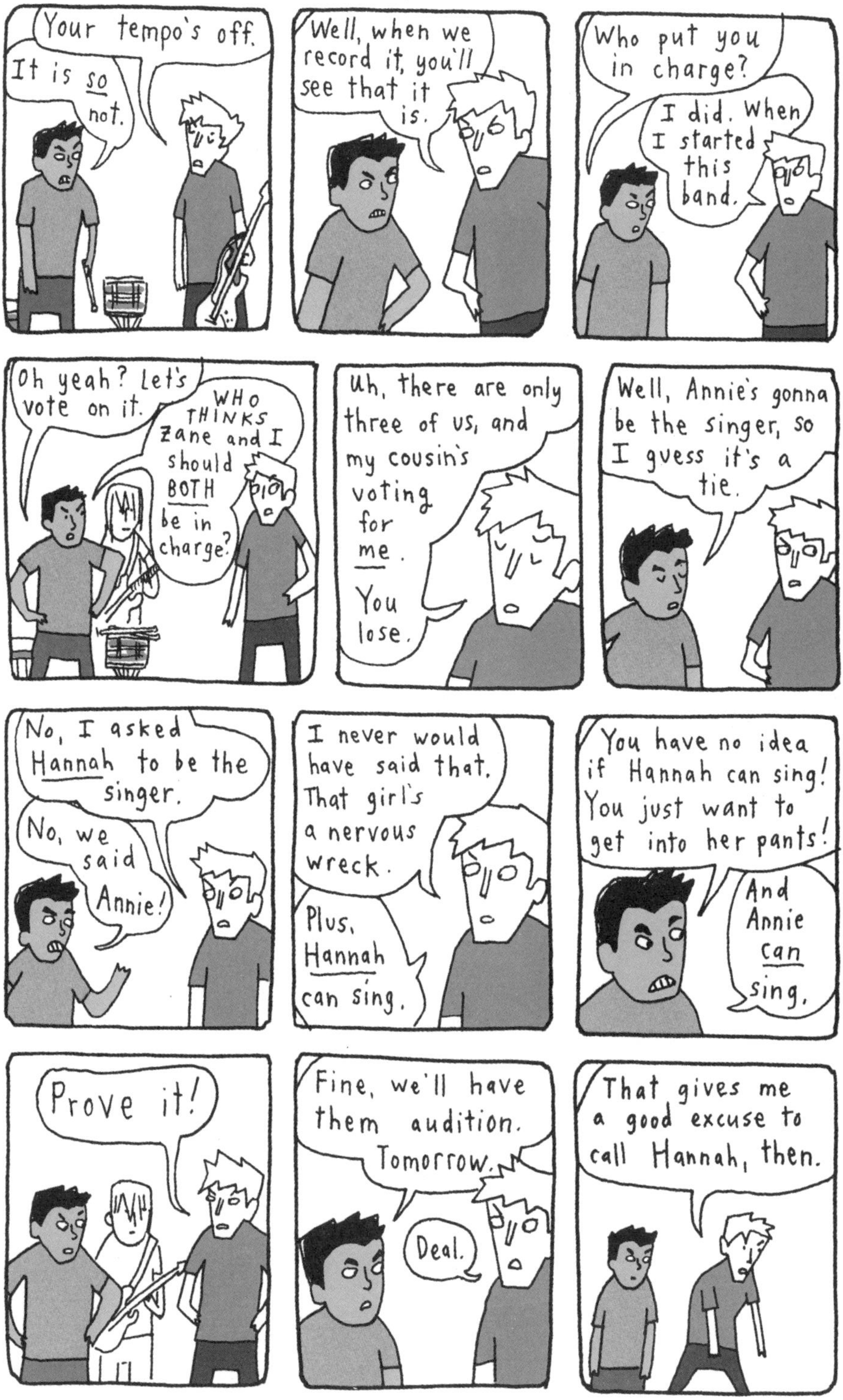
Your tempo's off.
It is so not.
Well, when we record it, you'll see that it is.
Who put you in charge?
I did. When I started this band.
Oh yeah? Let's vote on it.
WHO THINKS Zane and I should BOTH be in charge?
Uh, there are only three of us, and my cousin's voting for me.
You lose.
Well, Annie's gonna be the singer, so I guess it's a tie.
No, I asked Hannah to be the singer.
No, we said Annie!
I never would have said that. That girl's a nervous wreck.
Plus, Hannah can sing.
You have no idea if Hannah can sing! You just want to get into her pants!
And Annie can sing.
Prove it!
Fine, we'll have them audition. Tomorrow.
Deal.
That gives me a good excuse to call Hannah, then.

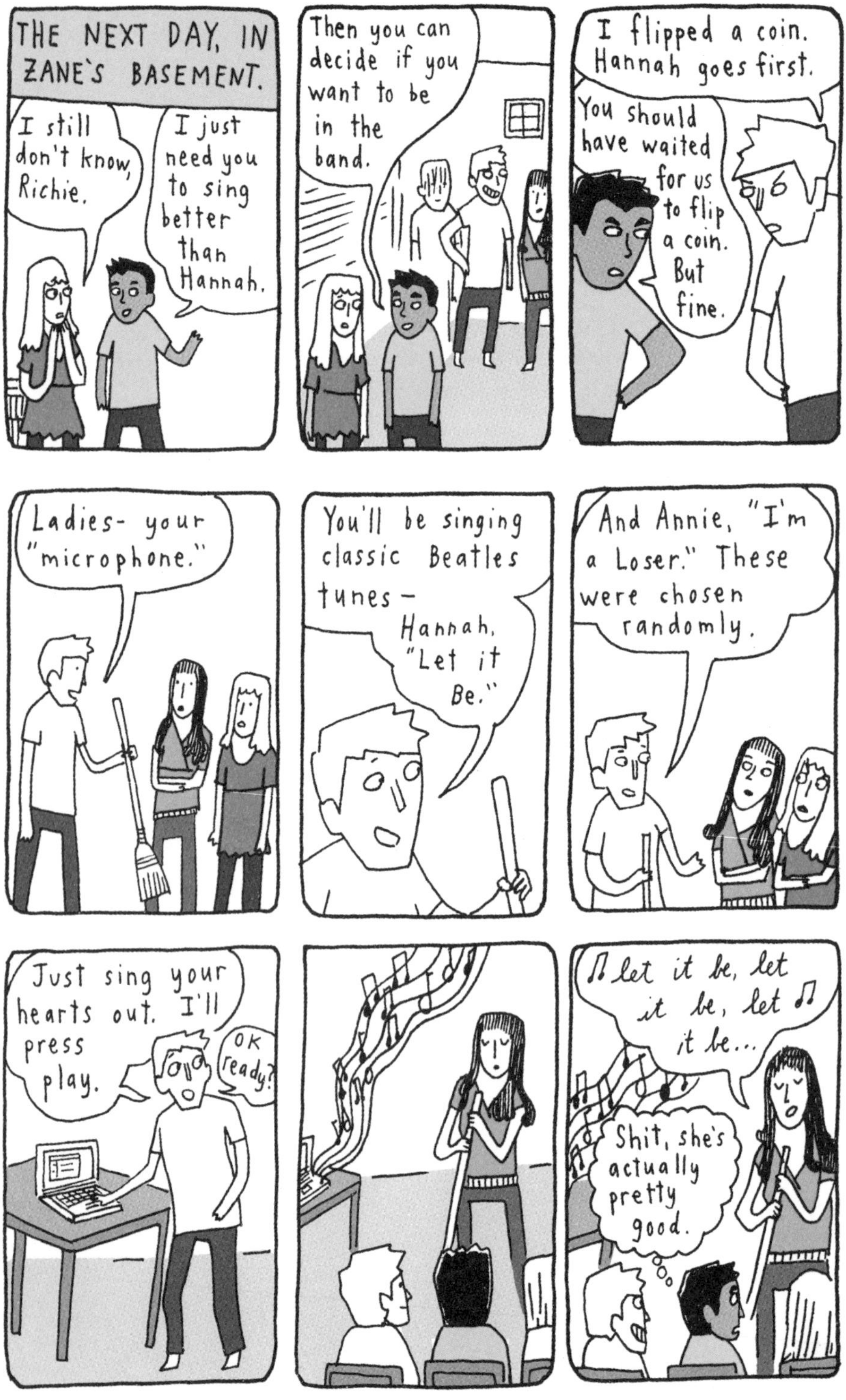
THE NEXT DAY, IN ZANE'S BASEMENT.
I still don't know, Richie.
I just need you to sing better than Hannah.
Then you can decide if you want to be in the band.
I flipped a coin. Hannah goes first.
You should have waited for us to flip a coin. But fine.
Ladies- your "microphone."
You'll be singing classic Beatles tunes—
Hannah, "Let it Be."
And Annie, "I'm a Loser." These were chosen randomly.
Just sing your hearts out. I'll press play.
OK ready?
let it be, let it be, let it be...
Shit, she's actually pretty good.

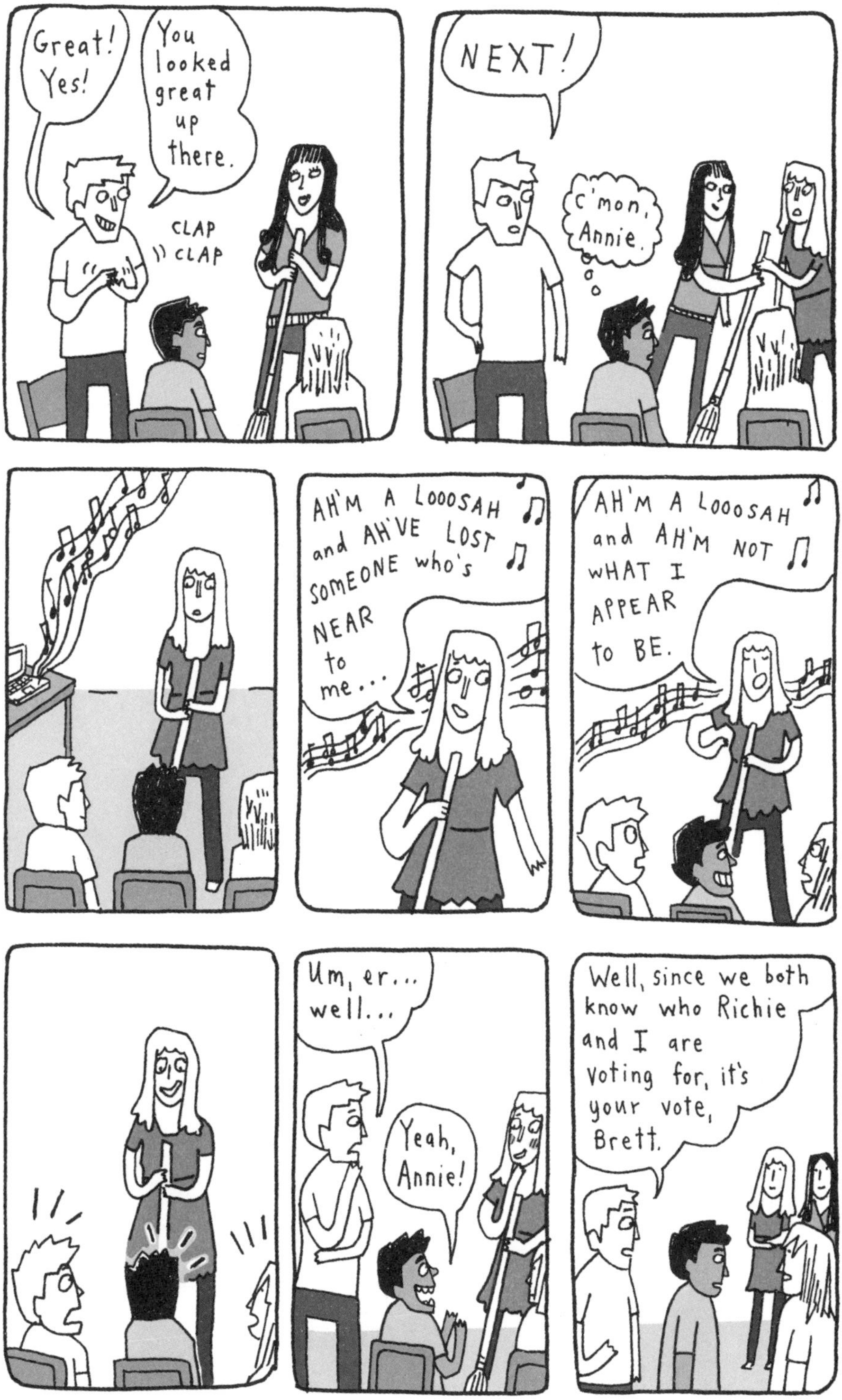
Great! Yes!
You looked great up there.
CLAP CLAP
NEXT!
C'mon, Annie.
AH'M A LOOOSAH and AH'VE LOST SOMEONE who's NEAR to me...
AH'M A LOOOSAH and AH'M NOT WHAT I APPEAR to BE.
Um, er... well...
Yeah, Annie!
Well, since we both know who Richie and I are voting for, it's your vote, Brett.

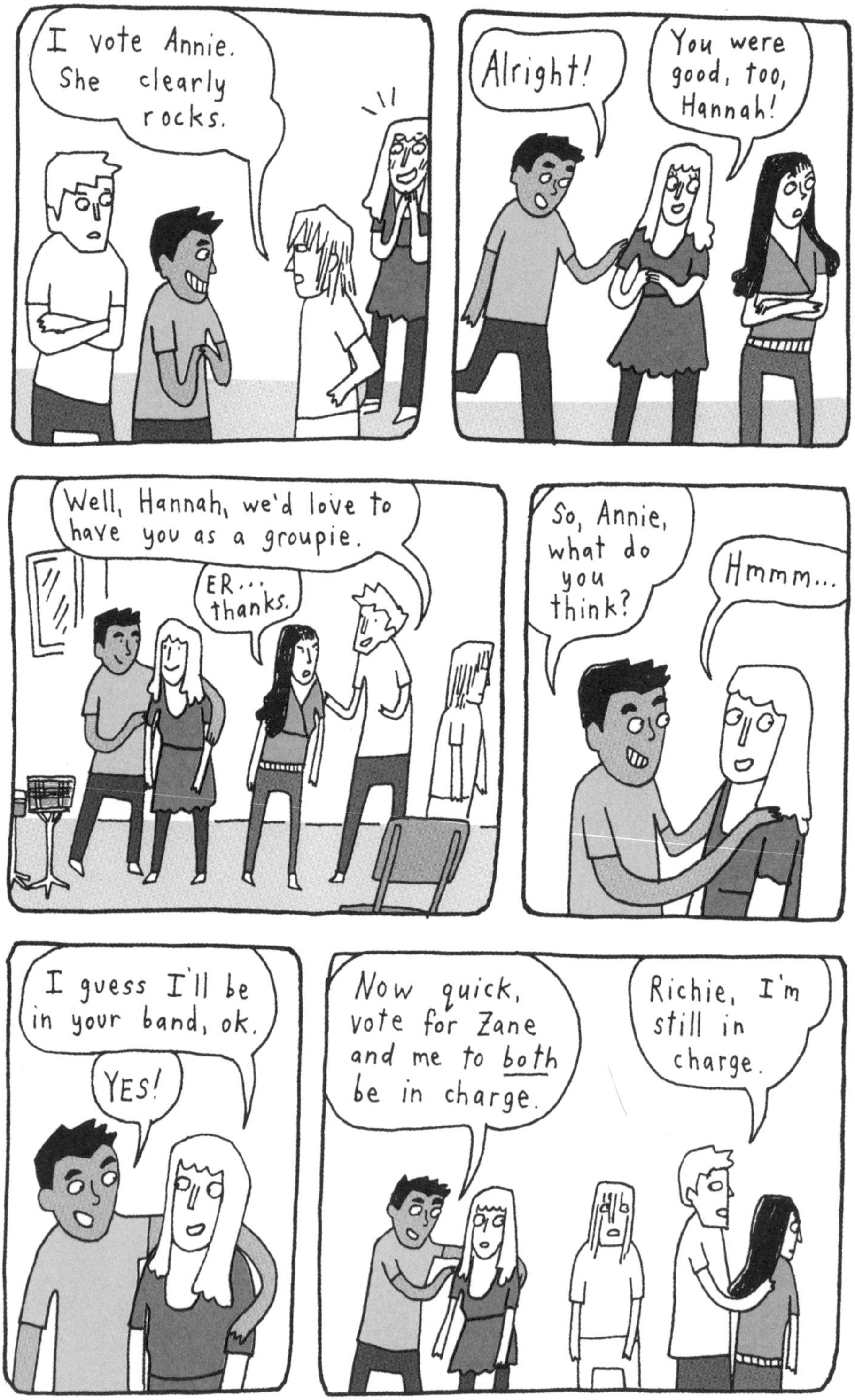
I vote Annie. She clearly rocks.
Alright!
You were good, too, Hannah!
Well, Hannah, we'd love to have you as a groupie.
ER... thanks.
So, Annie, what do you think?
Hmmm...
I guess I'll be in your band, ok.
YES!
Now quick, vote for Zane and me to both be in charge.
Richie, I'm still in charge.

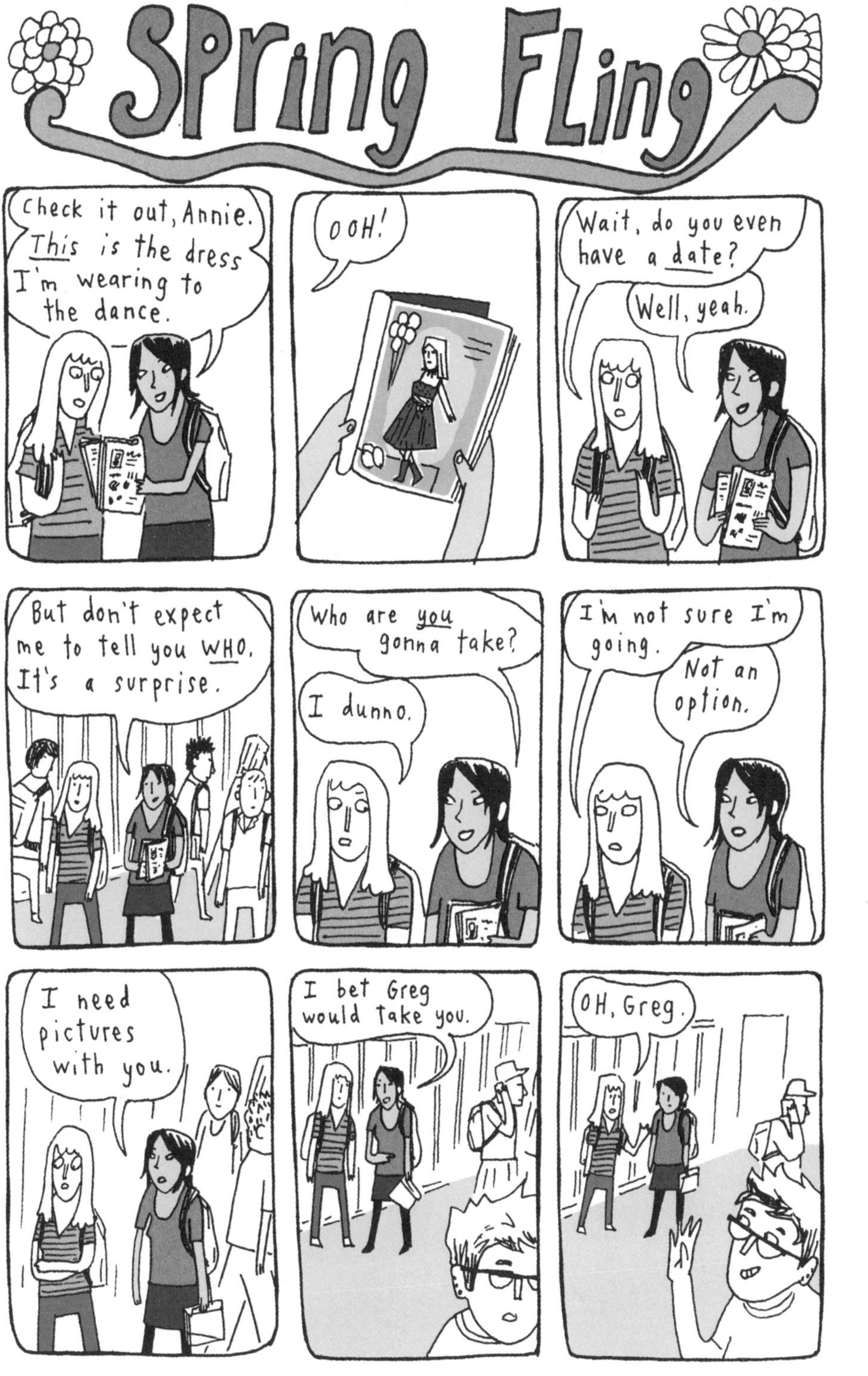
Spring Fling
Check it out, Annie. This is the dress I'm wearing to the dance.
OOH!
Wait, do you even have a date?
Well, yeah.
But don't expect me to tell you WHO. It's a surprise.
Who are you gonna take?
I dunno.
I'm not sure I'm going.
Not an option.
I need pictures with you.
I bet Greg would take you.
OH, Greg.

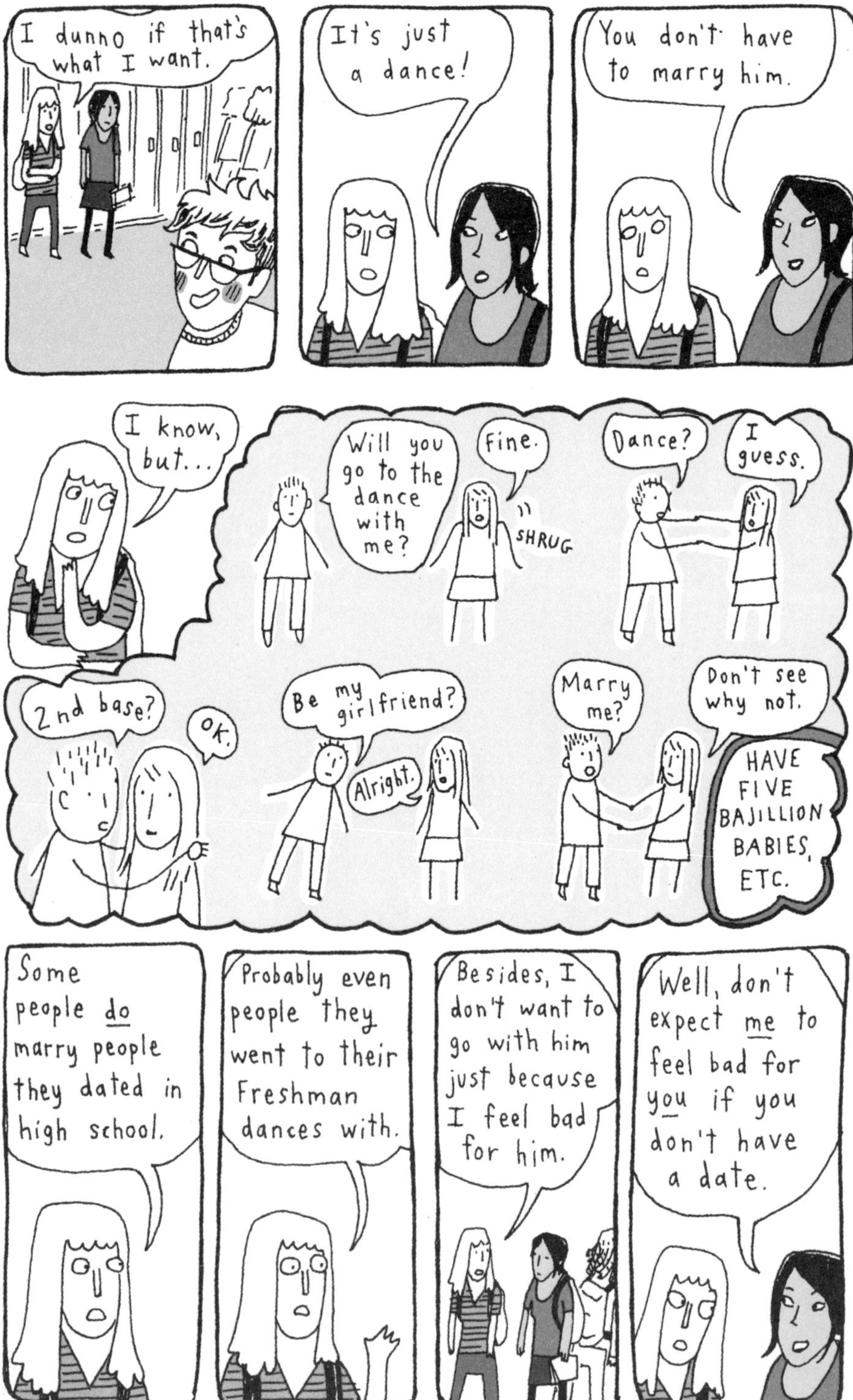

I dunno if that's what I want.
It's just a dance!
You don't have to marry him.
I know, but...
Will you go to the dance with me?
Fine.
SHRUG
Dance?
I guess.
2nd base?
OK.
Be my girlfriend?
Alright.
Marry me?
Don't see why not.
HAVE FIVE BAJILLION BABIES, ETC.
Some people do marry people they dated in high school.
Probably even people they went to their Freshman dances with.
Besides, I don't want to go with him just because I feel bad for him.
Well, don't expect me to feel bad for you if you don't have a date.

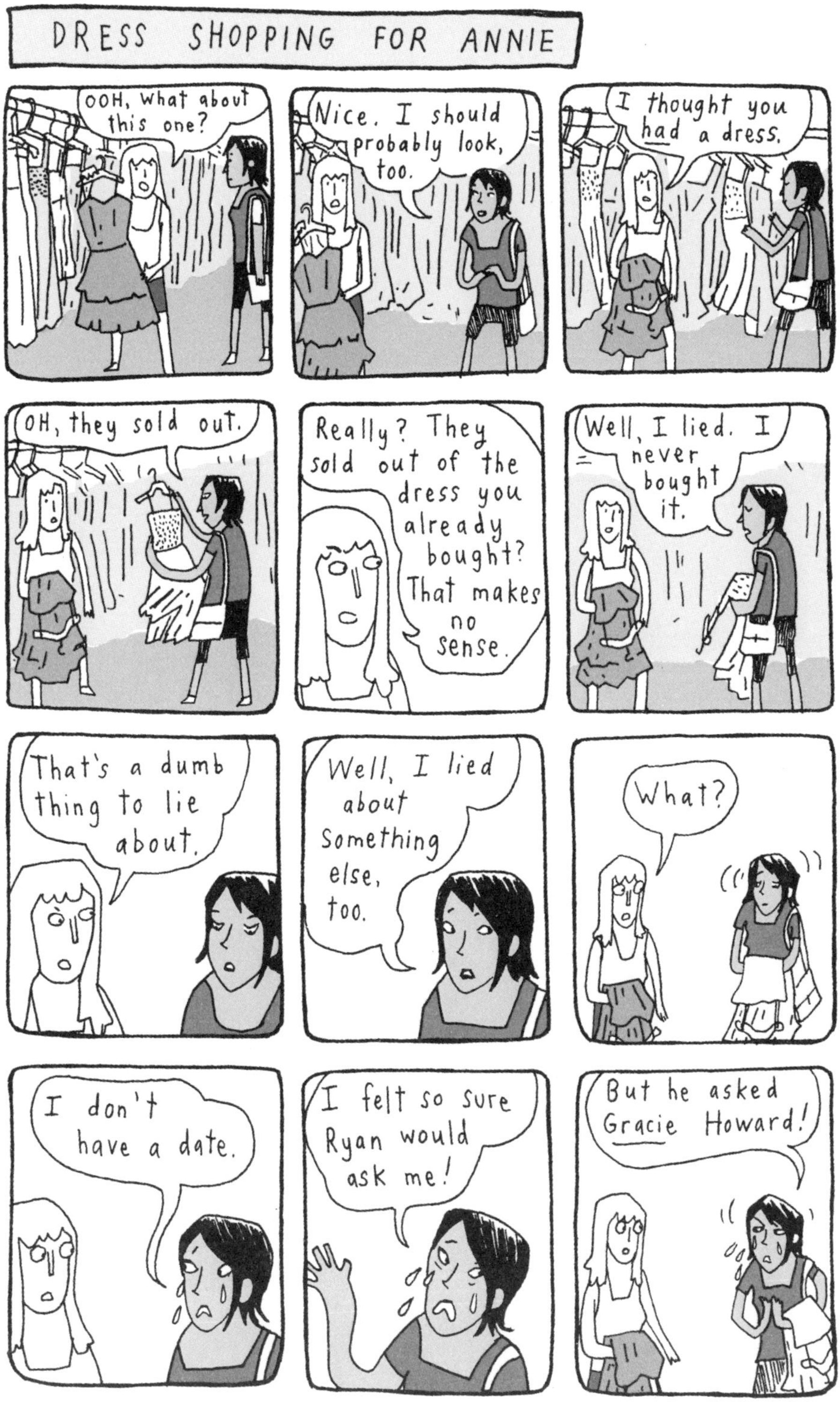
DRESS SHOPPING FOR ANNIE
OOH, what about this one?
Nice. I should probably look, too.
I thought you had a dress.
OH, they sold out.
Really? They sold out of the dress you already bought? That makes no sense.
Well, I lied. I never bought it.
That's a dumb thing to lie about.
Well, I lied about something else, too.
What?
I don't have a date.
I felt so sure Ryan would ask me!
But he asked Gracie Howard!

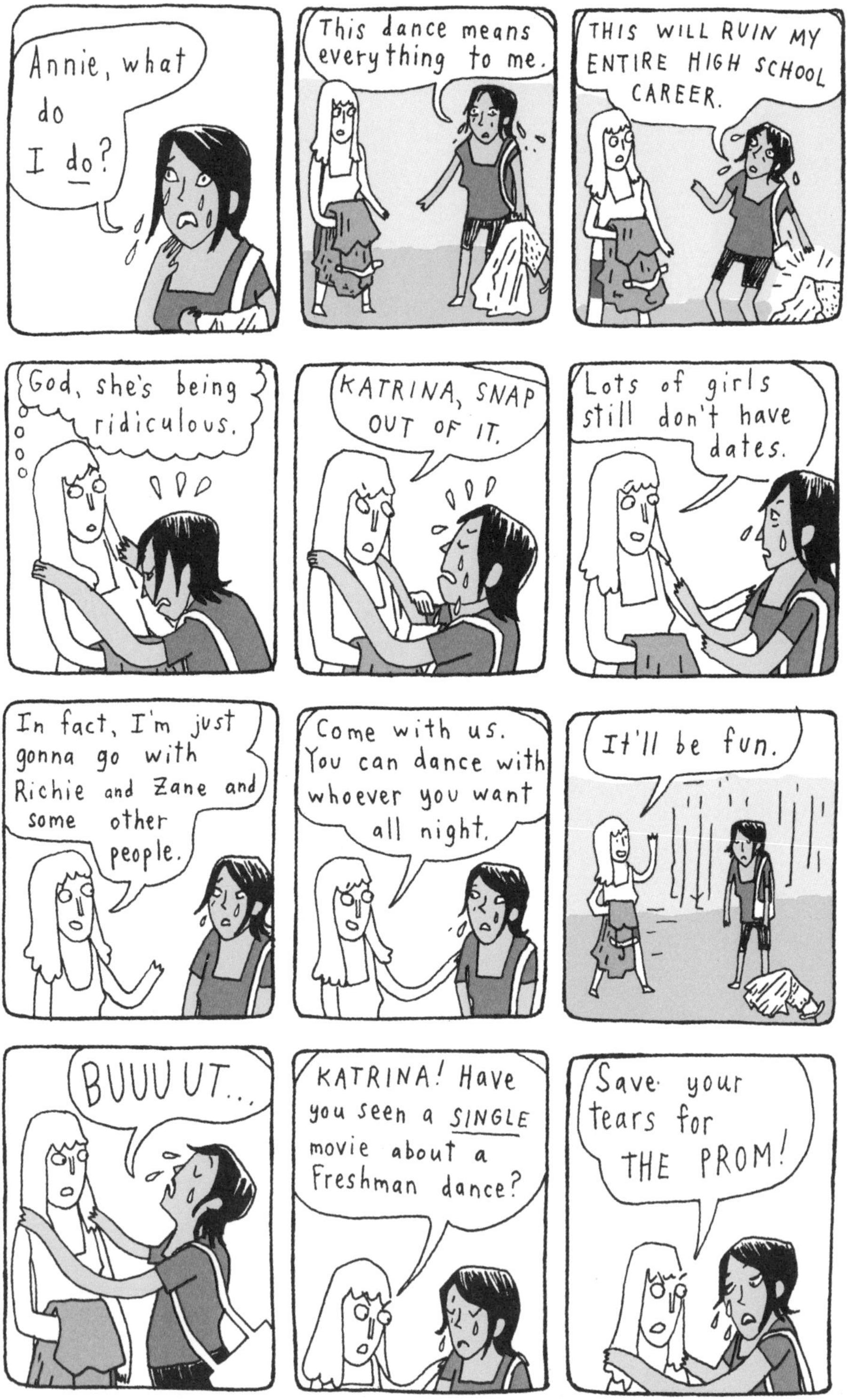

Annie, what do I do?
This dance means everything to me.
THIS WILL RUIN MY ENTIRE HIGH SCHOOL CAREER.
God, she's being ridiculous.
KATRINA, SNAP OUT OF IT.
Lots of girls still don't have dates.
In fact, I'm just gonna go with Richie and Zane and some other people.
Come with us. You can dance with whoever you want all night.
It'll be fun.
BUUUUT...
KATRINA! Have you seen a SINGLE movie about a Freshman dance?
Save your tears for THE PROM!

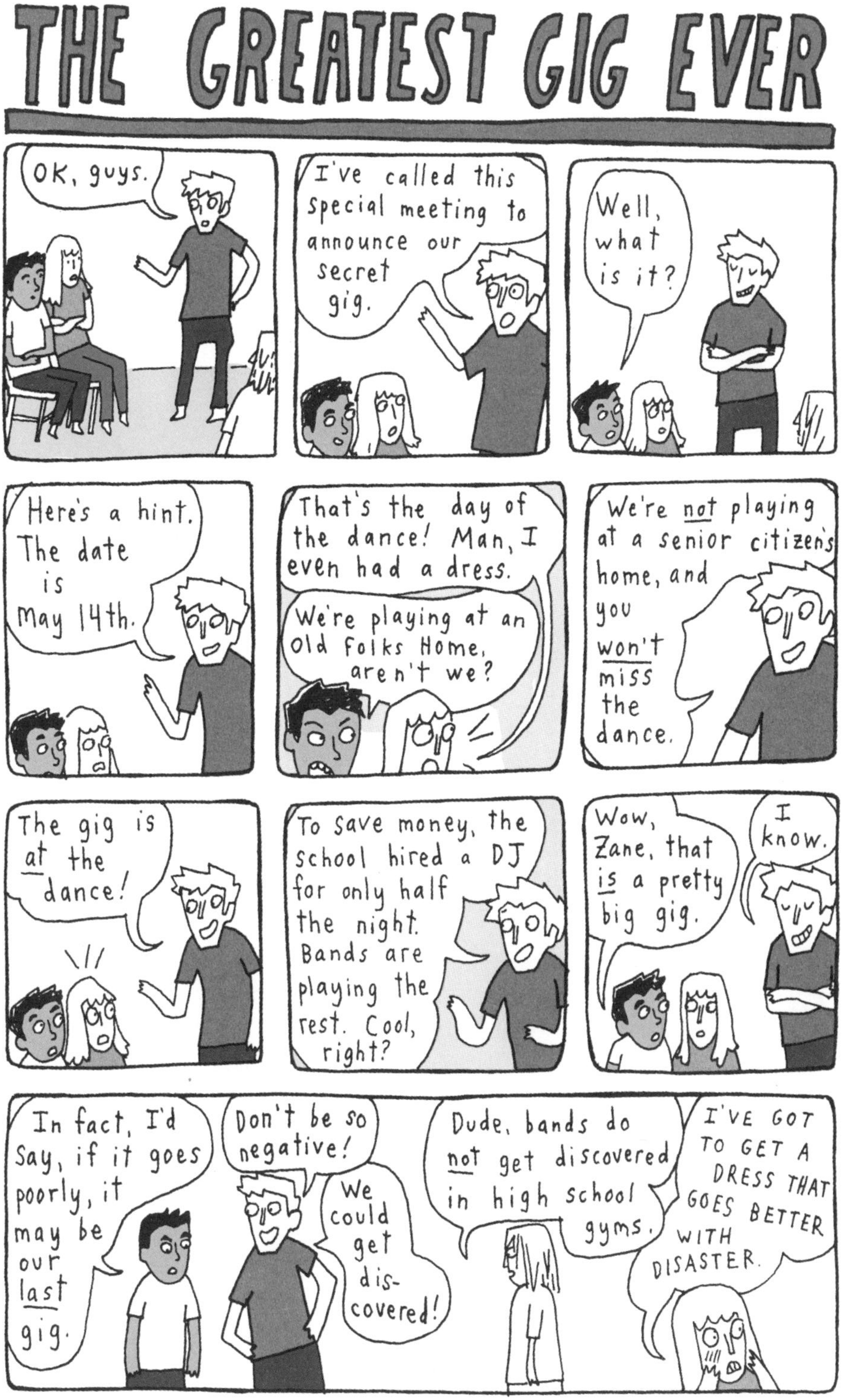
THE GREATEST GIG EVER
OK, guys.
I've called this special meeting to announce our secret gig.
Well, what is it?
Here's a hint. The date is May 14th.
That's the day of the dance! Man, I even had a dress.
We're playing at an Old Folks Home, aren't we?
We're not playing at a senior citizen's home, and you won't miss the dance.
The gig is at the dance!
To save money, the school hired a DJ for only half the night. Bands are playing the rest. Cool, right?
Wow, Zane, that is a pretty big gig.
I know.
In fact, I'd say, if it goes poorly, it may be our last gig.
Don't be so negative!
We could get dis-covered!
Dude, bands do not get discovered in high school gyms.
I'VE GOT TO GET A DRESS THAT GOES BETTER WITH DISASTER.

I KNOW YOUR SECRETS

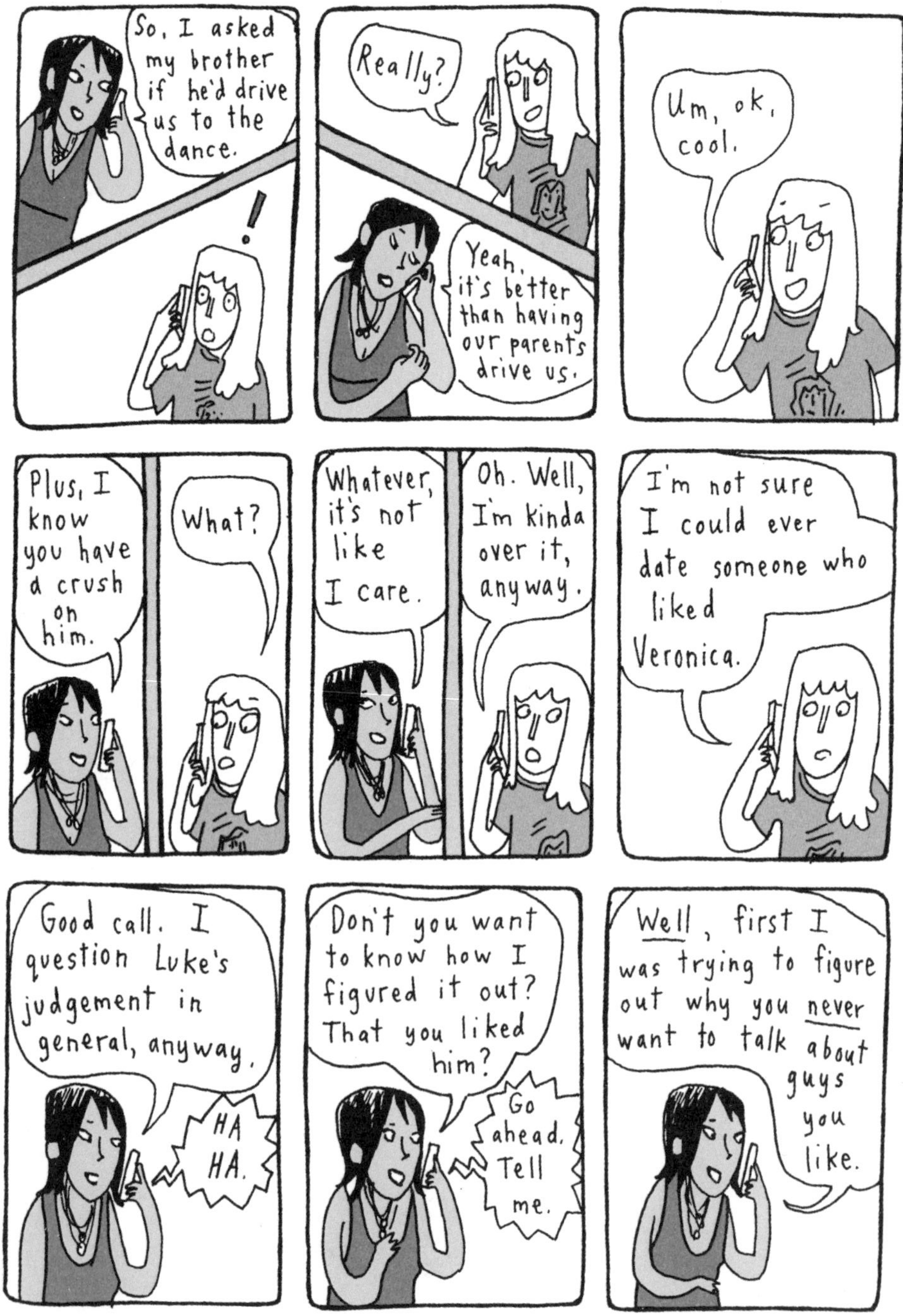
So, I asked my brother if he'd drive us to the dance.
!
Really?
Yeah, it's better than having our parents drive us.
Um, ok, cool.
Plus, I know you have a crush on him.
What?
Whatever, it's not like I care.
Oh. Well, I'm kinda over it, anyway.
I'm not sure I could ever date someone who liked Veronica.
Good call. I question Luke's judgement in general, anyway.
HA HA.
Don't you want to know how I figured it out? That you liked him?
Go ahead. Tell me.
Well, first I was trying to figure out why you never want to talk about guys you like.

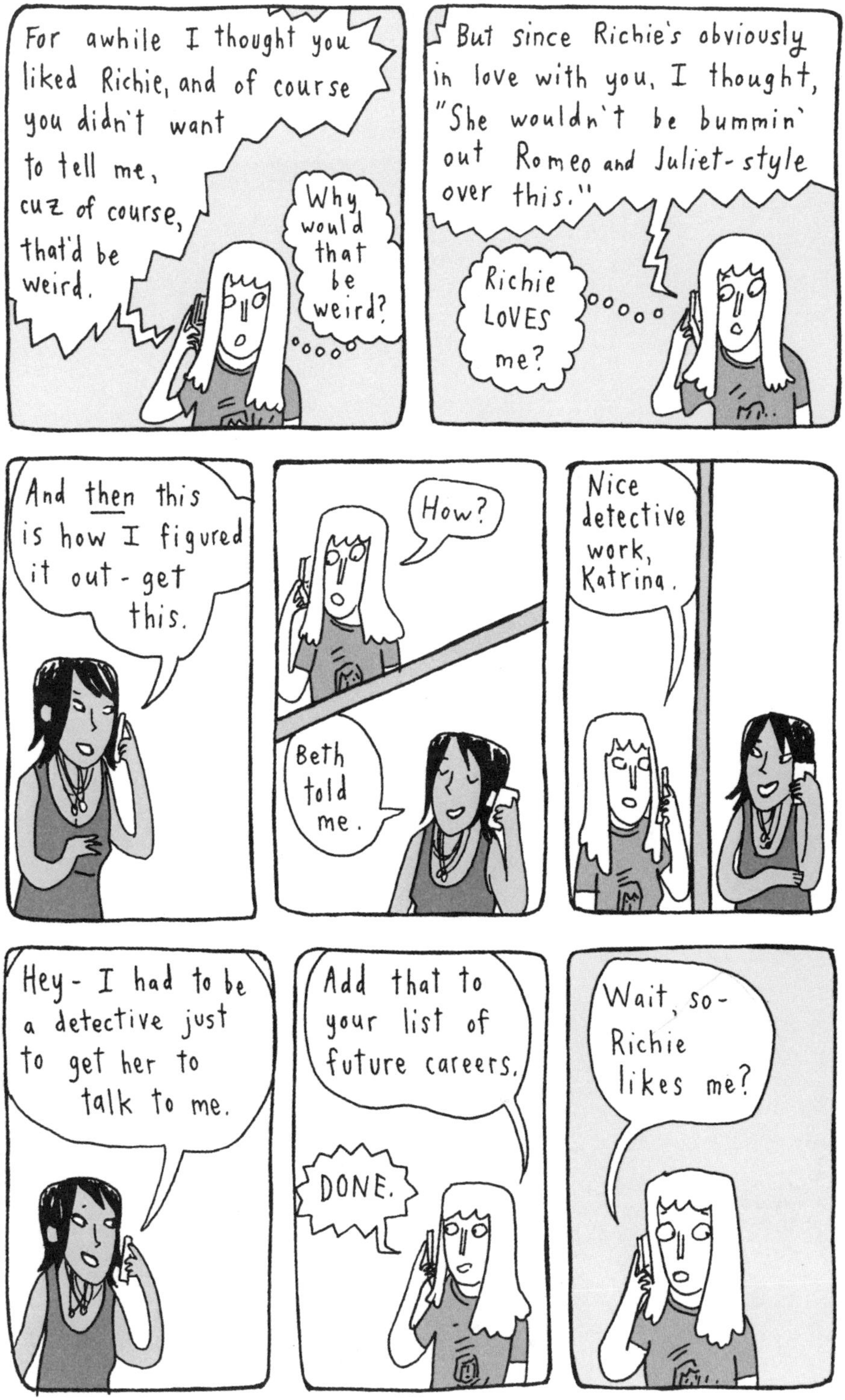

For awhile I thought you liked Richie, and of course you didn't want to tell me, cuz of course, that'd be weird.
Why would that be weird?
But since Richie's obviously in love with you, I thought, "She wouldn't be bummin' out Romeo and Juliet-style over this."
Richie LOVES me?
And then this is how I figured it out - get this.
How?
Beth told me.
Nice detective work, Katrina.
Hey - I had to be a detective just to get her to talk to me.
Add that to your list of future careers.
DONE.
Wait, so - Richie likes me?

Dance if You Want To

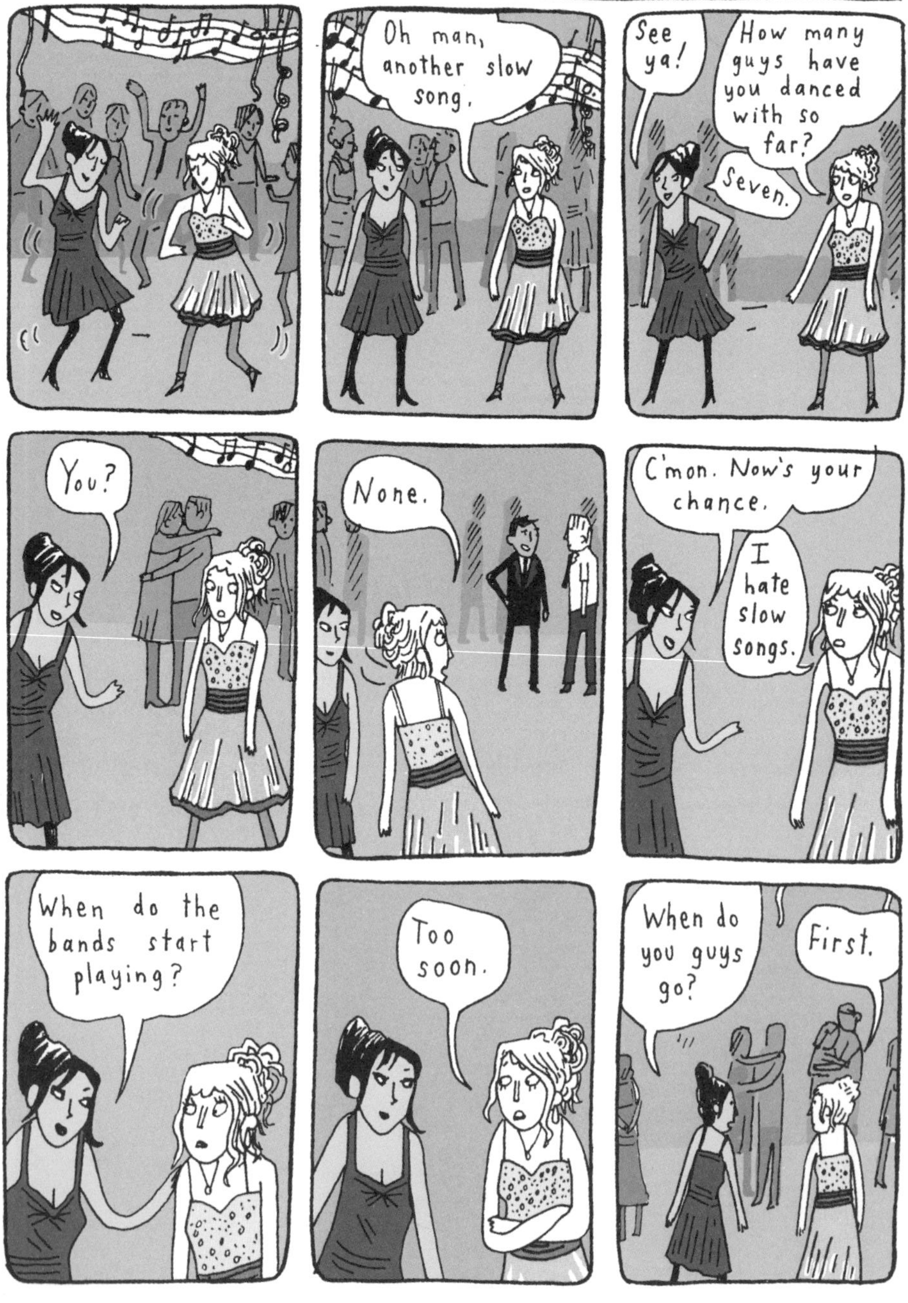
Oh man, another slow song.
See ya!
How many guys have you danced with so far?
Seven.
You?
None.
C'mon. Now's your chance.
I hate slow songs.
When do the bands start playing?
Too soon.
When do you guys go?
First.

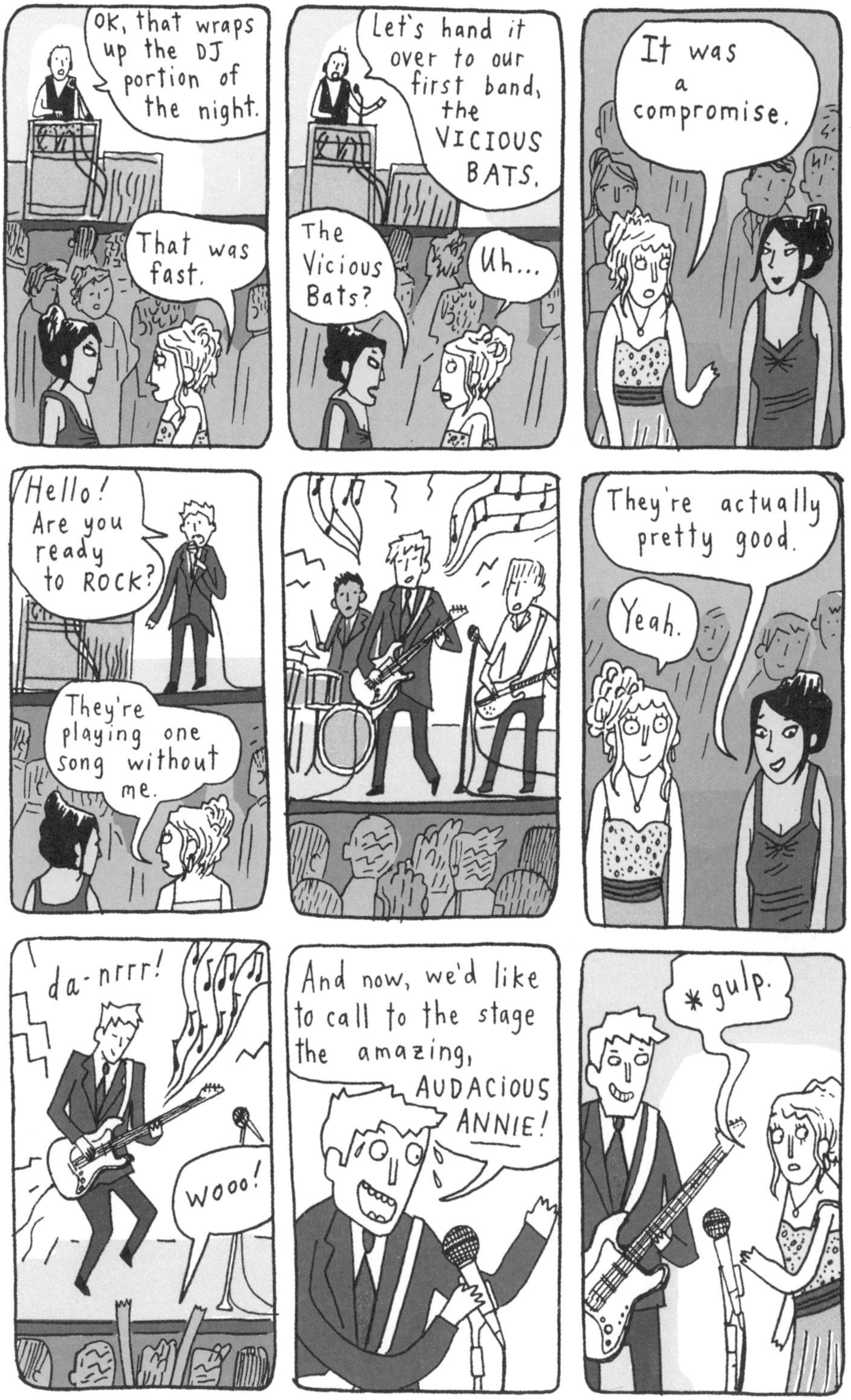
OK, that wraps up the DJ portion of the night.
That was fast.
Let's hand it over to our first band, the VICIOUS BATS.
The Vicious Bats?
Uh...
It was a compromise.
Hello! Are you ready to ROCK?
They're playing one song without me.
They're actually pretty good.
Yeah.
da-nrrr!
wooo!
And now, we'd like to call to the stage the amazing, AUDACIOUS ANNIE!
*gulp.

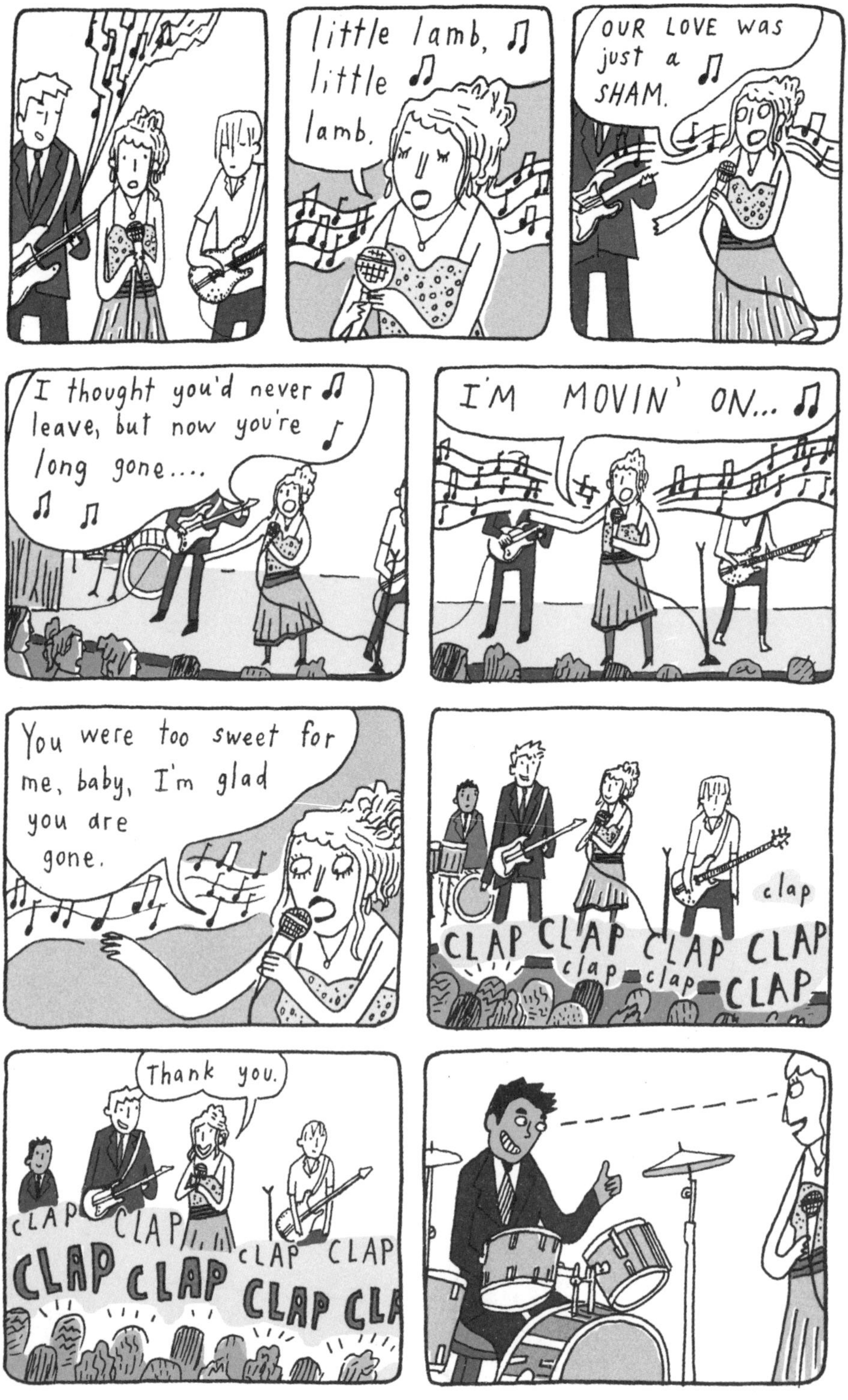
little lamb, ♫ little ♫ lamb.
OUR LOVE was just a ♫ SHAM.
I thought you'd never ♫ leave, but now you're ♪ long gone.... ♫ ♫
I'M MOVIN' ON... ♫
You were too sweet for me, baby, I'm glad you are gone.
clap
CLAP CLAP CLAP CLAP
clap clap CLAP
Thank you.
CLAP CLAP
CLAP CLAP CLAP CLAP
CLAP CLA

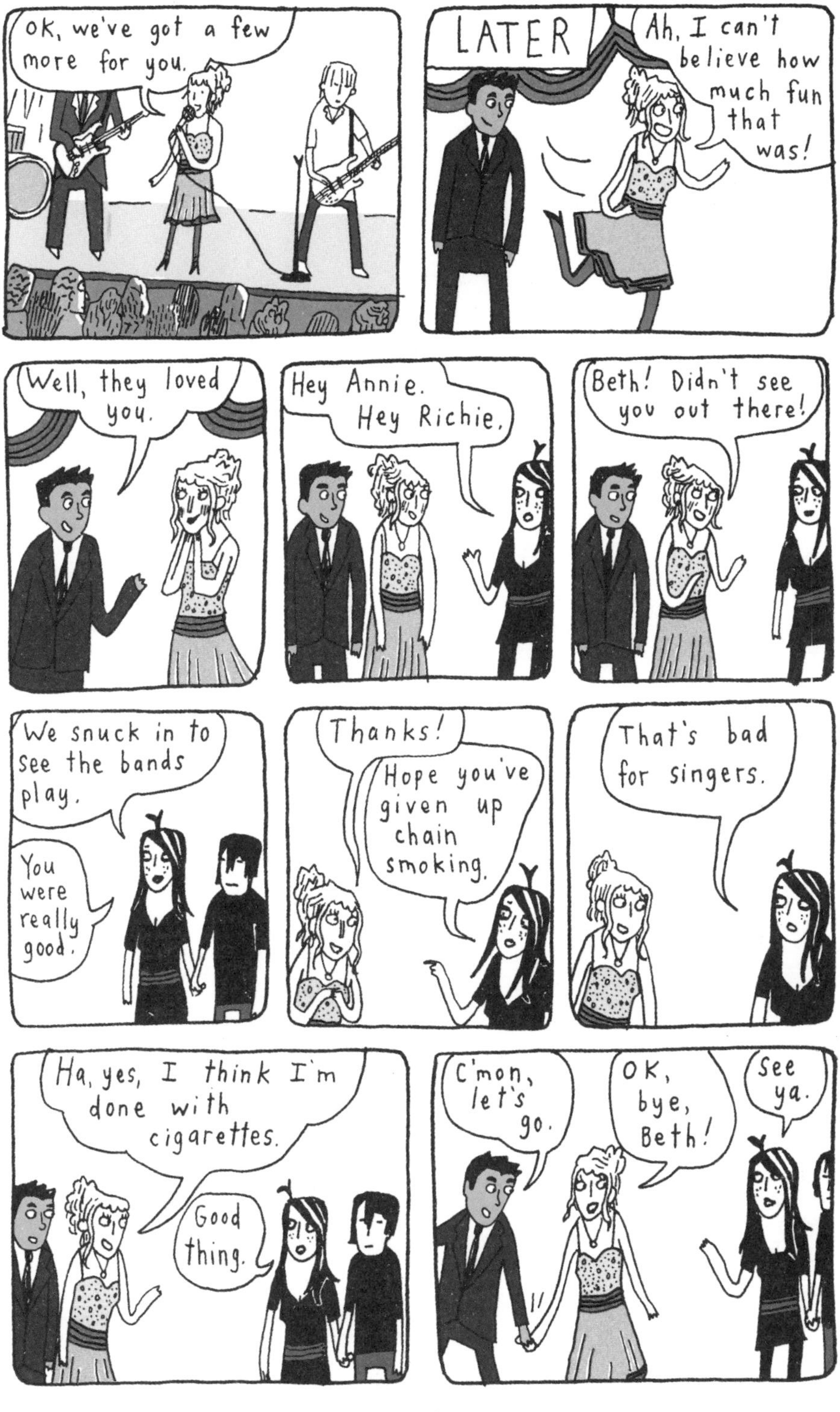
OK, we've got a few more for you.
LATER
Ah, I can't believe how much fun that was!
Well, they loved you.
Hey Annie. Hey Richie.
Beth! Didn't see you out there!
We snuck in to see the bands play.
You were really good.
Thanks!
Hope you've given up chain smoking.
That's bad for singers.
Ha, yes, I think I'm done with cigarettes.
Good thing.
C'mon, let's go.
OK, bye, Beth!
See ya.

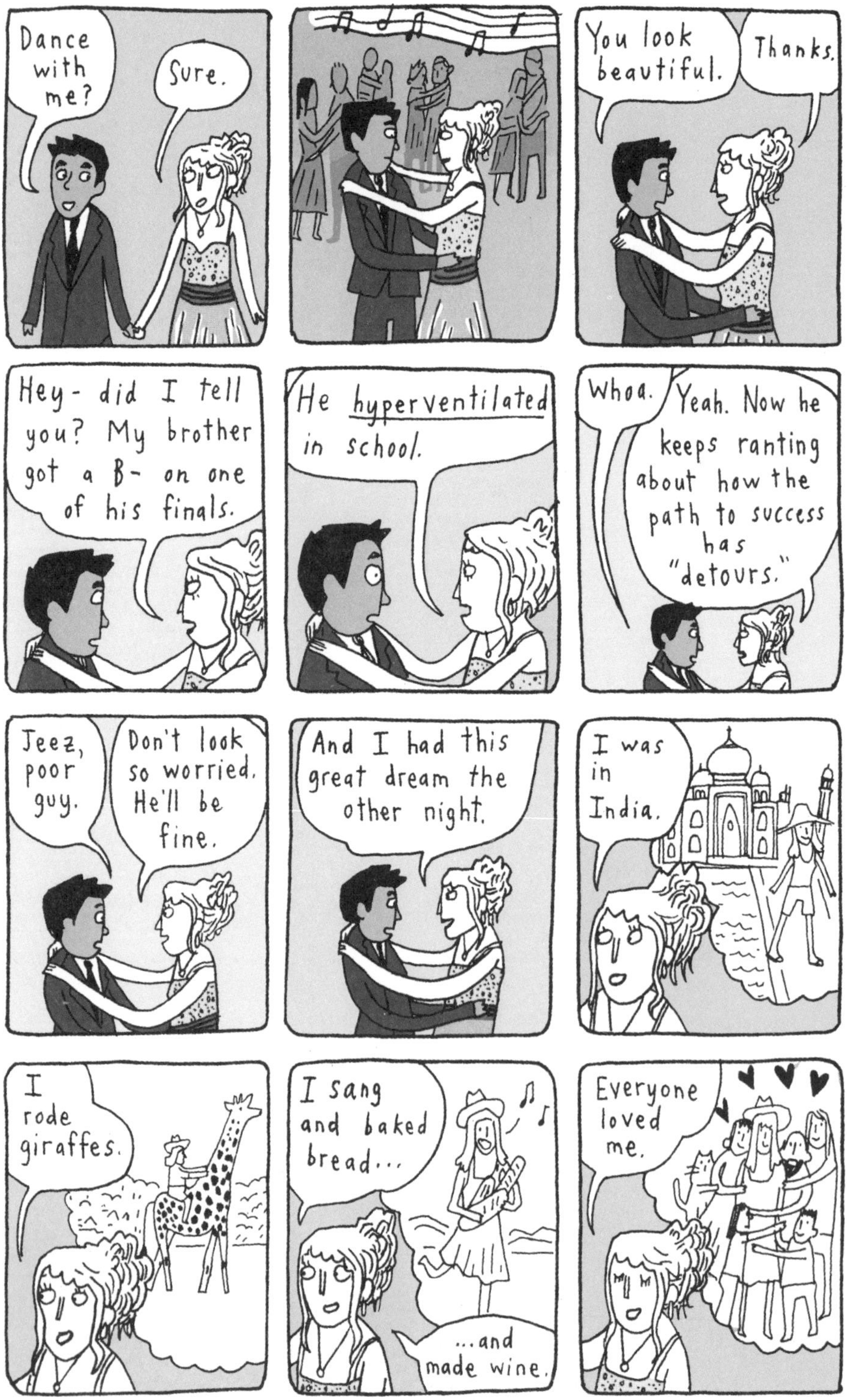
Dance with me?
Sure.
You look beautiful.
Thanks.
Hey- did I tell you? My brother got a B- on one of his finals.
He hyperventilated in school.
Whoa.
Yeah. Now he keeps ranting about how the path to success has "detours."
Jeez, poor guy.
Don't look so worried. He'll be fine.
And I had this great dream the other night.
I was in India.
I rode giraffes.
I sang and baked bread...
...and made wine.
Everyone loved me.

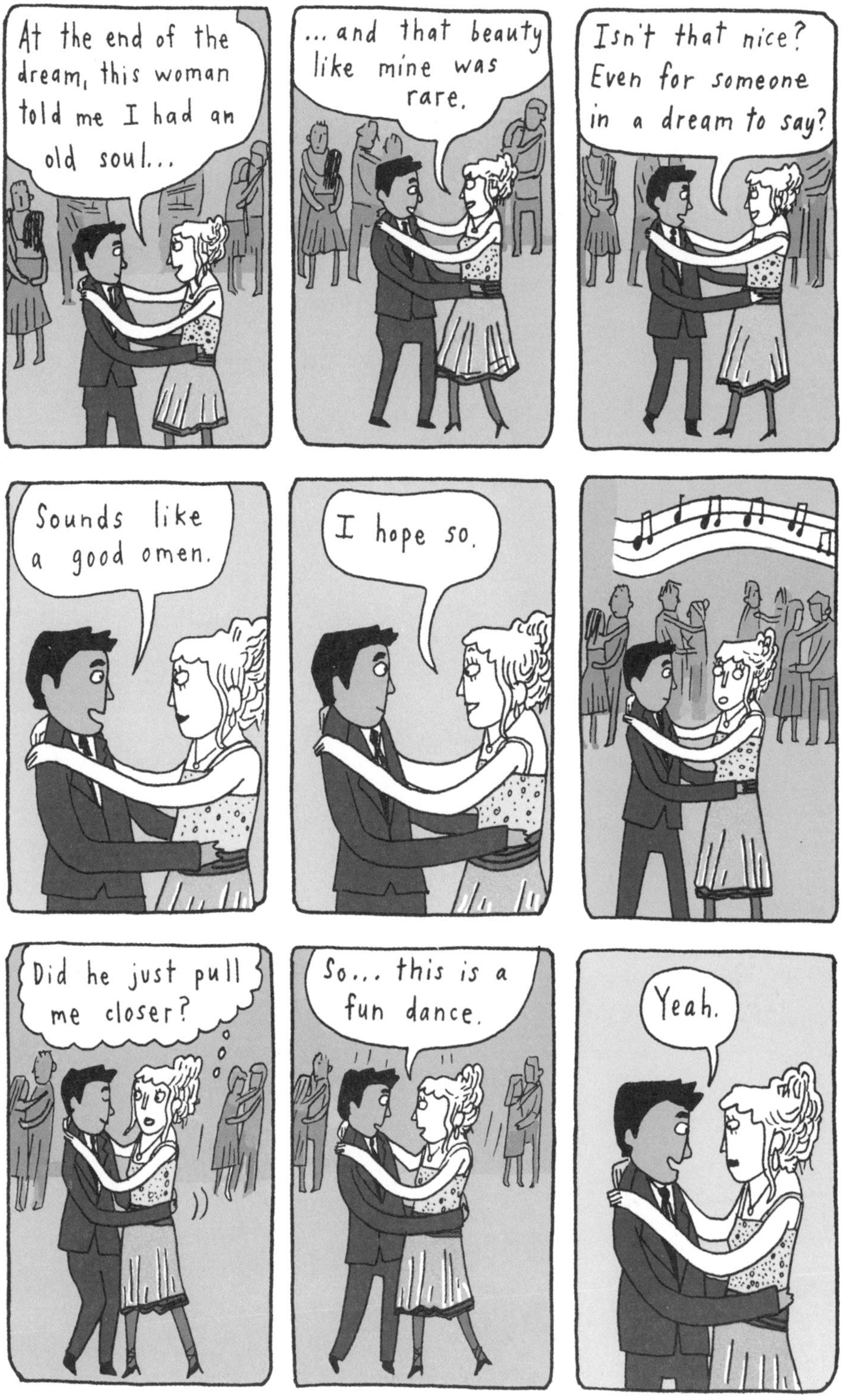
At the end of the dream, this woman told me I had an old soul...
...and that beauty like mine was rare.
Isn't that nice? Even for someone in a dream to say?
Sounds like a good omen.
I hope so.
Did he just pull me closer?
So... this is a fun dance.
Yeah.

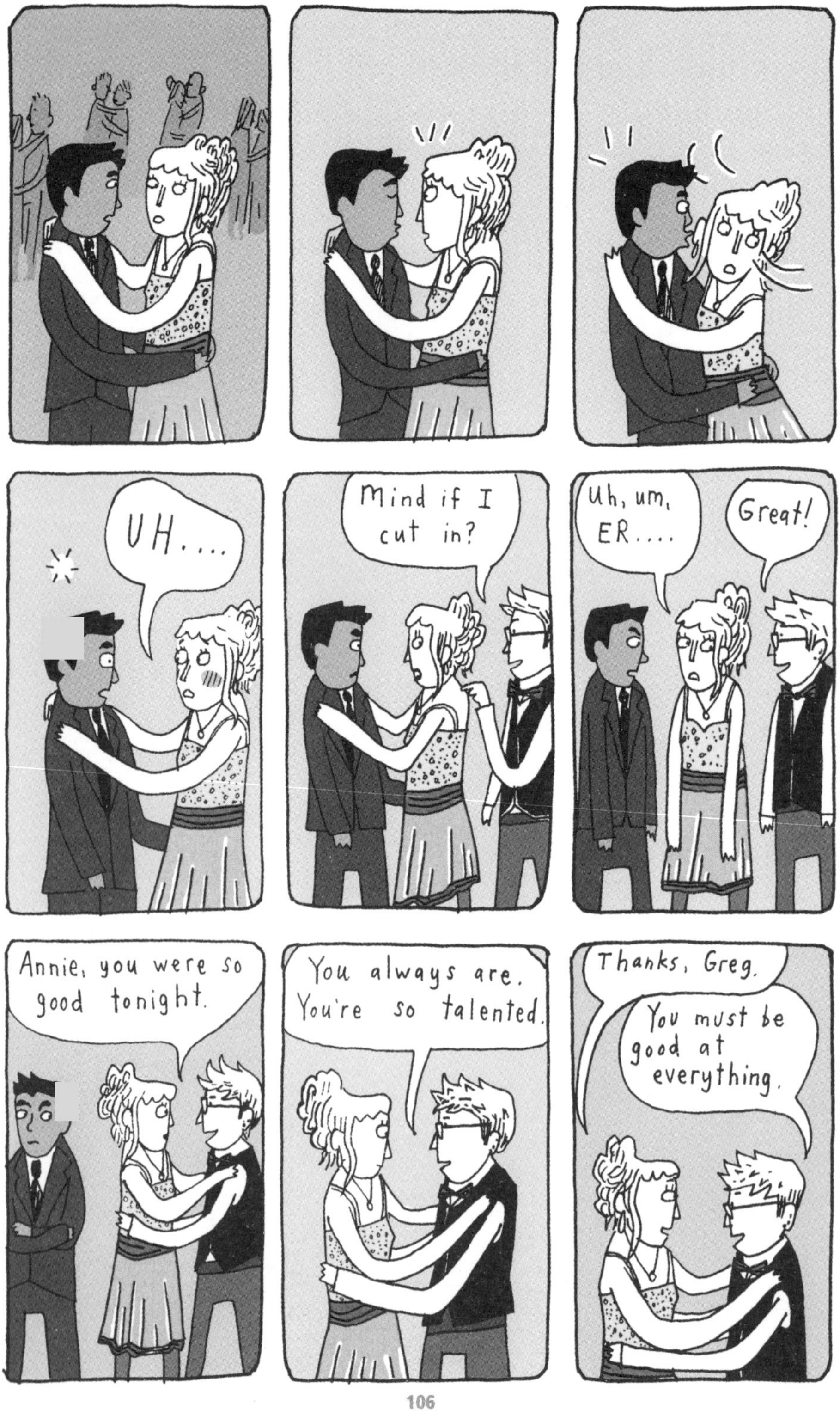
UH....
Mind if I cut in?
Uh, um, ER....
Great!
Annie, you were so good tonight.
You always are. You're so talented.
Thanks, Greg.
You must be good at everything.

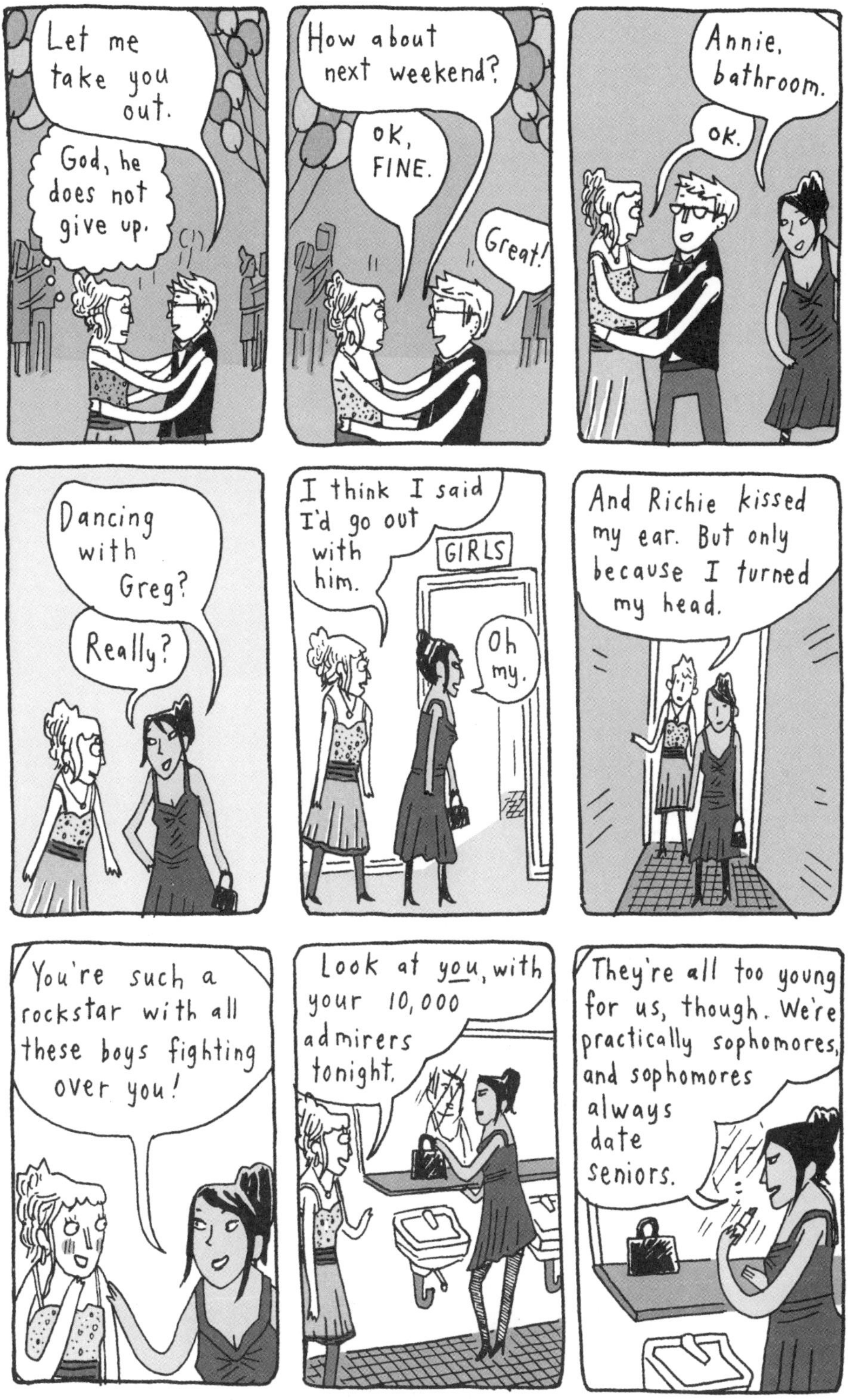
Let me take you out.
God, he does not give up.
How about next weekend?
OK, FINE.
Great!
Annie, bathroom.
OK.
Dancing with Greg?
Really?
I think I said I'd go out with him.
GIRLS
Oh my.
And Richie kissed my ear. But only because I turned my head.
You're such a rockstar with all these boys fighting over you!
Look at you, with your 10,000 admirers tonight.
They're all too young for us, though. We're practically sophomores, and sophomores always date seniors.

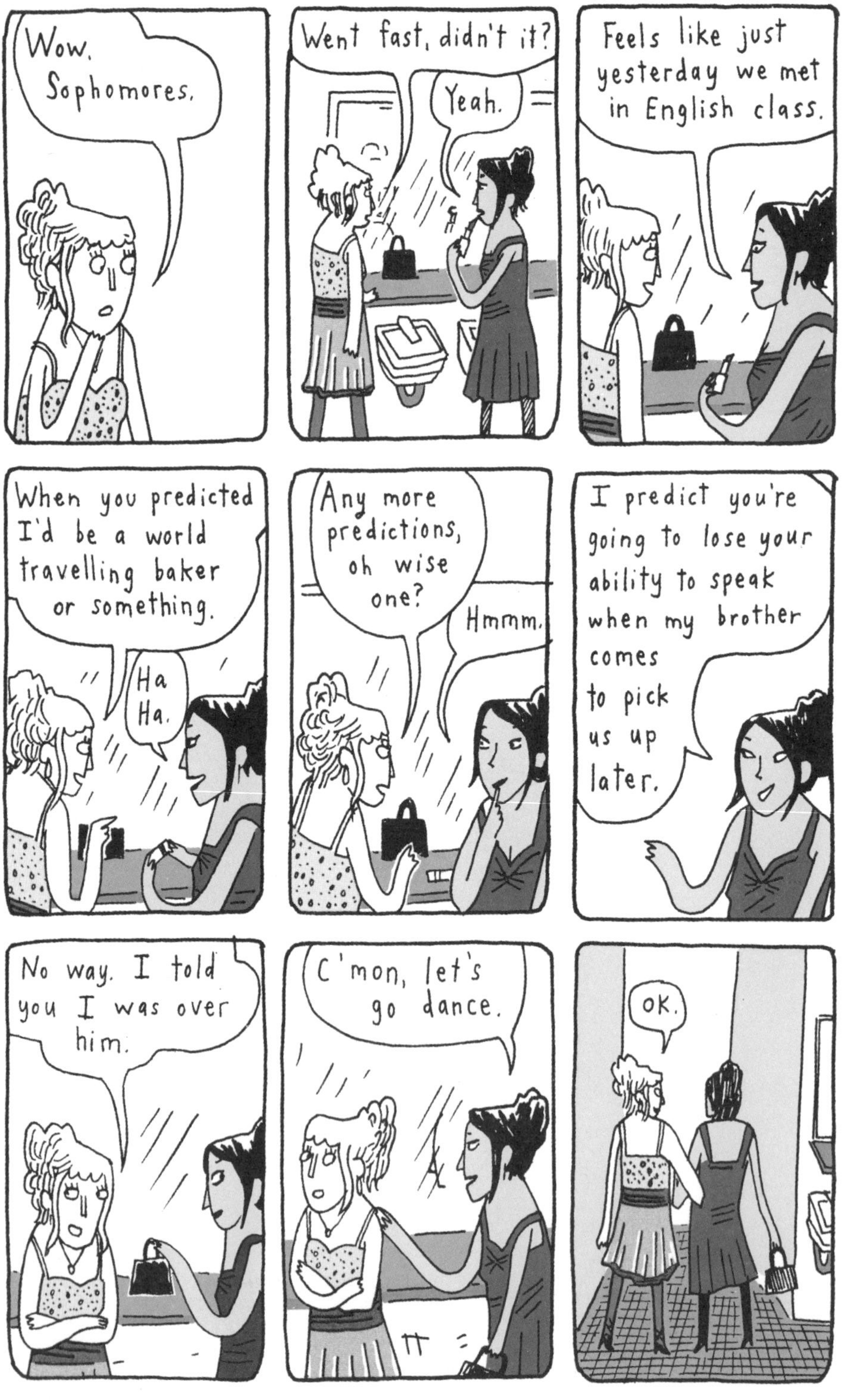
Wow. Sophomores.
Went fast, didn't it?
Yeah.
Feels like just yesterday we met in English class.
When you predicted I'd be a world travelling baker or something.
Ha Ha.
Any more predictions, oh wise one?
Hmmm.
I predict you're going to lose your ability to speak when my brother comes to pick us up later.
No way. I told you I was over him.
C'mon, let's go dance.
OK.

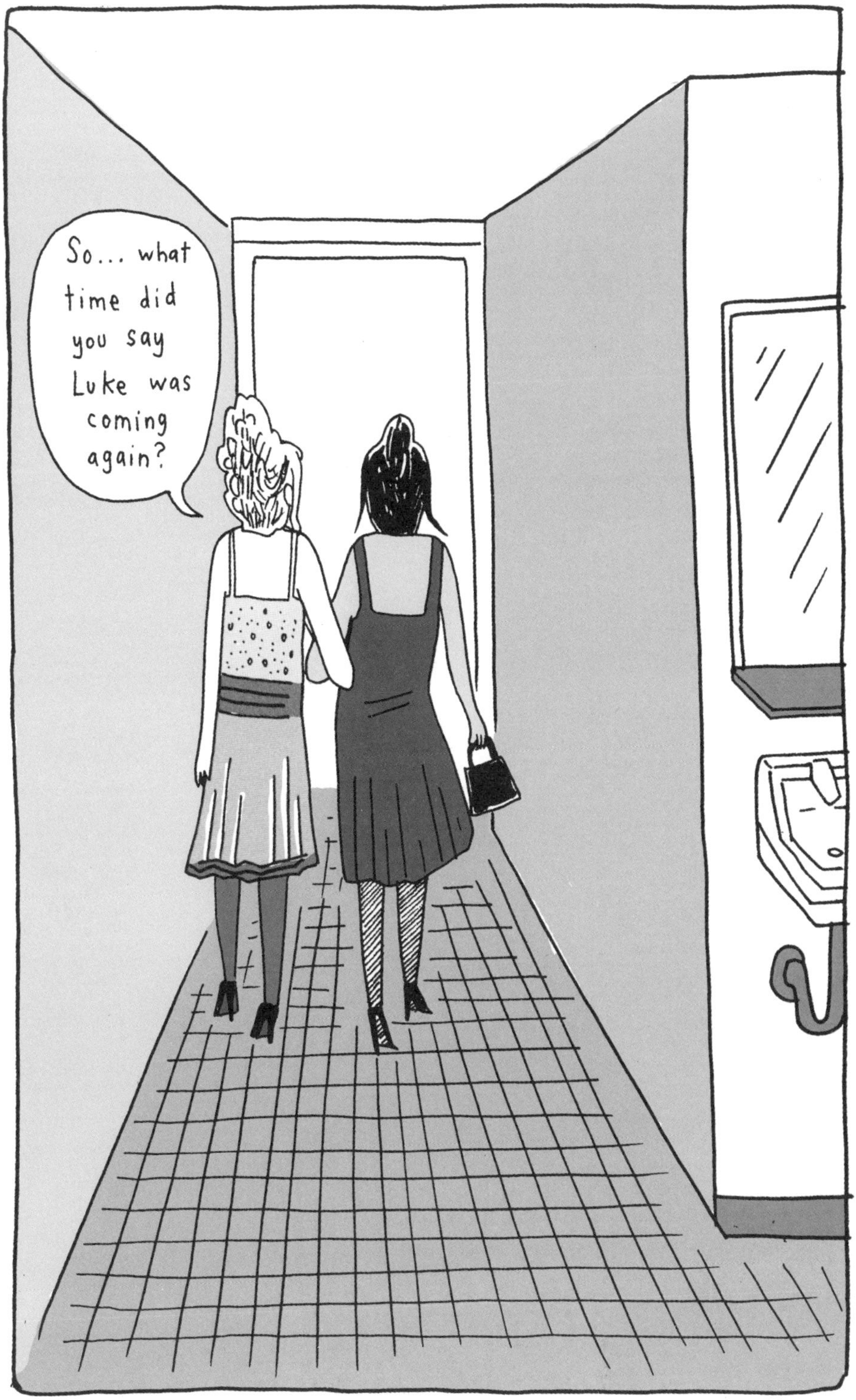
So... what time did you say Luke was coming again?

About the Author

Corinne Mucha is a Chicago-based author and illustrator. Among her credits are the Xeric award-winning graphic novel *My Alaskan Summer*, numerous minicomics, and the *Philadelphia Inquirer* comic strip etiquette column "Barnyard Etiquette."

© April Saul 2011

Author Acknowledgments

Thanks especially to my parents, Anne and Peter, for their endless support, encouragement, and enthusiasm. You guys are pretty special, and I'm lucky to have you. Thanks also to the fine folks at Zest for making this project happen, especially to Karen Macklin for her patience and editorial expertise, and Tanya Napier for her awesome art direction. Thanks to Heather Radke, for her wisdom, constant guidance, and reassurance, and Kate McGroarty, for being there to laugh everything off.

Thanks to all my fine friends in Chicago and beyond—including Alex, Dacia, Sam, Liz, Kandarpa, Kristin, Sara G., Sara A., Alyssa, Aaron, and Yaffa—who offered advice, support, love, laughter, and sometimes chocolate. Thank you to Ellen, for listening, and being a wise teacher.

I'm grateful to every employer who's understood that comics are a full-time job, but especially Paula, who helped make this book possible. Thank you also to Henry, for the vegetables.

And finally, thanks to Nancy Foster, who made high school so much more bearable.

Other Zest Books

The Look Book
50 Iconic Beauties and How to Achieve Their Signature Styles
by Erika Stalder with celebrity hair and makeup artists Christopher Fulton and Cameron Cohen

Queer
The Ultimate LGBT Guide for Teens
by Marke Bieschke & Kathy Belge

Freshman
Tales of 9th Grade Obsessions, Revelations, and Other Nonsense
by Corinne Mucha

87 Ways to Throw a Killer Party
by Melissa Daly

97 Things to Do Before You Finish High School
by Steven Jenkins and Erika Stadler

Girls Against Girls
Why We Are Mean to Each Other and How We Can Change
by Bonnie Burton

Crap
How to Deal with Annoying Teachers, Bosses, Backstabbers, and Other Stuff that Stinks
by Erin Elisabeth Conley, Karen Macklin, and Jake Miller

The Date Book
A Girls' Guide to Going Out With Someone New
by Erika Stadler

Sex: A Book For Teens
An Uncensored Guide to Your Body, Sex, and Safety
by Nikol Hasler